THE FACILITY

Also by Michael Mirolla

Novels:

Berlin
The Boarder

Short-Story collections:

The Formal Logic of Emotion
Hothouse Loves & Other Tales

Poetry:

Interstellar Distances/Distanze Interstellari
Light and Time

THE FACILITY

MICHAEL MIROLLA

A LeapLit Book
Leapfrog Literature
Leapfrog Press
Teaticket, Massachusetts

Cover image: *Birth Machine*, 1964, H.R. Giger. 115×65 cm, oil on paper
on wood. © 2010 H.R. Giger. All Rights Reserved. Courtesy of HRGiger-
Museum.com and HRGiger.com.

Michael Mirolla is a long-time admirer of Mr. Giger's work. The image
of the *Birth Machine* expresses all the right things for this book: futur-
istic, militaristic, and frightening.

Poetry Fragments at the start of each section taken from "The Endless
Instant" by Octavio Paz, translated by Denise Levertov

A LeapLit Book
Leapfrog Literature

Published in 2010 in the United States by
Leapfrog Press LLC
PO Box 2110
Teaticket, MA 02536
www.leapfrogpress.com

Distributed in the United States by
Consortium Book Sales and Distribution
St. Paul, Minnesota 55114
www.cbsd.com

Printed in the United States

First Edition

Library of Congress Cataloging-in-Publication Data

Mirolla, Michael, 1948-
The facility / Michael Mirolla. – 1st ed.
    p. cm.
"A LeapLit Book Leapfrog Literature."
ISBN 978-1-935248-15-6
I. Title.
PR9199.3.M4938F33 2010
813'.54–dc22

    2010028867

PART ONE

RE-ENTRY POINT: CONVERSATIONS WITH IL DUCE

The time is past already for hoping for time's arrival,
the time of yesterday, today and tomorrow,
yesterday is today, tomorrow is today, today all is today.

SCENE ONE: FINAL BEGINNINGS

The first time I use a gun. A 92 Model Beretta to be exact. Two shots to the base of the skull as he kneels before me. Then sit back while the creatures I've come to call The Scavengers clean up the resulting mess.

The second time I slit his throat. With a Bowie knife. I would prefer a stiletto but I need something with a sharp edge. Something that doesn't fall apart on the grind stone. Something that performs its duties with one clean slice.

The third time I try a noose, looping the rope across one of the exposed metal overhangs that give this place the look of a giant Lego set. Then kicking the chair out from underneath him. He jerks and struggles. Kicks. Wets himself. And it takes him much longer to die than I have been led to believe. I learn I have not positioned the knot in its proper place.

The fourth time, naturally, I electrocute him. Tied down to a shiny metal gurney with an array of electrodes. I pull the lever and there is a sizzling sound. He arcs up against his restraints and the muscles on his neck pop out with a snap before he shudders back into his chair and goes limp.

The next time . . . suffocation . . . drowning . . . poison . . . burial alive . . . plunging from the metal rafters . . . a perfect swan dive to the harsh floor below. . . .

Each time, I tell him it's nothing personal. That, if I have to kill him, I might as well make it interesting. For both of us. Otherwise, it's the same-old same-old. He looks at me with those big brown child-like eyes and says he forgives me. No, more than that. He says he loves me. He says that, if his dying is what I need to be happy, then he's ready to do it, however long it takes. Even an eternity, he says in his typically exaggerated manner.

Little does he know. Little does he realize that I follow right behind him. That I too splatter my grey matter against the nearest wall . . . feel the warm gush of blood pumping from my ruptured carotid . . . jerk like a deranged puppet beneath the mis-knotted noose . . . pound my fists and scratch in shallow-breathed desperation against the sealed coffin . . . the darkness . . . the lurching in the pit of the stomach . . . the last gasp sucking for air . . . the final evacuation . . . merciful, merciful relief. . . .

Only to find myself once again. Here. Popping up to the surface. Spitting out the fluids. Frantic to get a breath. Chest heaving with huge gulps. Of air. Walking naked. Bare-foot slip-slopping, flip-flopping. Wet. Cold. Shimmering. Shivering. Eyes darting. Following in the footsteps, the still slimy footsteps, of the one I am going to . . . lovingly, mind you . . . erase once more. Back to the start.

Scene Two: Getting In

Where to start. How about: *Getting in, I've been told, was easy for me; far too easy?* Yes, as good a place as any to begin. What did it take, after all, but the right colour-coded pass and a unique eye-print to match the one stored in the facility's central computer? Or so I've been told. Perhaps, it might have been even easier than that. Perhaps, they'd let anyone in who came knocking at the front door, genetic hat in hand, anxious for life without entropy, for eternal re-birth and re-generation. If only that someone now knew where the front door was.

Getting out is now another matter altogether. There was a time when, in order to leave, all you had to do was alert the nearest robo-guard and it saw you past the entry point—after a thorough scan to make sure you weren't trying to smuggle copyrighted genetic material to an unscrupulous competitor. But that, as far as I know, was the only way out, had always been the only way out: a metallic iris with a central point for the eye-scan. Zip—and it cycled open. Zip—and it cycled shut. Now, that exit route no longer exists. No guard—robotic or otherwise—will respond to your request. No matter how much you insist. Or cause a fuss. Or stamp your feet and throw a tantrum. Or even go on a well-planned rampage.

There are no guards left standing. Only pieces of guards stacked in dust-free, hermetically sealed storage rooms, occasionally jerking their spasmodic reflexes but incapable of ambulatory motion let alone asking or answering questions. The intercoms, the loudspeakers, the computers respond in mock-alive tones, pre-programmed to give a semblance of bustle and activity, of personality and character. But, like all mechanical things, they do a poor job of it, are sooner or later caught out—in the exceptions to the rules and the complications of grammatical constructions; in the illogical or fuzzy logical or downright contradictory that we humans are so proud of.

And the colour-coded pass and eye-print that allowed you to enter so effortlessly are suddenly useless for the outward journey, are nothing but excess baggage which you quickly discard, quickly toss back into the trunk with the rest of the superannuated junk: lockets of hair pressed between the leaves of well-thumbed crumbling books and passed down from generation to generation; a jar with an air-tight cap and half-filled with formaldehyde; letters of true and everlasting love sealed, for some arcane reason, with a bloody thumb-print; and other remnants of a past life.

There was a time when I used to think: Ah, but someone has to get out, no? The ones who run this place? The observers or controllers or whatever? Or are they, too, trapped in here? No, that doesn't seem likely, I said to myself, that doesn't make much sense. After all, they have families, hobbies, wants, needs, desires, a restlessness to see faraway places and do far out things. Don't they? So, despite appearances, there <u>must</u> be another way out. Yes, definitely. A back door escape hatch for when the foaming-at-the-mouth hounds are howling and clawing and digging at the front entrance.

All I have to do is find the persons in charge and either force the knowledge out of them or wait for them to make their inevitable move so I can follow them, watch as they begin to disappear and then throw myself at the invisible opening before it seals itself again. Or maybe there's some other way to communicate with the outside—telephone, computer network, e-mail, TV signals, via satellite. There must be something. Smoke signals. Tapping against the walls. Telepathy. Something. All I've got to do is find it. Work out the kinks. Get it going. Get on the right wavelength.

That's what I used to think—and, for all I know for sure, it might still be true. After all, the facility is huge and it would take a long, long time to search every nook and cranny, every tunnel, passageway, mountain and valley. Let alone every storage device, electronic path, digital communicator or neural net. As well, the entire array is constantly shifting, never staying put or in one place for long. At least not long enough for me to catalogue its contents in their entirety. Like keeping track of the number of ants as they dash along the jungle floor.

But, somehow, search as I might, I doubt I'll find anything new, anything that hasn't already crossed my path at least once. Somehow, it has become all too familiar for me. And that includes the possibility that the observers, controllers or whatever departed long ago, leaving the machinery to the machines. And me.

So here I am one more time. In what I call the "projection room." Sitting huddled up in my favourite pseudo-leather swivel chair. The one being held together with duct tape not so much because it keeps things from falling apart but as a means of holding onto something familiar, something recognizable. I'm wrapped in a cocoon of images and sounds. Some (the expression goes) as old—and worn-out—as the hills, being played over and over again; some newly created, wet behind the ears, at this very moment at the point of birth. They cover every square inch of the walls and ceiling. Constantly shifting, moving, being replaced, flashing in and out. Up to the minute. Up to the second. I feel sometimes that the images appear on the walls even before the events actually take place.

In one of the other chairs beside me, leaning exhausted, shiny bald head lolling as if his neck can no longer support such a massive, misshapen weight, is the reason I've entered once again this nightmarish circle: my student, my ever-renewed responsibility, my tongue-tied albatross. Is it my imagination or do they seem to be appearing more and more developed each time a new one comes out? Didn't the very first ones emerge like enormous foetuses, all curled up and amorphously gooey around the edges? Undifferentiated and leaking essential fluids? First rolling, then crawling along the floor and leaving a trail of putrid slime behind? Like mutant creatures who have spent too much time swimming in spent-rod pools. Now, their eyes are already open, their mouths wanting to chirp, their fingers eager to grasp.

The oversized baby in the chair beside me groans and smacks his gums together in his sleep. I pat his milk-white clammy hand. He grips mine claw-like, only the gross motor skills working. I sigh and look around. The room is window-less; the walls a play of liquid colour swirling and dancing about hypnotically. Like some type of late 20th century abstract art. Or the aurora borealis trapped within a jar.

Come, my friend, I say, standing up and taking him by the hand. *Let us arise and go now. We have many wonders to see.*

He is reluctant. Unsure. When he stands, his body shakes—and not from lack of coordination. He is afraid. This fear . . . this reluctance . . . this unsureness . . . is also new. The previous ones placed all their trust in me. Absolute trust. Without pause or hesitation. Their lives were literally in my hands.

Come. I slip his arm through mine and pat his hand. *There's nothing to be afraid of. Nothing. We'll do it together, okay?*

He nods, a beatific grin on his face. Odd with his teeth not yet in. A gummy grin. Then he frowns and shakes his head, tries to retreat to the safety of his chair. The place he considers his mother.

No, my friend. I pull him back towards me. Gently. And point to the walls. *There are no windows in this room. This room has no windows. We must go out to see. . . .*

R . . . r . . . r . . . room, he says, following my finger.

Yes. Room. I pat him on the back as I lead him out, knowing that positive re-enforcement is always a good thing. *Very good.*

Yes. There are no windows in this room and, from here, I can see nothing of the rest of the facility. But it doesn't matter. You could start anywhere in describing it. How about at the eerily lit central enclosure with its administrative offices and operating equipment? Where the bio-engineers peer out (or used to anyway) into a cryptic darkness and the cloning tanks glow with their own inner light of doubtful green? Where the heart of this abomination pulses ever so slightly, ever so carelessly, a spark here and a spark there?

My friend shrinks back. Tries to get back into the room. But the door has sealed behind him and it only responds to my palm print.

Nothing to fear, I say, leading him down the corridor. *All the ghosts are gone. Kaput. Nada. It's only you and me. Only me and you.*

Or we could start at the hollow, semi-circular spokes. Eight in all. Radiating out to the smaller, peripheral structures. Shaped like incredibly huge Quonset huts that stretch out as far as the eye can see.

He collapses to the floor and refuses to move. Curled up so that his arms and his legs are tucked in and he resembles a spongy ball. And, in fact, he does wet the floor, still excreting a glue-y liquid.

Come now! I say, becoming a little annoyed, unused as I am to this reluctance on the part of one of my protégés. *There are so many things to show you. So many things for you to see. And learn. You want to learn, don't you?*

He shakes his head back and forth, rhythmically, in tick tock fashion. I don't know whether he is responding to my question or simply decides that it is a good moment to shake his head.

Or we could begin with the mush-walled passageways between the structures themselves, a not-quite-closed ring connecting all but one of them—and that one accessible only from the central hub? Or the invisible "fence" around the outside edge of the facility, an impenetrable, unrelenting field of energy that gently but firmly bounces you back with exactly the same force you used to strike it? And don't go trying to dig beneath the fence or rocket over it either. The field forms a perfect sphere, a global encirclement. Impenetrable not only for tangible objects such as humans and hurled stones but also for Morse Code, radio signals and radiation. As well as fission, fusion and neutron bomb blasts, quantum particles, sub-space transmissions and anti-matter rays, too, for all I know.

You're trying my patience, I say. *Do you want me to drag you?*

He continues to shake his head. I notice a puddle forming around him. Yellow and brown liquid oozing out from him.

Oh, good Lord. Now look what you've done.

I reach into the nearest wall. It gives way with a whoosh. I pull out a hose, aim it at him and press the nozzle. A gush of water sprays at him, washing him down. I place the hose on the floor and it pulls itself back into the wall with a suck-a-suck sound.

Okay, I say, noticing that he remains curled up on the ground. *You win. Maybe another time.*

I place my palm against the projection room door and it opens. My friend scurries back inside, stumbling over himself, slipping and sliding to get back inside. I too walk back in, losing myself among the images flickering on the walls. The images multiplied in all directions.

Here I am again. Here you are again. Here you and I might as well not exist. Or you could be multiplied a thousand fold and no one would care, no one would ask: Who's the real you? Does that question have any meaning here? Thanks to the force-field's masking capabilities, I suspect that anything I do to the inside of these facilities will never see the light of day. I could destroy it utterly and no one would be any the wiser. To the outside world, this has always been an area of simulated non-being, a blank wall, invisibly blended into the slightly glowing slag heap background, just another product of mid-21st-century life.

My friend sits back down, a look of total calm on his face. Or is it a look of total blankness? Placid and flaccid. Without a care in the world. And so it should be. What does he have to worry about? To be concerned about?

There used to be an expression that was popular once: Memories make the man. This was normally mirrored by another expression: Once upon a time . . . The combination of the two was supposedly enough to trigger any of a series of neural patterns—from proud individuality to full-blown racial consciousness reaching back to the days when my primary occupation was to suck lice from the head of the dominant male and to make myself available for his various pleasures. It was the way to piece together what once was and never would be again.

But there's no need for that formula now, is there? I say, patting my friend's arm. *Not when we have projection screens—and video cameras whirring at this very moment, like visual bloodhounds. Not when we have stacks of cassettes to back us up, piles of laser discs, cases of digitalized film, layer upon layer of holographic images in containers the size of thumbnails. The repetition of the same experience ad infinitum—and captured from any angle you choose. Isn't that right?*

He looks up at me and smiles. As if he actually understands. Then the blankness closes in around him again.

So, what say we run the first tape, eh, my huge-eyed, pink-skinned, bald-headed, blue-veined friend? My fully grown baby? What say we get the show on the road? Here, sit up straight in your seat. Posture is important. Open your eyes. Look straight ahead. Start blinking. It's all there in the blink of an eye: birth . . . blink . . . life . . . blink . . . death . . . blink . . . re-birth . . . blink . . . Remove the protective mucus that keeps us from the truth, that holds back the flood of angst and anger. Rub those eyes real good with the back of your hairy knuckles. Hairy knuckles? Now there's a good sign. A sign of evolutionary progress. Be alert. Pay attention. Be thankful. Sit up straight.

This is for your own good. Believe me. I wouldn't be wasting my time, otherwise. Or yours. I wouldn't be racking my brain for new ways to bring it all to a climax, now would I? No, I'd just let you rot right here in this chair. I'd just let you melt back into the pool of slime and ooze, a quick slurpy meal for our dear friends, The Scavengers.

Scene Three: Into the Petting Zoo

Ready?

My own first memories of this place must always begin when I was a very young child and still living at home, not quite old enough yet for the communal boarding school that would swallow me and others of my age group for the next decade. It was something all families that could afford it did, public schools having gone the way of the household cat. In the meantime, I received my education via computer which connected all the children my age to the virtual central school hub.

During what we all had come to realize would be the last year of his long, long life, my grandfather often took me here. He called it the Petting Zoo—and that's how I came to think of it as well, complete with capital letters. Unfortunately, it was something I couldn't really boast about during the occasional electronic "Show and Tells." Oh, how I wanted to. How I wanted to shout it out for the whole world to hear: *I go to a place where there are all kinds of. . . .*

I remember several times switching on the camera and getting ready to describe the Petting Zoo. Ready to shock/impress my virtual classmates. But I never went through with it. My grandfather had sworn me to secrecy. He had warned me that, if I told anyone about the Petting Zoo and what went on inside, it would be the last time he'd take me there. And he would get into trouble. So, if anyone asked where I was going, I would tell them my grandfather took me to the park. And everyone would laugh because there was nothing to see in the park—except maybe some limp trees scarred with acid rain and the occasional homeless person staring out vacantly and waiting for the Kennel Kops to come.

When I mentioned this to my grandfather, when I told him that my friends laughed at us, he would take my hand firmly in his horny grip and say: *That is the laughter of fools. That is the same laughter I received when I told my fascist schoolteacher I was going to join my father with the partisans—and that we were going to defeat them. As long as the fools laugh, you are safe.*

Unfortunately, that didn't make me feel much better—especially since I had no idea what he was talking about when he spoke about fascists and partisans. Was that like some kind of cheese? I asked once. And it was his turn to laugh. Okay, I told myself, maybe I can't tell my friends about the Petting Zoo. But I can certainly make the park a lot more interesting. So I began describing all the animals I saw at the park with my grandfather. That brought even more laughter and ridicule. I guess I hadn't thought it through clearly. Everyone knew there were no animals in the park—unless you were talking about the remnant insects in the ground or the humans who had reverted pretty much to a similar animal state.

The year was 2030, long enough past the millennium for the excitement to have worn off and for the realization to set in that the transition from 1999 to 2001 had been little more than symbolic. One more really big number that sounds important and serves as a memory aid. In fact, nothing had changed very much really. The battle lines between the rich and the poor were a little more sharply drawn; the tiny pockets of resistance against the democratic right to shop till you drop were on their last legs, resorting to strip mall terror and the occasional blowing up of phallic symbol buildings; and, following the example of the American presidency in 2020, government by business proxy had become an accepted replacement for the outmoded one-person one-vote system.

There had been, of course, one unexpected millennial effect. That was the destruction of most of the world's free-roaming animals in the years between 2015 and 2025. By the end of 2025, anything higher than a member of the insect family was either dead or in the last painful throes. And, within a few years, the insects had filled in most of the niches left vacant: from beetle rats beneath the subway to beetle birds scavenging the sky.

I was only a year old in 2025 but I had seen the instructional materials enough times to have them permanently imprinted in my brain. While some took this as a sign of the coming apocalyptic doom (even if it was 25 years *after* the original predictions), the generally accepted scientific explanation was the suddenly ever-increasing mutation of the prions blamed for the original mad cow disease attacks of 2000-2001, followed by confirmed passage of the disease to other mammals several years later.

Those animals which hadn't gone off and died on their own were hunted down and destroyed for fear they would infect humans. Or they were placed in restricted areas with absolutely no contact with the outside world, places where they quickly wasted away without reproducing. Household pets were forbidden under harsh penalties including loss of job and property and potential prison terms which, amazingly enough, some were willing to risk to keep their beloved cats and dogs. Fortunately, several multinationals were in place and ready to supply the population with ersatz meat that didn't come with the risk of spongiform encephalopathy, meat created in the very shape in which it would be potted, cooked and eaten.

The disappearance of the animals most near and dear to humans led to a new push in the area of cloning. However, cloning was still a hit-and-miss affair, and the rules and regulations on the keeping of cloned material had to be very strict. I guess to make sure no human-made horrors escaped to ravage the unsuspecting citizenry. Not that that was much of a possibility—as cloned creatures had to follow pretty well the same physiological guidelines as the rest of "nature".

Abominations, of the animal variety at least, were just not in step with evolutionary processes or whatever genetic laws were actually in force. The only way to keep abominable genetic freaks alive was through an elaborate system of machinery and vast expenditures of energy. In other words, they'd have to bring their electro-mechano-genetic birth boxes with them, their umbilical cords dragging unwieldy, lumbering electronic wombs. So it wasn't likely that scaly, hydrogen sulphide-breathing, meant-for-the-moons-of-Jupiter beasties would be gallivanting around the countryside in the latest Jetson Family rocket cars. Not for long anyway.

But perhaps the real fear lay not so much in monsters but in the subtle changes that could be made, the tinkering and fine-tuning of the human engine itself. At any rate, while the bioethicists argued and the religious fanatics fumed (and occasionally blew up things), several cloning facilities had been licensed to start up and there was a fierce competition among them.

I remember well my father—an avid believer in the saving graces of technology even in such post-millennial times— checking out which of "The Body Shops" would make the best hi-tech investments. And the only occasion I can picture him smiling was on downloading the news that one of the facilities—the one he'd eventually bought stock in thanks to an insider tip—had succeeded in cloning a fully grown insect.

An insect! I remember him shouting. *We're going to be rich.*

Oh, there had been all sorts of cloning before this—sheep, monkeys, pigs, camels, what have you. But in those cases the creatures had been cloned at the sperm and egg level and then allowed to grow. Though why anyone would want to clone an insect when there were billions in the world was beyond me. And of interest to very few people, busy as they were trying to cope on a planet that was rapidly coming apart at the seams, a planet whose infrastructure desperately needed re-building—and not just the physical kind either.

But, even for a child (or perhaps because I was a child when I first saw it), the Petting Zoo represented something else entirely. It was—and, I presume, still is—a short walk from the end of the old subway line, about an hour's ride from the city where my mother and father had spent all their lives. Even then, not long after it came into existence, it was already practically invisible from

the outside—and placed squarely in the middle of tower-
ing and faintly pulsing slag heaps to deter any further
curiosity.

Nor has its internal layout changed in any significant way
through the years, despite my past attempts to rearrange it.
Each one of the buildings in the outer ring has its own eco-
system, set specifically for the kinds of animals it contains.
There are marshes, savannahs, deserts, forests and steppes,
as well as mountain, polar ice and salt water environments—
and even a section of a city sewage system so that the rats,
cockroaches and other creatures peculiar to such areas can
feel comfortable, if not entirely at home.

At the time, of course, I must have been too young to notice any of this—the layout of the buildings, the sustaining
machinery, the actual fact that the animals were cloned or
that each of the sections held a separate ecosystem. Nor did I
question the security measures which were, in any case, standard for the era. In fact, it was almost as hard getting into the
local meat reproduction shop—or any other business with an
electronic security system.

No, at the time, it must have been simply a place full of
vivid wonders and delights, a place where, in a matter of minutes, you could go from lush jungle to crackling desert, from
marsh walk to ice fields, from mountain top to sea-shore. You
only had to use the passageways connecting one building to
the next—the nondescript, dimly lit, faintly echoing passageways that seemed always slightly wet and slightly gooey to the
touch—and suddenly you found yourself in a totally different
environment, the miraculous changes taken for granted. At
least by me.

As you can see from the images on the screens, I got quite
a kick out of walking among and touching animals that had
long before become extinct in their natural setting, and
whose names I only learned much later: passenger pigeons
and ring-tailed raccoons; mallard ducks and the legendary
dodo. The most fun, however, was petting creatures that had
been considered dangerous in the wild: big cats, poisonous

snakes, crocodiles, hyenas, etc. But the ones in here were all tame now and incapable of hurting anyone—or so my grandfather had explained the first time he took me to the zoo.

There. (I'm pointing for the benefit of my newly hatched if overgrown baby). There we are now, sitting on a mountain ledge, a lunch of strong provolone cheese, rough bread and homemade wine spread at our feet, the wine my grandfather made through some mysterious alchemical process in the basement of our home and that I was only allowed to taste when alone with him. Even this far removed, you can almost feel the cool, crisp, recycled air, untouched by any form of pollution or impurity (bacteria, virus or prion) and scoured even more clean by the relentless scrub brushes of memory.

They roamed free once across the face of the Earth, my grandfather is saying in the faintest trace of an Italian accent he never lost despite more than seventy years away from his native land. Or perhaps to be used as an affectation. *To the farthest ends of it. They hunted for themselves and made their own laws. Or rather they did not need laws. They were cruel and unpredictable, hot-headed and did not care for church or devil. And filled with a lust for life.*

Predator devoured prey—and that is how the balance of nature was maintained. It was the natural order of things to live under the harshest conditions, to eat or be eaten—and to give up life with a shrug and without hope of ever coming back. No redemption.

He sighs, takes another gulp of wine, smacks his lips.

First, we took those environments away, literally pulling the rug from under them; then we began to fool around with the animals themselves, trying to shape them into what we felt creatures beneath us should be like. We had them just about trained when, as various bureaucrats and committees met to determine their fate, they played a nasty trick on us by getting up and vanishing. Poof! Just like that. A collective suicide without precedent in the history of the world: from pussycats to possums, periwinkles to parakeets. Their brains full of holes and their bodies no longer following orders, staggering around like drunken, emaciated sailors.

But we would not allow them to die. No, not that easily. Instead, as they plunged into oblivion we snatched their genetic material and placed it in air-tight, vacuum-sealed containers so that we could one day recreate them to our own image. If not quite in our own image. So, Faustino, my lad, what you see now is something entirely made up, something built just for you, just to be petted by you. Enjoy.

Although, thanks to these holograms, tapes and other projections, I have been able to listen to my grandfather time and again down through the years, to make him appear and repeat himself at will (a slave to my memory aids, a creature of infinite habit), that first morning I couldn't really understand, or be expected to understand, what he meant—especially the part about roaming free and killing one another and then being recreated by us.

For me—and I guess for anyone of my generation who had never seen an animal of this stature in the wild (or any animal larger than a subway rat beetle for that matter), this was their natural state, the only way it could possibly be. I said to myself (although I realize the language must be from later in my life, when my questioning and thought patterns were more systematic):

What creature in its right mind would want to try to make a life for itself in the midst of contaminated waste and trees that glowed? Or in marshes that had become little more than bubbly, acidic quagmires? Which of these would want to try to hunt down other creatures for food—a risky business at the best of times—when they have all the food they want right here?

These animals seemed happy and well fed, living in a kind of Edenic garden where they were protected from all harm. I couldn't imagine anything else—except perhaps the dark, boundless, metallic-edged chaos I sometimes experienced in my worst dreams. And what the connection between that and the animals was I only found out much, much later—when it was no longer of any use. When it is no longer of any use.

I remember clearly my grandfather taking me to this zoo at least once a week—and two to three times a week during that final winter and spring. The ritual was almost always the same. Stooped and balancing on a cane, he would come down from the upstairs room he had in my parents' house and say, in his reedy voice: *Siamo pronto, Signor Faustino?*

I nodded—swallowing my pride over being called "Faustino" rather than the more masculine or manly "Fausto"—and he would say: *Allore, andiamo, mio Faustino.* (To be fair to him, Fausto was his name as well. So maybe he was just trying to distinguish between us).

My mother would pull up my collar, slick back my hair, give us her customary, often contradictory, warning (*Don't talk to strangers on the subway; be polite to everyone you meet; and come straight home afterwards*) and send us off. All the while thinking we were on our way to the city's central park, which had a fountain in the middle that didn't work and the giant statue of a lion covered in green lichen. Her one concession to the anachronism that was her father-in-law.

The first morning inside the zoo, my grandfather took the time to give me a cursory tour through the seven peripherally connected sections, pointing out the various environments and areas of interest. Although the passageways between ecosystems had a rapid transit tube built into the walls for quick movement, my grandfather insisted we walk.

Good for the brain, he liked to say, taking a deep breath and pointing to the side of his head as if that would explain everything. *Il cervello.* When we came upon an animal, he called out its name—both in English and Italian—and some of them actually responded, coming right up to us and lying at our feet, including a snow leopard that slipped its muzzle beneath my grandfather's arm.

At first, I was afraid to get too close, let alone touch them. They had such big teeth, such tremendous jaws, such razor-sharp claws, such toxic venom. But they were also soft and warm. And, in their eyes, I could swear I saw a glint of utter love and devotion. There! Did you catch it? Hold on. I can replay it for you, if you'd like. See. It's not simply a trick of the light. Or the camera. It seems to come from inside. Ah, the old anthropomorphic spirit never quite dies, now does it?

Some of the creatures just will not come, my grandfather is saying as we sit on a rock outcropping, a cave entrance behind us and golden fields of waving grain before us. *No matter how often you call out to them.* He cuts a huge chunk of the cheese and plops it into his mouth. *But those are needed as well. I have given them the name of Scavenger. They are not quite like vultures and jackals, the old scavengers that once roamed the Earth, but they do the same kind of job.*

One of these days you will see them for yourself, mark my words. They are beneath us at this very moment, churning away. Can you hear them? Here, put your ear to the ground.

And I dutifully place my ear to the ground, then nod at the sounds of muffled rumbling beneath me. An angry buzzing sound that always seemed in a hurry to get somewhere else.

Yes, you can definitely hear them. They are free to come and go as they please. At first, the ones who run the facility did not truly understand what their purpose was—and spent a lot of time trying to get rid of them. Or so I have been told. Fortunately, they are not so easy to destroy because it was soon realized that, without them, all the rest would be lost as well. They had to be included whether we liked it or not, you understand? They had to be. Remember that the next time someone questions you about them. Say: 'They had to be included in order to secure our own proper dissolution.' Do you understand that? Do you? Repeat it after me.

I dutifully repeated the phrase, having never seen my grandfather so intense, so pumped up, before. At home, he would hardly say a word, would hardly acknowledge the family's existence and spent most of his time in his upstairs room, listening to ancient music (weird, drumless, unback-beated things he called "operas") on an antiquated recording machine while poring over strange, thick, leather-bound books that smelled of allergy-producing must and which no one in his right mind would keep around. Or in the little unheated room in the basement with its naked light bulb that swung to and fro, sending shadows in all directions, and where he spent his days transferring golden-coloured liquid from one container to another until he declared it ready to drink.

And, even though I <u>didn't</u> understand—not really as that would've been asking too much of me at the time—I knew then the importance of what he was saying probably as well as I know it now. And the words stayed with me, stuck to some overhanging ledge in my memory until they were jarred free more than 15 years later to come spilling out like an avalanche of loose ends that needed perpetual re-tying, perpetual propping up.

Even that very first time, I noticed that there was one section, one "Quonset hut" we hadn't entered—the one I later learned couldn't be reached except through the central building. When I asked my grandfather about it on that first ride home, he told me that's where they kept the creatures that hadn't been quite perfected, the creatures that still needed some work before they could be released to join the healthy ones.

(I immediately envisioned pathetic half-finished lions, crawling on forelegs only; one-winged or Cyclopic owls, spiralling and bouncing off trees; trunkless elephants, with a hole where the proboscis should be. Though later that night, as I lay in bed unable to sleep, these familiar semi-animals transformed themselves into more ominous, more lasting shapes: the true, milky-white horrors that only imagination can conjure up in the midst of nightmare).

And, before changing the subject, my grandfather promised he would one day show me that area as well. *To complete your necessary education. To prepare you both for the past and for what lies ahead. I have faith in you, my boy. In you—and in no one else. Remember that.*

But, except for that first morning, my grandfather only accompanied me through the zoo on one other occasion—and that was during our last, shocking visit together. The rest of the times, once we were past the gates, he would wave his cane in my direction (see, there he goes now) and immediately vanish down one of the passageways leading to the central structure, leaving me completely on my own to explore the peripheral buildings as I pleased.

The peripherals only, mind you, as any attempt to enter the passageways to the central area would be rebuffed by invisible barriers of the same type that encompassed the entire facility. When I asked him about this, he said it was to protect me from the operating machinery, a machinery whose hum I could detect but faintly if I placed an ear against the tunnel walls. (Or perhaps those were once more the Scavengers, making their way through solid metal).

Then, at the end of the day, we would meet again near the gates and go through the elaborate exiting ritual in reverse order of how it took place when we entered: the electronic body search, the eye-print and the pass-card.

Have a good day, the robo-guard inevitably called out in its robust, manly, newscaster announcer voice as the opening sealed behind us much like the iris on a camera lens. Except that, in this case, it vanished into itself and the only indication of anything being there was a minuscule slot into which to insert the coded card, followed by a tiny beam of light against which to place the eye.

On the way home, my grandfather would insist I recount all I had done and the animals I had seen—in minute detail. And I would describe for him the wonders that had appeared before me, the new creatures I had found, the old friends I had re-visited. I asked questions and he would answer most of them precisely, exactly, without hesitation. Those that he couldn't, he promised to look up in his damp tomes—and always had the answer the next morning when he came down for his breakfast of soggy cereal spiked with a splash of throat-burning liquor.

Brandy, he said one day when I asked. *Here, taste some. Very educational.*

And I shot it back as I'd watched him do and I choked and I learned that it burned your throat and my grandfather laughed and slapped his knee.

My favourite habitat was the marsh. A wooden walkway had been built across it so it was possible to come right up to the animals without disturbing them. It was also filled with hundreds of nooks and crannies where someone could hide out, could pretend there was nothing there but marsh animals, grass poking up through the water and stunted trees bending in the wind—just, I would imagine, like it had been in the days when such marshes actually existed outside the facility. From certain angles, even the permanent steel grey of the sky was hidden. At least, I see it that way in retrospect— and my size may have had a lot to do with it.

As for my grandfather, though he delighted in answering my questions and was justifiably proud of his knowledge, he would say very little about his own day, even if I pressed him, contenting himself with: *Today, I had a very interesting conversation. Very interesting and stimulating.* Or something similar, something along those lines. I assumed he meant with the zoo keeper—or with some of the other employees—and left it at that.

And the moment we reached the house, he would climb laboriously back up the stairs to his room, descending only for a quick supper which he always ate before the rest of us, noisily slurping his chicken soup like elderly men have a tendency to do and making satisfied grunts as he polished off a glass or two of the home-made wine, the golden liquid he kept in well-sealed bottles and which no one else would touch.

I wanted very much to ask my parents why grandfather went to the zoo so often. Maybe they knew something I didn't, something that would make me understand him better. But I couldn't do that without giving it away—or without having them laugh at me.

Zoo? What zoo? I could hear my father saying loud enough for grandfather to hear him. *Is there a zoo for insects now?*

Don't tell lies, Fausto, my mother would probably say before turning to my father: *That must be the influence of his grandfather.*

Besides, I think I realized even then that my grandfather was in enough trouble as it was with my parents without my childish input. Frequently, I would overhear them whispering to one another after he had returned to his room and the faint operatic strains of Verdi or Rossini (I only learned their names later) floated down to where we sat watching the gladiatorial game shows or interactive sports events on television.

The gist of their conversations was that "the old man" was nearing the end of his string and had started to imagine things, things that hadn't existed for a long, long time. There was talk of placing him in a proper home "for his own good," which really confused me because I thought that a proper home is what we had.

Dad thinks he's fighting a war, I remember my father saying one time, while not taking his eyes off the tri-V projection in the centre of the room. *He thinks he's a young man again, full of spunk and with a loaded rifle in hand. He talks about hunting down the fascist bastards and how he's tricked them once again. He keeps saying something about an eye for an eye.* At this point, my dad always shook his head. *The sad thing is that dad never fought in any war. He was only five when the war ended. He's confusing himself with his father.*

Oh you don't know the half of it, my mother added. *The other day he mistook the ersatz meat seller for an enemy soldier he claimed to have taken prisoner once. He wanted to know how he'd managed to escape so quickly, who had sprung him. And, worst of all, he spoke to the poor man in Italian. He said: 'Ah, now I understand. Si, capisco. That is not really you. That is only a disguise, is it not? Well, they should have told me before setting you free.' I nearly died. I had to apologize to the man so he wouldn't call the health services. That's the last time I take him shopping with me.*

But none of that seemed a reasonable explanation to me as to why my grandfather went to the Petting Zoo so often— unless, of course, he was under the impression the animals were long-lost comrades at arms, *amici* with whom he'd imagined sharing fox holes, trenches and night raids behind enemy lines. And maybe that's what he meant when he said he had "very interesting and stimulating conversations." After all, I myself found it enjoyable talking to the animals. Or simply passing my fingers through their fur, across their scales, over their feathers. Or rubbing my face against them as they warmed themselves in the sun. It was <u>real</u>.

Nor did my grandfather ever explain to me why he took me to the zoo but wouldn't allow any of my friends to come along, wouldn't even allow me to mention it to them.

Too dangerous, he said once when I pressed him. *And that is the last word on the subject. Do not ask me again.*

Or why, once inside, I never met any other visitors. I had seen zoos before on historical TV nature programs and I knew they had been places where people went to see animals—behind cages and high metal fences, of all things, because they were considered dangerous. Here there were tame creatures roaming free—thousands of them and some so rare they hadn't been in existence for hundreds of years—but no people.

If the word got out, I could just envision the line-ups rushing to get in, the tube transports packed to the gills, the various vendors selling everything from gooey hallucinogenic candy to sticky virtual reality action games. In the true business enterprise spirit that ran everything. But, except for my grandfather and me—and a few shadowy employees whom I glimpsed only from afar, flitting among the machinery in their spectral colours, I never saw anyone else. And the shadowy employees represented a collective *deus ex machina* that later vanished for want of miracles, I guess.

I should have suspected something was wrong then and there. Nobody in his right mind would pass up an opportunity like that—not when there were huge line-ups for the Subway Rat Beetle-Chomping contests, the Homeless Street Running and Trampling competitions, and other highly appetizing features of inner city life in the fourth decade of 21st century.

Scene Four: The Eighth Ring

I've left the projection room and my sleeping friend behind—but the video cassettes and holographs are still running, still pushing the story forward. And the camcorders are faithfully filming future episodes. Despite his seeming inertness, my student is even now gathering knowledge, filling his head with facts and figures, memories and impressions. And he's getting faster at it each day—or each time a new one comes out.

As for me, I have all the knowledge I need for the task at hand. Just the right amount, in fact. Too much leads to paralysis, the urge to sit and reflect, to consider a potentially infinite series of pros and cons like the quintessential double helix with one strand forever facing the other and locked in mutual dependency. Leads to the inevitable questions. Questions like: What do you get when you film one camera filming another camera filming. . . ? Where does it begin? What is slow motion and what is speeded up? Which one is the original action and which the imitation? Is there any such thing as progress?

Stasis. I know. I've been down that road before. The road to Hamlet, Zeno and paralysis. Good for levitation, perhaps, and so levity . . . but not much else.

A paradox, my grandfather said one morning when, in my customary way, I knocked on his door to advise him breakfast was about to be served—and he'd better hurry if he wanted his brandied porridge.

Dio cane! He stood up slowly, creakily. *A real ball buster. How is it possible that time advances, moves ahead, speeds on, yet we are going in circles?* He leaned on me. *We are going in circles, are we not? It is tomorrow but I am in the same place I was yesterday.*

Yesterday. I remember very well—like a sudden, quick, illuminated, searing flash in an otherwise absolutely dark room—the one time, the one and only time my grandfather took me with him to the eighth section. I remember it as if it was yesterday. Isn't that a bit of a joke? I guess part of the reason for its vividness is that it coincided with another event that left a similarly indelible flash: my grandfather's death. On the other hand, it might have actually been yesterday for all I know. All one giant indivisible yesterday stretching backwards forever and no way to get past it. No way to peek behind the curtain to see what is real and what isn't. No way to any longer subdivide the infinite moments into parcels that humans can handle without their brains exploding.

It was one of those spring mornings when the temperature fluctuated wildly between summer heat and mid-winter cold—in keeping with the tendency to sudden inversions of air at that time of year (having, no doubt, to do with the holes punched in the ozone layer or acid rain from Arctic Sea oil gushers or something like that—in other words, the prevalent worries of the outside world). April 28, to be exact, a date that meant nothing then but would become significant soon enough.

I knew something was up the moment my grandfather came down the stairs. My mother rolled her eyes when she saw him—but she didn't say anything to him and instead left the room shaking her head. He had on a peaked, black army cap of some kind and some sort of shabby, frayed military uniform topped with a greatcoat that dragged beneath his feet. It would have been an impressive sight except that everything was too big and smelled of mothballs and old sweat.

I guess I have become a little smaller, he said with a wry smile, looking down at where his feet should be and the overhanging greatcoat. *Shrunk, is that the word? Just a bit. But it will have to do, will it not? At least for this time around. If my superiors do not like it, they can lump it. Bah. I was never one for the military niceties. Enough saluting and marching! Give me a rifle and an enemy to shoot, porco dio!*

It was then I noticed he was walking upright, without his stoop or customary cane. Even more astounding was the fact he had shaved and had trimmed his moustache in the middle of the week. Ordinarily, that was unheard of. He shaved once a week—punctually at 8 a.m. Sunday.

I didn't blame him for his reluctance to do it more often as he had allowed me the honour of watching the shaving ceremony one morning. It was a frightening experience. First, he turned on the hot water tap full blast until the entire bathroom steamed up, fogging glasses and mirrors alike so that he had to constantly wipe them clean with his handkerchief. Then, using a coarse-haired brush, he spread some foamy material on his face, material he himself had whipped up in a wooden bowl with the same brush. Finally, he flashed what looked like a blunt-ended knife-blade to scrape away at it, occasionally nicking his flesh and drawing little droplets of blood. And, when he was finished scraping, he slapped some foul-smelling liquid on his face and winced.

All the while, he whistled a tune I recognized from one of his hopelessly outmoded recordings—again one object scratching the surface of another when the rest of the world was civilized enough to use lasers, both for shaving and music playing.

It is called Bella Ciao, *he said without my even asking. Remember it well as it might come in handy some day in your own guerrilla battles, your own wars against would-be universal oppressors and destroyers of the human spirit.*

Later, I learned it was a song the Italian partisans had adopted as their own during the so-called last Great War. Or last Just War. Or last whatever. Before the business of war became so obvious that patriotism had to express itself in the buying of a new set of sofas and a double dose of Disneyland. Before it was Wal-Mart sponsoring one side and Home Depot the other.

At the time, his shaving habits were of more interest. I asked why he used such a dangerous-looking instrument rather than the very convenient and safe depilatories preferred by my father and other men of his generation. He shrugged and said: *Habit. Abitudine. I got used to this in the mountains during the war. Just like those records that make your teeth grate.*

That may have been—but I'd never before seen him clean-shaven in mid-week so he couldn't have been all that used to it.

Andiamo, ragazzo, he said, even his voice no longer reedy and with a resonance that would have made a bureaucrat-cum-CEO proud. *We have a lot of work to do this morning.*

As we walked out the door, I distinctly remember my mother rushing to the phone. She was whispering urgently into it. And, just as ominously, she'd forgotten to give us her usual warning and send-off.

The other passengers on the subway stared openly at my grandfather. The more timid ones moved aside when he opened up the greatcoat to reveal what even I, despite my childhood ignorance, recognized as a gun in a holster. A massive gun in a holster. But some reacted by reaching for their own carefully concealed weapons.

I had seen on my TV pre-school program the results of these subway battles: bodies pumped full of exploding bullets, limbs blown away at close range, chests with holes you could drive a truck through. It was all part of our social studies imprinting on how to avoid mutilation and "cessation of life functions."

The idea, I learned later, was to bombard you with images of horror at a very early age so that they'd eventually repel you—originally suggested in an obscure movie from the mid-20th century called *A Clockwork Orange.*

Did it work? I don't know. In any case, it still took two to tangle and my grandfather obviously had other things on his mind. He simply paced back and forth across the entire length of the subway car, paying no attention to the other strategically positioned passengers. Nor to me, for that matter. It was the first time he hadn't spoken to me on the way to the zoo. Usually, he would give me hints about where to go to find the best animals, the ones off the beaten path, the strays, the unique creations. That's how I'd discovered the almost completely hidden lair of the snow leopard—the most beautiful and majestic creature I've ever seen.

Coincidentally, a man called Leopardi, Giacomo Leopardi, was one of the greatest poets ever in the Italian language, my grandfather had told me, as we stood in front of the cave and watched the animal sunning itself in the artificial light, licking its great paws as if it didn't have a care in the world. *His words were literally like leopards gliding across the page.*

And he would lift one hand up towards the sky and begin reciting one verse or another: *Or poserai per sempre,/Stanco mio cor. Perì l'inganno estremo,/Ch'eterno io mi credei. Perì. Ben sento,/ In noi di cari inganni,/Non che la speme, il desiderio è spento./Posa per sempre. Assai/Palpitasti. Non val cosa nessuna/I moti tuoi, nè di sospiri è degna/La terra. Amaro e noia/La vita, altro mai nulla; è fango il mondo./T'acqueta omai. Dispera/L'ultima volta. Al gener nostro il fato/Non donò che il morire. Omai disprezza/Te, la natura, il brutto/Poter che, ascoso, a comun danno impera,/E l'infinita vanitè del tutto.*

And sometimes, perhaps for my benefit, he would repeat the verse in English: *Now will you rest forever,/My tired heart. Dead is the last deception,/That I thought eternal. Dead. Well I feel/ In us the sweet illusions,/Nothing but ash, desire burned out./Rest forever. You have/Trembled enough. Nothing is worth/Thy beats, nor does the earth deserve/Thy sighs. Bitter and dull/Is life, there is nought else. The world is clay./Rest now. Despair/For the last time. To our kind, Fate/Gives but death. Now despise/Yourself, nature, the sinister/Power that secretly commands our common ruin,/And the infinite vanity of everything.*

Now, there is a man I would not mind speaking to. There are no more poets these days, no more use for them or their words. Everything has become literal. Or used to sell automobiles. What I would not give to hear his voice.

Perhaps someday he might just get his wish, but that morning, we travelled in silence. Rather, I remained silent while my grandfather hummed the entire way. I had no trouble recognizing <u>Bella Ciao</u> this time. My grandfather hummed it as if he were practising for something, head in the air, seemingly inspecting the graffiti on the ceiling of the dilapidated car.

I looked up, too, hoping to find something there that would help break the code. The only legible writing spelled out in a childish scrawl: 'Kelly D. eats mutant beetle rats for breakfast.' No enlightenment coming from those quarters. Or the walls either which were covered in 3-D, stylized male and female sexual organs, some floating blithely and others coming together in every combination possible.

I looked back at my grandfather. At that moment, all I could think was: *My parents are right. Grandpapa has definitely gone over the edge. It's cloud-cuckoo land for him.* An expression I'd obviously heard on the morning pre-school program but which didn't make me feel any less guilty for having used it.

However, he seemed anything but crazy as the friendly robo-guard at the zoo double-checked his card and eye-print. In fact, he acted very sure of himself and bristled with high spirits. I accompanied him as I always did to the edge of a tunnel that led to the central building. Then I prepared to bid him good-bye for the day, off on my own adventures. A visit to the marsh beaver dam, perhaps, to see how it was coming along. Or up on the eagle's aerie with its two fluff-winged eaglets just about ready for flight. Or even a sewer crawl to check in on how the cockroach brigade was doing. Last time I was there they'd built a miniature city made of paper, almost a perfect duplicate of the real one outside. Back in the projection room, you can see me waving at him—and turning away.

Good-bye? he said, preening his waxy moustache with one hand while holding me with the other. *Oh no. Today, you do not get off that lightly. Today, you are coming with me. Oggi, lei viene con me. No more fun and games, my lad. Today, we are going all the way.*

And with that he took my arm and pulled me through into one of the tunnels leading to the central area. I immediately sensed a change—in atmosphere, perhaps. Or in the increased hum of the machinery. Or maybe it wasn't anything that physical or tangible at all. Maybe it was the words of my grandfather about creatures that weren't quite ready for the outside world (translate: the light of day or the proper light of human congress).

All I knew for sure was that I didn't feel completely comfortable there as those night-time shapes came back to me with hardly any effort on my part. Ready to spring out through the not-quite-solid walls, the wet-to-the-touch and liquid-y-oozy walls.

Do not be afraid, my boy, my grandfather said, sensing my reluctance. *There is nothing here that can harm you. Absolutely nothing. Come along.* He held my hand in his strong grip. *All you have to do is pretend you are back inside your mother, waiting to be born. That is all. You stay with me now and do just that.*

Somehow, that advice and that image didn't help relieve my anxiety much as we made our way up the truly womb-like passageway (or at least what I imagined a womb would look like) towards a green glow in the distance.

The light at the end of the tunnel, my grandfather said with a laugh.

Nor did meeting the occasional creature—obviously newborn, still wobbly and licking itself furiously—make it any better. They would appear suddenly out of the gloom, shimmering like lost souls: some with their eyes still shut; others mewling in a pitiful way and sniffing us up and down.

In fact, my only comfort—and a cold one at that—were the robo-guards, floating slightly above the ground on their magnetic pads as they hummed by on their rounds. No matter how non-human and downright deadly they looked with their red-beam laser eyes and pincers and screwdrivers and soldering kits, at least they were doing something useful—whatever it was—and weren't about to change shape or melt down or gobble me up.

At one point, we passed along the very edge of the central structure, a peripheral walkway that circled it completely. Where we stood, we could look through Plexiglas openings down into a series of gigantic tanks—the green glow I'd seen from a distance. Their contents gurgled and quivered like jelly in the murk as discharges of what I equated with captured lightning ripped through them.

And there were things in them, things that occasionally forced their way partially to the surface before vanishing once again. I wanted to turn away, to catch my breath, to touch something "normal"—but I couldn't. It was as if I had been caught in a vortex of magnetized filings and forced to aim one way only. My face pressed against the Plexiglas, I stared fixedly, as if in a trance, trying to clear up the images that were all fuzzy about the edges.

But each time I almost succeeded, they would vanish or dissolve again—like some not quite caught bit of action on a videotape which you hope, upon repeating, will allow itself to be captured. Will become clear. Will come into focus. But it doesn't. No matter how many times you look.

That is where they make them, my grandfather whispered, mercifully breaking the spell. *And above there—you see it? Suspended from its metal umbilical cord?—that is the control room. The central nervous system, if you will. It is full of computers and electrical equipment and stuff like that, like an eye that never closes. Argus, was that not his name? Only this Argus not only watches over the wool, it actually creates it. Maybe one day you will get to go inside and see how things are done, the alchemy of it all. You might find it not only fascinating but necessary for any future well-being.*

I mentally shook my head. No way. No way was I going to allow myself to be dangled like tender bait above those tanks. No way was I going to risk that. This was as close as I wanted to come—no matter how "fascinating" or "necessary" they might become. Whatever those words meant.

Then, just as quickly, we had turned the corner and were inside the eighth enclosure. It was completely unlike the others. There were no environments and ecosystems here. Instead, this consisted of line after line of long, rectangular structures sectioned off by corridors that ran the length and breadth of the building. These structures—cold-looking and steel-grey in colour with giant transparent ducts sticking out from them and leading to even bigger tubes along the ceiling—were not only placed side by side but stacked on top of each other as well.

Every 10 metres or so, there was a door with a letter and a number on it, made visible by some type of LED sensor or natural spotlight that tracked back and forth across it. At the end of each 50-metre section, open elevators glided silently up and down, stopping according to their own indecipherable patterns.

But, no matter where you were, you could still see through to the other levels because the floors weren't solid but rather made of metal grills spaced a centimetre or so apart. I noticed, with a lurch of my stomach as the elevator shot up several levels, that they stretched out below us as well—and gave the impression you were suspended high above the ground, just one more part of the grid pattern.

But, of course, there's little point describing it. It's all there on video—even if the image can never get the real feeling of terror across: the burning hollowness in the chest; the accelerated thump-a-thump of the heart beat; the leaden deadness of the legs; the cold-sweat, hair rising from the nape of the neck; the feverish working of the brain as it fills in the blanks. As it tries to compensate for lack of proper sensory stimuli.

Welcome to monster row, my grandfather is saying in the video—and I immediately jump, the sound echoing through the building. He is laughing. *No, no. There is nothing to worry about. Only a joke. All the doors are locked. See.* He is trying the door nearest us. It won't open as he rattles it and presses the various coloured buttons along its side. *All the doors but one, that is. The one for us.*

Let's hope those doors stay that way, I find myself thinking. A robo-guard clangs by us, making its rounds. It stops for a moment to scan us, then continues, red eye-band flicking in turn against each of the numbers. I watch it disappear—and then re-appear on the level below us. It doesn't need an elevator and there's no danger of its falling either.

This way, my grandfather says, as he takes me by the arm. *And watch your step. It is a long way down.*

We are crossing before several of the rectangular structures. Despite my grandfather's assurances, I expect any moment some deformed, slobbering, nightmarishly a-glow creature to come oozing out of the dark, trailing gobs of radioactivity—all the monster-movie horrors packed into one. And hungry to boot. To my way of thinking at the time, nothing could be worse than that. But there are no monsters to behold. There is nothing but the sound of our shoes on the metal grating—and the whirring of the occasional guard on one of the other levels.

Eccoci qua, my grandfather is saying as he stops before a door that looks identical to all the rest—except for its unique fluorescent letter and number, of course. *Siamo arrivati.*

He knocks lightly, then passes his card over the flashing, coloured buttons. *Remember now. Do exactly as I say and, above all, do not be afraid. There is no need to be afraid.*

The door slides open. Don't be afraid, I keep repeating to myself. No need to be afraid. Nothing to be afraid of. Yet, I cringe and hunch my shoulders, ready for the worst. Trying to decide whether to squeeze my eyes shut or keep them open. I keep them open. Then shut them. Then open them again halfway, ready at a moment's notice to slam them tight.

At first there's relief—followed by disappointment. A child's disappointment. It's no monster's den, after all, full of maggoty meat, foul stenches and the half-eaten carcasses of its victims. Mental remnants of all those alien monster movies where humans are little more than fodder for some parasitic species' reproductive process. Rather it has the appearance of a poorly lit office of some kind with a large and somewhat rusted metal desk and several rickety chairs the only furniture. Looking back on it, a low-level bureaucrat's modest office, perhaps, in a mid-level government agency, next in line for renovation. Always next in line. Waiting for the papers in triplicate to be processed by the bureaucrat one level above.

There is a man sitting on the other side of the desk. Actually, as you can see, he isn't so much sitting as leaning over with his head cradled on the desk so that all you notice at first glance is the top of his head.

I remember most the perfect gleam of that bald head, the perspiration dripping from it in rivulets, the thick cords of muscle that twitch at the nape of his neck—and the fact the man is sobbing, crying very much like a babe lost in the woods. Sobbing with no effort at self-control.

Shape up, my grandfather is saying sternly. But in Italian, not English. And his voice, as always, acquires a new precision and lilt when speaking the language of his youth. *Otherwise, you'll have red rings around those famous hypnotic eyes of yours. That wouldn't do, now would it? They'll lose their effectiveness. Besides, I've brought someone for you to meet. Someone who needs to be acquainted with you. So look proud now.*

The man lifts his head from the desk and wipes his eyes. Yes, you may have noticed he's very familiar—a more developed version of my drowsy friend in the projection room perhaps. He looks at me and smiles weakly. I smile back but he has already turned away towards my grandfather, as if anxious not to miss out on any of his words.

Do you know what day this is? my grandfather is asking, gently, calmly, and always in Italian. *What special day this is? Do you, my friend?*

The man stands up and shakes his head. He is wearing a fancy uniform, with medals across his chest. Sharp-fitting and nothing like my grandfather's moth-eaten one. He has on newly polished riding boots, fitted into recently pressed khaki pants which bulge out sideways at the thighs. He carries a small whip—a riding crop, I believe it is called—which he occasionally slaps against his pant leg so that it makes a snapping noise.

Everything about him seems majestic, cocky—from the upright, stiff-backed way he walks to the bemused tilt of his head. Only his face gives away the fact that he has been crying and that he is very frightened, perhaps even more frightened than I am.

After sharply pacing the room several times, like a mechanical toy, he stops near my grandfather. I check for signs of disguise. I've heard that monsters could lurk beneath the most innocuous forms, could burst out from the chest of the most ordinary-looking human. But, if there is a monster in there, it is perfectly concealed, perfectly moulded into the vessel of flesh that contains it. Has become one with the host.

No more lessons like last week, please, he is saying in a whining, pleading voice, a voice not at all suited to his bearing or dress and one which I was to hear countless times in the years to come. *I can't take much more of that. I couldn't sleep all night after you left. Promise me you won't show me anything like that again. You must promise!*

No, no, my grandfather is saying pleasantly, patting him on the shoulder. *Your lessons are officially over. I have taught you all you need to know for the time being. In fact, there is only one thing left to complete your education. Or should I say re-education? It is something we provide for all our students sooner or later.*

A test? the man says stiffening. *Are you going to test me? I've got perfect recall, you know.* He taps the side of his head with pride. *I remember everything down to the last detail. Important or not.* He pauses for a moment and then seems to sag. *That's what hurts, sometimes. All those awful memories. All those evil, despicable things I'm supposed to have done. How could I? How were such things possible?* He looks up hopefully. *It is a test, isn't it? Nothing more than a test?*

Yes, you could call it that. A test of your manhood. My grandfather takes him by the arm. *Come. Sit. Here, in your chair. Make yourself comfortable.*

The man allows himself to be led back to his chair. At the time, I remember thinking (or perhaps it only struck me the second or third time around): It has to be a game they're playing. There's this big, strong, muscular he-man in the prime of life being led around by my tiny, emaciated grandfather, my grandfather who can hardly hold himself up most of the time. It has to be a game. The kind adults play, the kind that are so hard to understand.

Now, my grandfather says. *Relax. Think of this as a holiday in the Lake Como region. You have taken a break from your terribly busy schedule. It is a wonderful day, a day to be sipped like fine wine, to be savoured as one of the few remaining before the cruel axe falls.*

My grandfather takes a step back before continuing:

You are in a fancy villa with your wife in one bedroom and your number one mistress in another. You have just finished with them and they are sighing with post-orgasmic pleasure, calling out your name in tiny, love-propelled voices. And you, you stand at the castle window, bare chest out, drinking chilled champagne, eating aphrodisiac oysters and looking out across the Lake.

Really! the man says, brightening. *That sounds like fun. Did that actually happen to me? Did I really do that?*

Of course, you did. You loved them both equally, did you not? Not a millimetre of difference in the feelings you had for them. Or do you not remember?

Yes, yes. Of course. How could I not remember? I was torn between them, wasn't I? Rachele and Claretta. Those were their names. I loved them both. No! Correct that. I <u>still</u> love them both. Passionately! I want them right now. Bring them to me this very instant!

He slams his fist on the desk and tries to look fierce—but even I realize it's just an act, something he's seen someone else do perhaps. The man in the mirror with the fancy uniform and the new riding crop.

That is the spirit, my grandfather says, patting him on the shoulder. *They did not call you the stallion stud for nothing, did they?*

Damn right, they didn't. I earned that title fair and square. Worked my way through those women like a hot knife through creamy butter.

You are right, my grandfather says, hand still on the man's shoulder. *Now, look at my grandson over there. His name is Faustino. A good boy. Although he prefers 'Fausto' in the modern style. Give him your best pose. Hands on your hips, chin and chest thrust forward, and that little cat and mouse smile you are so famous for. After all, he is going to be your final and most important witness.*

To my greatness?

If you wish, to your greatness.

My grandfather stands behind the man as he gazes fixedly at me and smiles. It is an awkward, lopsided smile, not at all natural, a smile that needs plenty of practice. My grandfather is now leaning over the man and whispering something in his ear.

The smile vanishes; the man suddenly becomes very agitated. He is shaking his head vigorously, as if denying something. Then, he stands up in a burst of rage, hurling the chair back so that it slams against the wall and the sound echoes throughout the room. I cringe, afraid he'll attack me.

You bastard! he screams at my grandfather, cutting the air with his whip. *You insubordinate swine! Unpatriotic traitor! How dare you countermand my direct orders! No one disobeys me! I'll have you shot for this.*

Me first, my grandfather is saying, a slight grimace on his face making it impossible to determine if he is smiling or angry.

And, pulling the long-barrelled pistol expertly from its ancient, ratty holster, he fires twice at point blank range—right through the man's skull.

Scene Five: Machinery & Machinations

I smile at the camera whirring above me, following my every move. Then I make rude faces and gestures at it, expose myself before it. Childish, I know. But I don't care. These cameras have always both fascinated and irritated me. The way they record everything—and yet see nothing. It's a bit like staring into the tanks that form the core of the facility.

Yes, I have access to the entire compound now—including the central area and the eighth enclosure. All the tunnels are open to me; all the tubes available to whisk me from one end to the other in a matter of seconds; all the doors swing out of my way at a touch. "Swing," of course, being a figure of speech.

So why am I so untouched by it all? Is it because nothing I do makes any difference? Because no action of mine can cause any harm? Or good, for that matter? But how is such a thing possible? I don't know. Perhaps, this isn't the real core. Just a decoy. Perhaps all the switches and buttons are fakes. Very good replicas that pretend to work like the real ones. All for my benefit. All to make me feel comfortable in my confinement—like providing a series of open cell doors in a prison to give the impression escape is possible.

But something has to be real, no? I must be able to do damage—even if only to the illusion. And why haven't I yet come across those who run the facilities? Why do I get the feeling they're here but always beyond reach, just beyond my touching? That one day I'll push my fingers through a liquid wall and there they'll be—all smug and comfy? Making detailed ticker-tape notes of every single event, and sipping tea or whatever it is cold-hearted, ever-so-ruthlessly-logical scientists sip?

It's not for lack of trying, I assure you. I've examined every square millimetre of these facilities that I possibly could; pushed myself right up against the force field like a mime leaning on a wall only he knows is there; discovered where the robo-guards were stacked—like cordwood, they'd say in the old days. Except that some of these still twitched, still instinctively tried to solder something for old times' sake. Or to scan an eyeball. Each exploration was an adventure, a way to pass the time, a glimmer of hope. But that's all. Nothing more.

Ah, but I'm getting ahead of myself. Look there. Right now, right at this moment, a creature is rising out of the nearest tank. The cameras are focusing on it, capturing its still wet body, its dripping nakedness, recording it for future use—and allowing me to examine it on the nearest monitor. Here it comes. Right on time.

I slide out of the way, into the shadows. I wouldn't want it to see me prematurely (although I've done just that in the past and it has made no difference—or none that I could tell). After passing through the drying stalls and stopping to select a uniform, the baby-blue form-fitting unisex outfit that goes by the name of clothing around here, it steps into one of the giant ducts that shoots it along a see-through tube across the ceiling.

I don't need to follow it to know where it's going—or what it means. It means that the one back in the projection room didn't make it, that without me it shrivelled and wasted away. So this new one will wait for me in that dimly lit office—always in the same office behind the same numbers. It'll wait for me to lead it out into the projection room, to show it the ropes, as it were. To teach it the tricks it needs to know for its limited survival.

Or perhaps it'll be the one so advanced it won't need me to teach it how to survive. Perhaps it'll walk out of the office by itself. The other offices, I've discovered, although they too open to me, yield no secrets. They're duds, false fronts, façades with nothing behind them. At least, they have been until now. But one never knows in here. No one knows when they too will become fleshed-out and real.

Real?

Today, I know exactly what happened on that first April 28. Why, how could I not? I review the details daily, go over them with a fine tooth-comb, frame by frame: stop, reverse, slow, fast-forward. Again and again. I circle around the holographic image from all sides—not to mention top and bottom. I jump into the middle of it and join in the explanation.

But, at the time, those events so traumatized me that, for fifteen years, I remembered nothing about how my grandfather and I got home again. Or the echoing sound of the bullets booming within that office. Or the grey matter and bits of bone that must have splattered out against the nearest wall of the cubicle. Or even if I screamed or fainted or just stood there in a state of total and utter paralysis while tiny wheel-like, armour-plated creatures emerged from the suddenly porous floor and proceeded to cut up and devour the dead man's body, leaving nothing, absolutely nothing behind. Not the tiniest bit of brain or drop of blood.

The Scavengers? The very same creatures that wouldn't respond to our call? That ensured our necessary dissolution? How was I supposed to know any of that? One moment, I was watching a puff of smoke from the barrel of an antiquated gun; the next I was at home in front of the TV, the volume on the organ-transplant game show (*Use It Or Lose It*) down practically to nothing so as not to disturb my grandfather who was lying gravely ill in his room.

I realized the situation was serious—hopeless even—when my father came home early from his work as a government accountant. He would never have done that under ordinary circumstances, always making up some excuse about how busy he was, how he shouldn't be disturbed during his actuarial calculations unless it was a dire emergency. As well, both my parents tip-toed around the house. They whispered; they cried; they shrugged their shoulders. This was definitely a dire emergency. At one point, while my mother bawled her eyes out over some uneaten chicken soup, my father called me over and told me I could go in and say hello if I wanted—but not to expect too much.

When I entered my grandfather's room, I could hardly bear the stench. And it was coming directly from where he lay in bed, pathetically stained sheets pulled up to his throat, and a black patch over one eye. That patch was something I'd never seen before. But I took it as just another symptom of the sudden deterioration and decay. On a par with the smell. How could I know the eye had been lost many years before and was now part of my grandfather's machinations? Or of even deeper cycles of control and torment that would go spiralling down through the ages, often chasing their own tails?

Ah, Faustino, he said in a low, barely audible voice, motioning with his permanently crooked index finger. *Come closer. Come sit beside me.*

He patted the bed. I hesitated for a moment, then took a deep breath and approached. Around me, the walls seemed to vanish, replaced by an endless dark. A velvet empty dark.

Good, good. They wanted to call an ambulance for me. He snorted. He was having trouble breathing, let alone talking. But he continued, taking deep breaths between words and phrases, taking gulps of air, each less effective than the previous. *Can you imagine? I told them it was a waste of time. I would kill myself first before allowing them to take me to a hospital. They have machines in those hospitals, machines that can keep you alive forever. Forever! And without your permission either. Did you know that?*

I swallowed hard and shook my head, although I <u>did</u> know about the machines in some vague childish way.

Well, I have seen them, he said, suddenly regaining some of his strength and his voice. *They are like mechanical cocoons, spinning their webs round and round you. Turning you into something you are not. Something so unnatural not even your own mother would recognize you. Oh God, the horror. No, not me. I am going to die right here and there is nothing they can do about it. Nothing! But, before I go, I want you to understand something.*

He leaned back on his pillows for a moment, filthy pillows encrusted in spittle and God knows what else. Then he continued: *We are accomplices, you and I. Got that? Siamo dei*

*complici. And you have been given an opportunity like no other. It
is important you understand the significance of that. Do you, Faustino? Tell me that you do.*

Yes, grandpapa, I said, not because I really did know what
he was talking about but in the hope that agreement would
allow me the quickest exit out of that rapidly vanishing room,
a room defined only by the odour of death. For what else
could that stench be but my grandfather rotting from the inside, about to burst like a wormy cabbage—or about to reveal
his alien core?

*Good, good. My little Faustino. I always knew you were the right
person for the job. In fact, the only person. Is that not right?*

Yes, grandpapa.

Closer, he said. *Come closer.*

I inched forward. His fingers—looking like pieces of gnarled
oak—reached out blindly towards mine. I pulled my hand
away, suddenly no longer anxious for the feel of my grandfather's rough grip, the warmth of his blood pulsing through
those ravaged arteries and beating against my own.

It is up to you now to finish what has been set in motion.

What?

He suddenly jerked up in bed, good eye blazing. *You must!*
A blast of his fetid breath blew my way and I almost fainted.
Promise me you will!

Yes, grandpapa, I said, getting weaker by the moment—
as if he'd sapped me to gain his few moments of renewed
strength. Now, even the floor was spinning away from me,
swirling and twisting like toffee being pulled apart.

Your parents have proved useless for the task, he said, sighing
and falling back on the pillow. *More than useless. They live in
a very small world, afraid to make a move if it has not been pre-
programmed. Afraid even of taking the subway, of all things. They do
not know what war is, let alone the ultimate battle. I could not very
well have taken them to the zoo, could I?*

No, grandpapa.

*No, of course not. They would have seen it simply as one more
miracle of modern technology, of man's control over his world. That*

son of mine in particular, too busy with his calculations to make any sense of what is really important. So I have left everything to you. Do you understand?

I nodded, thinking: What is this "everything" he's leaving for me? The gun, maybe, safely back in its holster? That would indeed be a swell thing to have.

Good. You will not get it right away, of course. But rest assured it will be there for you when you come of age. I have seen to that. I have seen to it all. He tapped the side of his nose. *They did not call me La Volpe for nothing, you know, in those days when life was still worth living. And worth dying for.*

He shut his eyes. Or eye, rather. I waited for him to say more. To explain, perhaps, what this "coming of age" was or when it would take place. Or even to simply dismiss me with a wave of the hand as he would normally do when he was busy poring over one of his stinky tomes. But, after half a minute or so, I could see he planned to do neither so I eased myself on tiptoe out of the room—and glad of it, too.

My grandfather died later that evening, insistent to the end that he wouldn't be displaced. But, because my parents were so embarrassed by the idea of having someone voluntarily die in their house, they requested that the ambulance only remove his body in the middle of the night—when the neighbours were in bed. The unnatural hum of the robot stretcher woke me up, however, and I saw the outline of his body then, beneath the odour-absorbent red sheet, being lowered down the stairs and out the front door. I remember waving weakly as he floated by.

The following day, after my father had gone to work, several very serious-looking men came and carefully labelled and crated all my grandfather's belongings: papers, books, records, tapes and whatever else they could find. My mother tried to convince them that some of the stuff was junk and ought to be thrown away—his old razor, for example. Or the moth-eaten clothes in the back of the closet. But they said that wasn't possible. They had their orders. Nor would they tell her where it was being taken. I watched from the upstairs window as they loaded everything on a truck and sped away, splashing mud to all sides.

While my mother was still busy on the computer phone, passing the news on to ever more-distant relatives, I sneaked into what had been my grandfather's room. It was horribly empty—except for a small pile of dirt that had been swept to one corner. I sifted through the dirt and found a tiny scrap of paper and the needle from one of his recording machines. I wrapped the needle in the paper and put it in my pocket. Suddenly, I wanted my grandfather to return. I wanted the room back the way it had been. I wanted time to stop, to reverse itself. And I thought that, if I concentrated hard enough, I could make it happen.

But my mother did exactly the opposite—and she won out. She spent the entire day scrubbing the room clean from top to bottom with some mighty powerful disinfectants. Then, she hired a carpenter to open up one of the walls, the one in common with the master bedroom, and had a desk, computer and shelving installed. It was to be my father's long-awaited study so that he'd no longer have to do his income tax calculations and stock predictions on the kitchen counter.

As for my grandfather's room in the basement, I sat on the stairs and watched my father's giant shadow pour all the wine down the drain and then carry the glass containers to the recycling bin. Then, he returned with a gauze mask on and sprayed the room with some type of disinfectant. When I asked at supper why he had done that, he mumbled something about cleanliness and disease. To me, however, it seemed their way of removing every single trace of my grandfather, even the odour of his memory itself.

And, for the next fifteen years, it worked. For the next fifteen years, the image of my grandfather was that of an eccentric but sweet old man who had taken me to a place full of extinct animals, perhaps almost as extinct as his kind had become. Sometimes in my dreams at the boarding school a nightmare room would crop up (filled with glinting wheels within wheels) and I would wake up uneasy, covered in perspiration. But that was it—until a registered letter arrived for me at the university where I was in my last year of an economics degree and already engaged to be married. The letter requested that I present myself at a lawyer's office—my grandfather's lawyer—to receive my "inheritance".

That meant interrupting my studies and leaving Evelyn, my fiancée, behind to travel back to the town where my parents still lived. I called them to find out what this so-called inheritance might be but they couldn't help me. My father advised me instead to stay put, to ignore the whole thing. After all, it couldn't have been more than a few musty books. Or a few crates of records that could no longer be played as all the machines were either obsolete or in museum showcases. My mother warned me that the trip might be dangerous— lots of strangers infesting the roads between cities—and that I was taking an unnecessary risk leaving my fiancée behind unprotected, open to the proposals of any unattached man who might fancy her.

Same old father; same old mother.

But something in the letter reached out to me over all those years. Maybe, it was something as simple as seeing the name "Faustino" again. Or just a way of breaking up the monotony of too many years doing the same thing, too many years filled with well-orchestrated, mapped-out plans for the future. Or maybe I just wanted to defy my parents whom, deep down, I'd never forgiven for their treatment of my grandfather's body and the places he had inhabited.

In any case, I decided I owed it to my grandfather to at least honour his last wish, to at least see what he had to offer before going on with my own life. Besides, partly due to the fact my parents never spoke of him and would change the subject when his name came up and partly because he'd left such an impression on my five-year-old mind, there was an aura of mystery surrounding him that I couldn't resist, a feeling that things had been left hanging. It was time to clear the air, to set the record straight, to get to the bottom of things—whatever that meant.

SCENE SIX: THE RETURN

I've triggered some sort of alarm by climbing to the edge of the nearest tank. Lights flash; doors clank shut and open again; sirens make shrill sounds all around me. So what, you say? If there's no one there, what good does an alarm do? And you would be right. I imagine there was a time when robo-guards would descend on an intruder from all directions, when doors would seal and laser weaponry slither out, ready to blast the unauthorized and probably contaminated object to kingdom come.

Or, at least, the masters of this place would come out to see what the problem was, who or what had dared disturb their Buddha-like existence set in contemplation of the higher order of things. There <u>had</u> to have been such a time. But there's no longer any need, I suppose. My entry was an accident—albeit a carefully planned accident—and no one else now has the means or desire to get in.

The alarms are remnants of a long-crystallized past, a game I play with the facility. And it knows this game intimately. The alarms squeal, buzz, wail and ring each time I blast a monitor. Or get too close to the cloning tanks. Or hurl half a robo-guard from the top of a metal mountain. Now, they're sounding because they think they know what my plans are. *No, no, no!* they seem to be screaming. *That's not the right thing to do! That's blasphemy! That's against the laws of nature!*

But they'll grow tired and turn themselves off soon enough. It's all pre-programmed, you see. I sit on the platform, looking down at the murky, opaque liquid, the little green webbed fingers that reach up towards me. Or is it the light they desire, the promise once more of photosynthesis? I'm no longer frightened of these tanks and what may lurk within them. After all, this isn't where the real horror's found, now is it?

In fact, creation is quite prosaic, I say to myself. Then, because I like the sound of that, I repeat the words out loud for the benefit of the ever-watchful cameras: *Creation is quite prosaic—be it the stimulation of ultra-violet light through green muck or the explosion of little wigglers in search of eggs.*

My grandfather's legacy came in the form of a small trunk-like wooden box, covered in faded stamps, over-written addresses and his name in huge, bold, capital letters: **FAUSTO GIULIO CONTADINO.** A palimpsest, I think the term was, parchment used and re-used down through the centuries. The box was the same one he'd carried with him, my father said when he saw it, the day he'd set sail for the "New World."

That's what my grandfather had always called it, his only name for it. Or rather: *La Terra Nuova.* The place of new beginnings for old, jaded, worn-out souls tired of the parochial squabbling and the small-town mentality of the "Old World". A clean slate and no ties. The reality was often very different: a world as closely jealous and tight as the old, a world where others had already made their mark and weren't willing to share with newcomers, especially newcomers who'd fought against them only a few years before.

I don't know what I expected to find inside the box—valuable stocks and bonds, perhaps; antiques now worth millions; the key to some treasure trove or the secret to a better world. Maybe even the rocket fuel ingredient or hyperdrive formula that would make me wealthy beyond my dreams, that would allow me access to one of those orbiting colonies for the mega-rich and ultra-powerful and where life was rumoured to be one unending drug-induced orgy.

There was nothing of the sort. In fact, about the only thing that in any way fit the description was my grandfather's gun, oiled and ready to use. Some antique dealer might find that valuable. The rest: a tightly-sealed Mason jar half-filled with a clear liquid and labelled "Formaldeide" in my grandfather's meticulous scrawl; a badly faded photograph showing a half-dozen or so men, rifles in hand, standing triumphantly over what looked like the mutilated body of another; a circled newspaper ad asking for people to take part in some sort of genetic experiment; an envelope with my name on it (always "Faustino"); one of those musty, leather-bound Bibles with the traditional lockets of hair pressed between the front cover and the first page—two of them, with tiny hand-written labels that read "Joe" and "Rosa"; and a small cigar box that would normally have held jewellery but in this case contained an artificial eyeball, a plastic card and a slip of paper with the words "Bella Ciao" written on it.

I tore open the envelope:

Caro Faustino,

Now you know the whole story. That man I shot was, of course, Benito Mussolini, Il Duce, vicious dictator and self-styled Don Juan deluxe. Since I was responsible in part for re-creating him, it was my duty to kill him. It was my duty to educate and then exterminate that Benito Mussolini as quickly as possible, before the world discovered his existence, before he once again walked the Earth, head held at an insufferable angle and a danger to all decent folk.

You must understand that, caro Faustino, when I first saw that ad in the paper, I did not know what to expect. At the cloning centre, quite a bustling hive of activity at the time, they said they were looking for people willing to take part in an unusual experiment. I told them I was the man for that as I was always looking for unusual things to do. To put it simply, they wanted some of my genetic material so they could reproduce me, somewhat like they had done to the animals. Immortalized. A guaranteed non-extinction.

I thought about it for a while and was actually tempted. Who would not be? But then I decided against it. I suggested they were wasting their time reproducing someone like me. An insignificant nobody. Un niènte. What they needed was someone who had made an impact, someone the world would instantly recognize. And I told them I had something better than my genetic material for them. I had an actual piece of Benito Mussolini, the preserved flesh of my countryman. They did not ask me how I had obtained that piece, how I

*had stooped down and cut it off the still quivering body, how I had
stuffed it into a jar to keep it from rotting. They simply jumped at it,
endless hunger in their eyes, their hands so shaky they could hardly
hold the jar steady.*

*You are probably asking: 'Why? Why would I do something like
that? Why would I help in an experiment to bring someone like that
back to life, especially since I not only fought against Il Duce but was
actually involved in his assassination at Giulino di Mezzegra that
fateful April 28, 1945?' Yes, my proudest moment. I was one of those
who piled his body on top of 12 others, including that of his mistress.
The hatred we felt that day was unrelenting.*

*And perhaps that is the reason I wanted to see him alive one more
time—to once again feel that pure unadulterated hatred. It would
give me something to live for after all those years of merely existing,
of wandering about like an eternal stranger. And I did experience
that surge when I confronted a man who not only looked like Mussolini but, in some essential way, actually was the late dictator re-
incarnate.*

*That is, until he opened his mouth to speak. I discovered then he
was nothing but a blank copy, simply a container. There was emptiness inside him—not malice. He was clean, innocent, unconcerned.
A slap in the face to the entire human race, to those who had suffered
so horribly under his boot and had fought so nobly to destroy him the
first time. So, pretending I was helping them conduct a study into the
nature of evil (even if only second rate), I agreed to use my information to re-fill him, to teach him all the atrocities 'he' had committed in
the name of la patria and fascism.*

*Each time you and I went to the Petting Zoo, I showed him docu-
mentary footage of the war, footage so dangerously collected and so
zealously guarded. I read him detailed and gruesome descriptions of
what his secret police had done to their fellow countrymen, of the
Fosse Adreatine, the discovery of horribly mutilated bodies all with
their hands tied behind them and a single bullet to the back of the
skull. I talked about my own experiences in the mountains, hiding
from Nazis and fascist Italians alike.*

*And then, when he was once again the Mussolini we all knew
and hated, the arrogant, posturing, egocentric Duce with ever-faith-*

ful wife and lengthening string of mistresses, when it was once again the same date all those decades later, I shot him. With you as my witness. And I was sure that day I would never get out of the facilities alive. After all, I had just assassinated their most prized possession, a creation worth more than all the snow leopards and passenger pigeons put together. Or so I thought. But they acted as if nothing had happened, as if it were just another day at the clone farm.

It was only after we got home that I realized what had really taken place. If they had one, then. . . . You get the picture. But it was too late for me. When they let me walk out of that facility unharmed, with the robo-guard's pleasant 'Good day to you and your grandchild' ringing in my ears, I knew I was done for, that I had failed, that I would never be allowed back. And that is where you come in.

Indeed, that's where I came in—never to go out again. My grandfather's story was so incredible, so beyond anything I'd imagined possible, that I just had to check it out, despite the fact that my sources all told me the facility had been closed down years before.

Violations, my father said. *Serious, very serious violations. The directors were charged with unspecified crimes. It's all classified. I tried pulling some strings to get to the bottom of it but was told in no uncertain terms it wouldn't be healthy for my career. So I stopped asking.*

But that only made me more curious. So, after sending an e-mail pouch explaining the situation to my fiancée (little realizing at the time it would be my last communication with her), and with my grandfather's wooden box and Evelyn's love letters under my arm, I headed for the subway. My parents—looking more aged and forlorn than ever—pleaded with me to forget the whole thing.

At the last minute, when he realized I was determined to do this, my father offered to drive me. But I could tell he was scared shitless just standing out on the street like that. I'd hate to see what he'd look like after an hour's ride to the slag heaps, to "the end of the world" as he'd so often called it. So I held out my hand and thanked him anyway. He looked at my hand for a moment before taking it.

Be careful, he whispered, looking around. *No one seems to know what's out there, not even the department bigwigs.*

I'll be careful, dad.

And try to make it back for dinner, he said as he turned to re-enter. *I know your mom won't rest until all this is over.*

Shouldn't take long, I said, as jauntily as possible. *Give Mom a hug for me.*

Did he? Give her a hug, I mean. I don't know. Knowing him, probably not. Too embarrassing. A pat on the shoulder, maybe. Or a re-assuring shrug. Someday I might find out for sure. Ha! That's a laugh, isn't it?

The subway hadn't changed much in the 15 years since I'd last taken it: a little more greasy, a little more dilapidated, a little more grinding. The rat beetle collectors were still poking about in the tunnels with their nooses, looking for that one specimen—the albino, the wingless, the double-headed—that would give them instant credit during the next chomping tournament. But, as usual, most of the catch was very ordinary-looking: squealing, fiercely objecting insects blinded by the sudden lights.

As for the subway car itself, it could easily have been the same one—with the graffiti so thick now there was no way to make out individual phrases and the other passengers sprawled about as if this were their permanent home. I kept one hand on my grandfather's trunk and the other beneath my coat, on the trigger of the gun. In my pocket was the eyeball, my grandfather's fake eyeball, unseeing but still sending out its coded electronic messages, and the pass-card. The keys to another world, if not necessarily a better one. And one that couldn't very well be expecting me.

How long ago that was now, I don't remember, although it would probably be very easy for me to find out. One of the things I do remember is that, despite my initial fears, I had no problem whatsoever getting in. And the fact that the cameras whirred and started tracking me the moment the iris shut, closing off any view of the outside world. At the same time, I realized right away something was wrong, that my father may have been correct in his assumption the facilities had been shut down. Or an attempt had been made to do so.

For one thing, there were no robo-guards to greet me, friendly or otherwise, and no sign of anyone else being on the grounds. In fact, I had the distinct impression everything had only started up again the moment I stepped beyond the force field—like some amusement park where the rides are dormant until a visitor breaks an invisible beam. So maybe I had been expected after all. Or someone like me. But what disturbed me even more was that I could see no mechanism for getting out again. The iris had vanished completely, without the tiny slit as guidance. When I placed the pass-card over the spot where the iris had been in the past, nothing happened. And my grandfather's eye didn't help either.

Oh well, I'm saying to myself the first time this happened (can't you see me saying it to myself?), I might as well get this over with. Then I'll worry about getting out, about getting on with my life—a steady job with the government, marriage, children, a vacation home on one of the more affordable orbiters. Or at least a time-sharer with a bunch of office pals.

There I am, safely inside one of the tunnel tubes, whooshing towards the eighth enclosure, a determined look on my face. Along the way, I decide to stop at my favourite marsh. It's a disappointment. Everything seems so different now, so prosaic and unmagical. Totally lacking in magic. By standing up, I can look across the entire walkway, removing any sense of mystery. And the animals that come up to me all have an air of tiredness about them, as if they've become resigned. Or handed in their resignations—for the second time.

I guess that's what happens when the creators lose interest, shrink into the background. For the second time. Fur falls off; wings atrophy; limbs become arthritic. I decide it's best if I don't pay the other animals a visit: my favourite leopard, the emus, the humped-back whales. Perhaps their eyes will no longer glint; perhaps they've turned cold and cloudy like marbles. Or like the eye I carry in my pocket, my grandfather's trick for getting around those who first started up these facilities.

Or maybe he didn't trick them after all. Maybe they were aware all along what he had in mind. After all, they must have known that his eye was artificial, a stray-bullet legacy from his partisan days—or so he claimed, although as my father pointed out, he would have been barely a child at the time. And they must have known that the eye could be passed from person to person. So, they pretended not to catch on. It was part of their elaborate trap.

Somewhere on high, swinging on their leisurely machinery, sipping their artificial tea, they're laughing right now at my grandfather's expense. How could a peasant warrior have ever hoped to outwit the combined forces of post-modern technology? I was there because they'd wanted me there and because they had plans for me.

On the other hand, perhaps I was the one who'd changed and the creatures might be exactly the same as I remembered them, bright-eyed and bushy-tailed and eager to please. When they become too many, too packed in, the tiny creatures, the Scavengers, emerge uncurling from the ground to devour the dead ones along the edges. I can't make up my mind which is worse: eternal decay without death or life filled with sudden and random munchings. Best to avoid them in either case.

In the projection, I'm standing undecided in front of a familiar door. I find it easily amid the maze of identical doors and levels because the number, long forgotten, springs suddenly to mind (that overhanging ledge again). I take a deep breath and walk in, not bothering to knock.

Il Duce is up against the far wall, hands thrust straight in the air and literally shaking in his boots—the only things he's wearing. Thigh-high, pliant leather boots. Two naked women cower in the corner, arms about each other, strategically covering one another's private parts.

You haven't come to shoot me again, have you? he says in Italian, barely keeping his voice under control.

I didn't shoot you last time, I say, the words difficult in a language that I haven't spoken in years. In fact, I'm surprised I can still remember it.

Please, he says, reverting to English as he gets down on his knees in front of me, head bowed in a posture of utter submission. *I haven't done anything. Those atrocities, those aren't mine. You know that better than I do. Those memories were put there. I was made to have them. You must understand that. And I had no choice but to accept them. You can't imagine what it's like being a total blank. You'll grasp at anything. Can you shoot a man for that?*

No, you can't shoot a man for that, the younger, more beautiful woman—later I learn her name is Claretta—is saying in a timid voice. *He's the man I love. Doesn't love count for anything these days?*

I love him, too, the other—Rachele—says. *He's a great man. He's changed the course of history. He's made the trains run on time. He's given Italian men back their pride. All the women want his babies. He'll create a race of super-Latin lovers to re-populate the world. There'll be peace and prosperity everywhere.*

That's right, Claretta continues. *Haven't you noticed the world is empty? It's time to re-populate, don't you think?*

I look from one to the other. With each word, they become more bold—and no longer bother covering up. They come at me from opposite directions, obviously meaning to do me harm. Confused, I place the pistol in the Mussolini's ear, feel the tip of the barrel fit snugly in his ear. The women gasp and hug one another—like heroines in a melodrama. I pull the trigger; the man recoils with the anticipated shock. But it isn't to be—this time. I've made sure the hammer falls on an empty chamber. And there's only a click.

I'll be back, I say. *You can count on it. Your days are numbered.*

I close the door behind me and lean against the nearest wall. Suddenly, I'm shaking and covered in sweat, thinking: How was it possible for my grandfather to pull the trigger so coolly, without panic or remorse? Without even a second thought, it seemed? Was it that hate he'd talked about in his letter? If so, it was an emotion felt towards a pseudo-Mussolini, a fake sociopath, a papier maché megalomaniac with too much blubber around his waist and lips that quivered like a little girl. But then again, my grandfather was himself also a fake, relying on second-hand emotions.

Despite my threat to Mussolini and his women, I'm determined not to return to that room. I spend the rest of the afternoon searching around in the area where the opening is supposed to be. But I can't find it. I look for something that will allow me to communicate with the outside world—phone, modem, radio, radar, satellite dish, anything. They exist—in large numbers and around every corner. But there's no sending out signals or messages. The only sounds and images are from inside—e-mail messages from one computer to another; satellite shots of the various eco-systems; static hum on the radio. I think: *Well, it looks as if I won't be making it back for dinner, after all. Maybe tomorrow I'll have more luck.*

But I don't have more luck that day—or the day following. In the end—a week, a month, six months later—I find myself back in that room. The man called Mussolini is panting heavily, arching back, belly slapping against Claretta's as the two make passionate love on the floor. The other woman, Rachele, is lying in the corner with a contented look on her face and doing her toenails. Mussolini looks up when I enter and, without consummation, immediately pulls out to take his customary kneeling position before me and to personally direct the barrel of my gun into his ear.

How many more are there like you? I ask.

Like me? He looks up coyly. The make-up on his face is running because of the sweat. *I don't understand. I'm the only one. There are no others.*

You're lying! I scream—and smash him across the back of the head with the pistol butt. He falls face first, a trickle of blood sliding from the wound. The two women let out a simultaneous yelp and make as if to come to his aid. *Don't move! You're as guilty as he is.*

I beg of you, Mussolini says, clutching at my foot. *Don't hurt them. They mean no harm. Hangers-on, that's all. All they want is a taste of power. It's only natural. The human thing to do.*

You'd better tell me what I want to know then before things turn nasty. Exactly how many Mussolinis are roaming around this place?

But . . . but there's only one of me. There can only be but one. Isn't that so, girls?

They both nod.

So, you've seen no others? All three shake their heads. *Good.* I replace my gun and head for the door. *I'll be back soon. Then, we'll talk some more.*

And talk we did—after I myself had learned everything I could, spending night and day in the projection room. I told him all about his life, from his birth in the village of Predappio in 1883 to his ignominious death in 1945, slaughtered like a pig and then hung by the heels from a scaffolding in Milan; from his ascension to power in 1922 at the head of Fascist troops marching into Rome to his removal in 1943 by King Victor Emmanuel.

I told him of his campaigns in Ethiopia and Spain, of his alliance with Hitler, of the countless letters written by his many admirers—especially the women ("Dear Benito: I have saved my maidenhood for you. You're the only one who can deflower me"), of the mistresses (*more than one?* says Claretta with a frown), the sycophants and intellectuals who vied for his favour.

So, am I Mussolini now? he asked after the final film had been shown, the final atrocities laid out before him, topped off by pictures of his head being propped up by a bayonet, flies burrowing into his nostrils to lay their eggs.

It's now or never. I've told you all I know.

He stood up, cutting off the image of the celluloid Claretta as the camera panned across her, half-naked and also dangling by the heels—while the Claretta in the room wept in the corner, her head on Rachele's shoulder.

Funny, he said. *You tell me I'm Mussolini. But I just don't feel like him. In fact, I don't think I'd know how it would feel to feel like him.*

Don't be a fool, I said. *You're going to keep coming out of those tanks until you __do__ feel like him.*

That's impossible, he said. *No two men can occupy the same memories.*

Are you quite sure?

Well. . . .

But for the longest time, I couldn't find the final piece to the puzzle, the thing that would make him realize who he was. We got so far, to the point where he had all the knowledge necessary, all the gestures needed, and yet there was something missing. And there was no way I could pull the trigger if he didn't believe he was Mussolini, if he didn't believe he was the man who'd committed those atrocities—thus forcing me to accept that truth as well. Even then, I wasn't sure I would be able to do it. Wasn't sure I had my grandfather's visceral hatred and contempt to guide me.

Over and over again, I analyzed the videotape of that first time, that first visit with my grandfather. I was looking for something my grandfather had done, something out of the ordinary. Nothing. I questioned the computer at length. It answered patiently—as it always did—but never what I wanted to hear. It claimed it knew only what it had been programmed to know. And who had programmed it? Why, I had, of course. I said I remembered doing no such thing. Perhaps I, too, had been programmed, it suggested. To forget I had programmed it. And we kept going in circles.

In my frustration, I pulled out my revolver and opened fire on the nearest terminal. The terminal fizzed and shorted, throwing up on the screen a garble of electronic gibberish—long sequences of numbers, strange symbols, backwards writing and ever-changing formulae. From the title, which repeated itself several times in the course of the scrolling, I was able to recognize it as the actual program for the creation of the Mussolinis, the program that directed the tanks in the putting together of Il Duce's DNA sequences and chromosome combinations.

I was about to fire another bullet into it, to put it out of its electronic misery, when I noticed, right in the middle of a string of commands, the words *Bella Ciao* flashing out at me in all their obviousness. Jesus, I said, as I pumped the screen and surrounding area with bullets, setting off yet another string of alarms, how could I have been so stupid?

The next time I visited the dimly lit office, both Claretta and Rachele flung themselves at me while Mussolini sat without expression at his desk. It was as if they sensed my discovery. First, the two women pleaded, calling on our shared humanity. Didn't I, too, have a mother? They realized their mistake the moment they'd spoken the words. In desperation, they offered their bodies in exchange for sparing him.

I thought of my fiancée back at the university and the guilt I would inevitably suffer. Nevertheless, I immediately accepted. They were good, very good, especially when they worked in tandem. But I saw no reason to make sparing Mussolini a condition for my sexual satisfaction. After all, I could have them anytime I wanted—and Mussolini couldn't do anything about it.

That's exactly what I said the next time I visited Il Duce, the two women in tow. I described to him in minute detail what I had been doing with his wife and mistress. Better yet, I brought in videotapes of our long nights together, our wild and dramatic couplings within sight of the tanks.

You have a good technique, he said. *Very tender and yet aggressive at the same time. I myself tend to be a little too hesitant when it comes to the crunch, the final je ne sais quoi. Don't you agree, Claretta?*

Well. . . , Claretta began.

Idiot! I said. *The real Mussolini would have made me swallow several bottles of castor oil by now. Then, he would have shoved a greased bayonet up my ass. And, after the wounds had festered and gangrened, he would have fed me to the pigs he still kept on his ancestral farm in Predappio.*

But Mussolini wasn't to be moved. The man who once had boasted that every woman in Italy had the hots for him now sat there like a flatulent eunuch. Until, of course, I leaned towards him and whispered gently in his ear—exactly the way my grandfather had done so long ago. The same look— a combination of twitching frustration and volcanic hate— crossed his face.

You'll pay dearly for this, he said, picking up a letter opener and rushing blindly towards me.

I guess I will, I said—and fired.

At that moment, at the moment I pulled the trigger, I realized Mussolini wasn't the only one who couldn't control himself, who was linked to an inescapable destiny. There was no way I could not have fired. *Bella Ciao* worked on both of us. I turned and, before the rage subsided, put Claretta and Rachele out of their miseries as well.

Then I waited for the Scavengers to come rolling out, their metal carapaces rattling along the floor as they extended themselves to their full lengths, their hooded eyes glistening and occasionally looping out on springy stalks. It was over in a matter of seconds.

Scene Seven: The Truth

How many times had I done that now? There's no way to tell really because my gun is always fully loaded and looking as if it has never been discharged when I wake up in the morning. If I hurl the weapon away, it finds its way back to my side—or one like it anyway. In here, cloning guns (or food or computers) is child's play. And each time, after I've eliminated a Mussolini, another can be seen rising from the tanks, still wet, flopping towards the intake ducts to take the eliminated (assassinated? murdered?) one's place.

There's an endless supply, recycled no doubt by the Scavengers. And it doesn't help if I incinerate the body before the creatures have a go at it. Or burn the entire room to the ground, sparks falling countless levels through the wire mesh floors. No new flesh is needed for the regeneration. I assume the genetic imprint—provided by my grandfather in that sealed Mason jar—has long ago been fed to the computers.

Each time a new Mussolini is born, you can see the DNA molecules being replicated on the screens, flashing in three-dimensional increments till they click into place. Always the same, with never an aberration, never an imperfection—except for the built-in ones needed to create human life. And Claretta and Rachele? I can only assume some part of their genetic pattern was stuck to Mussolini when my grandfather did his hatchet job all those years ago.

At the same time, my quest to discover what happened to the original directors and employees of the facility continues. Once, using a cherry-picker contraption to manoeuvre up close, I tried to get into the room above the tanks, the room that my grandfather had pointed out to me long ago as the control centre. I searched for an opening but there was no obvious way to enter—only a series of windows through which I could see wall upon wall of monitors, each one showing a different part of the facility, tracking in the eerie silence as the control room moved back and forth over the tanks.

Several cameras had even been placed within the tanks themselves. Occasionally, half-formed yet still amorphous creatures swam up to them, peered into the lenses, their faces even more distorted than usual. In the middle of the room, an empty chair, one of those captain's chairs, spun slowly. After a fruitless attempt to smash one of the windows (sledgehammer, gun, even ramming the cherry picker itself), I settled back and watched the comings and goings of the latest Mussolini and his entourage, which was growing larger by the minute.

Now, he had a series of mistresses, poets who declaimed his genius, intellectuals writing learned tomes on the advantages of fascism, historians re-writing the past. All the trappings, in other words, of the dictator. Okay, so maybe Rachele and Claretta were the only "real" persons in his entourage, the others mere holographic images thrown off by the Mussolini's personal projector. But none of that helped me. Nor did the fact that I was often witness to the intimacies of which even hardened dictators are capable, the soft gestures, the loaf of bread shared with a peasant family from his paternal village, the genuine delight in discovering another Alpine mountain stream—even in the dire days of the ill-fated Republic of Salo when Il Duce was a hunted man. No, none of that brought me any closer to what I wanted to know, to a resolution of my own situation.

That's when I went on my first wave of calculated destruction, hoping to hit the "eject" button, the lever that would shut off the energy shield, the switch that would blow everything sky high—making the inside and the outside one again. But nothing ever happened. In my frustration, I took sledge-hammers to the tanks, placed explosives in the passageways, slashed the thickly-wrapped bundles of electrical wiring. I even managed to sever the umbilical cord that held the control room high in the air, sending it toppling into the tank below it. To no avail.

I went to sleep with the smell of devastation and ruin in my nostrils, with the thought that the force field had collapsed at last, had tired of my misfit vandalism and finally yielded for the sake of peace and quiet, if nothing else. I dreamt that my way was clear to the outside world, a world where I could once again taste the acid rain water on my tongue, soak up the cancer-causing sun, breathe the asbestos-fibred air, look up at the unattainable space colonies in all their blinking, star-twinkling splendour.

The morning, however, brought only disillusion. Nothing had changed. Nothing has changed. It's as if the facility is actually made of some sort of three-dimensional onion skin. You manage to strip one layer off and another immediately takes its place—identical down to the last detail.

When I'm not in one of my periodic fits of destruction, I'm busy asking myself: What's the point? The facilities are sealed off. There's no way to communicate with the outside world. These Mussolinis will never see the light of day, never get to play John The Baptist to Hitler's Christ. Why not let them go beyond their April 28's? Better still: why teach them their names in the first place? Or whisper the words that obviously serve as a triggering mechanism, bringing all the memories together like a ragged bundle of twigs, the *fascio* that gave the original movement its name? Why not leave them a *tabula rasa*, blank, bumping into objects they can't place, dancing to the tune of memories that flicker just beyond reach, lacking the proper connections to make any real connections?

There are times when I think I know why. As a moral, responsible human being I can't take that chance, I tell myself with the utmost conviction. The risk is too great. One of these Mussolinis—the one sitting in the projection room, the one heading for the eighth enclosure, the one now being born—could find a way out, could be let out. Or it might be all of them at once. And it wouldn't matter if he (they) were repentant or not, if he (they) had learned his (their) lesson from history, if he (they) found himself (themselves) up as Nobel Peace Prize nominees. The truth is that particular period is one scar that won't heal, that can't be allowed to heal.

Several times, a proto-Mussolini has asked me to grant him forgiveness for what his genetic forefather did, absolving himself of blame.

I have these two women to love, he'll argue. *That's more than enough for me. You can have the power if you want it. It's all yours for the taking. All of it: the armies, the bureaucrats, the conquered lands, the obsequious poets, the brutalized peasants, the lackey, kiss-ass intellectuals. Especially those lackey intellectuals. I've really had my fill of them.*

That's impossible, I say, somewhat sadly. *I have a racial memory to uphold. We have always executed our tyrant dictators. Or driven them to suicide. You had the privilege of serving as an example, almost prototypical. You can't ruin that now. Besides, you have an image to live up to—even if you did go down on your knees like a dog before the partisans executed you. Even if you befouled yourself and felt the purgative powers of every single drop of castor oil you forced down the gullets of your opponents. Even if you had your balls removed and cast to the genetic winds—to end up here in this unique version of hell eternal.*

But, lately, however, I've come to the realization that's only part of the reason—an excuse really. The truth is that the Mussolini clones are little more than a distraction—somewhat like the reconstructed animals in the other enclosures, the friendly cockroaches and cuddly cobras, the koala bears and lemurs. Cute toys. In the dark nights when I've managed to escape (beneath a computer shell or some other place where the cameras can't find me), it has struck me that Mussolini isn't the real enemy. That honour must go to the facility itself.

Why do I say that? The thoughts hurt. They resist clarity. But I know it has to do with nightmares. It has to do with the original claims of those who put these facilities together—and then so conveniently made <u>themselves</u> extinct. It has to do with the assertion that they did it to keep things alive for eternity, to ensure that we wouldn't go the way of the dodo. Or the household cat.

But—and once again the ideas are painful, fuzzy, with a tendency to vanish with the artificial light of day—the actual result seems to be the eradication of memory, the making obsolete of the very concept of memory. And no one outside this force field is aware of that—if they still exist, if they're still out there. Only those trapped inside know what's going on. The ones who can do little about it, the ones who are actually contributing to its success.

Of late, I have done my best to ensure that my own memories won't go astray. That's one of the reasons I tolerate the video-cameras and spend a great deal of time talking into laser disc machines, expressing my thoughts and feelings in detail. Just as I'm doing this very moment. I've even broached the subject with the latest Mussolini, introducing a new parameter into the equation of dictator and executioner—with not entirely felicitous results, I might add.

You mean, he said, *that you, too, don't know everything that's going on?* I nodded. *You hear that, Claretta, Rachele. Our lord and master isn't all-powerful after all. He's asking <u>me</u> for information now.*

You don't say, Claretta said in a mocking tone I hadn't heard before. *Well, maybe then we should stage a little revolt. What do you think, Rachele?*

We're all in this together, I said as I backed out of the room— and just ahead of a flying vase.

That was the last time I ventured into that room. Instead, I kept an eye on our budding revolutionaries through the video-cameras. And that's how I discovered, at last, the true extent of the horror facing me. I had been sitting in my favourite chair in the projection room for several days, watching Mussolini seething and boiling, plotting and planning. At long distance, I had continued feeding him information about himself, continued the necessary educational process, although that part of it was becoming less and less necessary.

I want my own memories, he suddenly screamed one day, after ingesting one more piece of unsavoury history—this time about the slaughter of hundreds of Romans by the Nazis as reprisal for the killing of German soldiers in a parade ground explosion. Each at point blank range; each with their hands tied and with a bullet to the back of the head. *This is all bullshit. It has nothing to do with me. Absolutely nothing.*

While Claretta and Rachele clapped, he flung open the door to his cubicle and rushed out. He stamped his feet against the metal grating; his voice echoed down the empty corridors. With a swing of his whip he smashed one of the spotlights.

You bastard! he yelled, fist in the air. *I don't give a shit about the millions who died. Or that I'll die. But give me something fresh and clean. Something I can discover for myself. You have no right to stuff me full of your shit-encrusted history. Come on. Come out here and face me like a man. Let's see who's really in control here.*

He reached over and started punching the buttons on the door beside his. At first, I paid no attention, busying myself with the newly-formed creature in the chair beside me, who, as usual, was having trouble wiping the mucus from its eyes. The rooms, I had long ago realized, were duds—as blank as this newborn Mussolini slobbering over itself.

There, there, I said, handing the creature a Kleenex. *Isn't that better?*

The creature smiled and nodded. You're so cute, I said. Maybe this time I'll spare you.

And then a familiar voice caused me to turn towards the screen, caused the hair to rise on the back of my neck. The voice was that of my grandfather. He was inside the room Mussolini had flung open, sitting at his desk, the antique desk covered with leather-bound books. The crackly sounds of *Va, pensiero sull'ali dotate* from Verdi's *Nabucco* were coming over his ancient recording machine. How do I know? How can I be so sure? From having heard it over and over again. From having analyzed each verse, each note. My grandfather looked up, smiling—whether at Mussolini or me I couldn't be sure—and said: *Andiamo, ragazzo. We have much work to do this morning.*

I wanted to scream, to claw away at the videotape machine, to trash everything in my way. How dare they! This was obscene. Some things are sacred, aren't they? If not, what's left? It was even worse when the video camera pulled back for a wide-angle view. For, along the entire line of open doors, my grandfather looked out, image after image identical in every detail, making a mockery of individuality and memory both—before shrinking back to one image. Still one image too many.

I felt myself sucked up in the vortex, unable to move, record piled upon record, some simultaneous, others like films within films, stories within stories, going back to the beginning of time itself and turning everything into flimsiness, without substance, without hope of ever realizing itself. Not just the Mussolinis. No, not just Il Duce. We, who had been teaching him who he was, were ourselves in danger of becoming nothing but figments.

Perhaps we had always been figments—more creations of the facility. Perhaps there was nothing outside the facility. Perhaps all the memories from the very beginning had been faked—the smells, my grandfather's bony grip, my mother and father, my neglected fiancée and her passionate love letters sealed with a bloody thumbprint, the dilapidated subway with its mutant beetles and even more confused humans.

And it struck me that it had all been a wonderfully elaborate set-up. It wasn't Mussolini these people wanted. It was me. I had been too vain and egotistical to realize it, too proud of myself and the power I thought I wielded. They didn't need me to teach Mussolini about himself. All they had to do was plug him in. It was me they'd set out to capture from the very beginning. And I'd been lured in by my own grandfather. Or some copy who smelled, laughed, talked, walked and listened to music just like the real one had done—if there had ever been a "real one" in the first place.

I don't know how long I sat there in a state of shock, the

frightened creature beside me trying to snap me out of it, shaking my arm and calling out my name—the few words he'd learned so far. When I finally awoke, the image of my grandfather was long gone, replaced once again by duds, by blanks, by ciphers. And I knew precisely what I had to do.

What I have to do.

No more smashing of tanks, blowing up computers, detonating Quonset huts. No more hunting down and shooting of Mussolinis—or pitiful facsimiles thereof. No more filling their heads with useless knowledge, a knowledge that bounces to the far end of the universe—and back. Their memories have been lost already. Can no longer be retrieved from the contamination around them. All I can do now is attempt to preserve mine.

Scene Eight: First Endings

And with that, I plunge in—conscious of the irony that, to hold on to what I have, I'm obliterating myself in the very broth of creation.

Even more ironical is the fact I'll soon be rising from that broth again—and, for the longest time, not know who I am. Or, more importantly, who I've been.

That's all I can say for sure. That's all I'm certain of.

PART TWO

THE SPIRALLING TRAP

Between sleeping and waking, I hear an incessant river running
between dimly discerned, looming forms,
drowsy and frowning.

SCENE ONE: DREAM SENTENCES

A hand-like machine (alternating with a machine-like hand) claws at the contours of Fausto's face. It pulls his suddenly elastic flesh up through dull layers of sentience, strip by epidermal strip. Delicately, with exaggerated care, the hand/machine separates the skin tissue, peeling it away and rubbing the web-thin membranes back and forth between its cold, metallic fingers, its cold, finger-like clamps. Like someone testing for promised quality in a piece of cloth.

Fausto tries to scream but his mouth warps before it has a chance to do his bidding. His lips erupt into crimson flowers that in turn burst into violet flames. His tongue, severed from its pink, nourishing root, flaps uselessly like a trapped bird at the top of its cage. Thick and fleshy. Grey and uninspiring.

Now the hand that has been clawing, the fingers that have been peeling, turn into needles dripping blue acid, burning pits of flesh where his eyes should be, leaving him blinded, the sockets two black hole corrosive pools that devour whatever comes near. The world skews inside out—literally—and all he can see is what lies within: moist blood-red caverns filled with pendulous, pulsing, self-enclosed nodules that hang suspended from their roofs, vibrating ever so gently; bony tracts and canals that, shrinking, threaten to collapse entirely and suck the air out of him; raw, spiked cavities that plunge straight down in hopeless twists and turns.

It's at the end of one of these terrible plunges that the various sections of his brain come into view: reticulate, convoluted, overlaid with redundant circuitry and appendages long ago shut off. And, as he nears what he suspects as somehow being central to his essence—a glowing, neural core packed together so tightly the separate parts have little definition or distinction—he finds himself wondering how this standing apart is possible, how this internal journey could be achieved, how he could be seeing what he is seeing when what he is seeing is himself seeing . . . himself. Or the core seeing the core. And he knows this isn't possible. That this self-seeing hasn't really been achieved. That the core can't really be perceived by the core. That he needn't be afraid of getting lost because he will be waking soon. Any moment now. He'll be waking to the truth.

And, before the thought vanishes (somewhere within the density of that very dense core), he does wake up. The scar tissue falls away from his eyes, falls away to scuttle into the maws of creatures he recognizes from somewhere else—but where exactly? Another dream perhaps. Or the same one remembered in a different way, from a different angle. It doesn't really matter, now does it? The important thing is that he's now awake. He's now fully awake and no longer at the mercy of bad-tempered dreams. Or the effects of severe acid indigestion.

The young child Fausto (also known as "Faustino") lies ever so still in bed, breathing hard and covered in slick films of sweat, layers of film that spread several inches on every side of him. He lies still, staring straight up, only eyeballs swivelling from side to side. Slowly, he passes nervous fingers over his face, almost afraid of what he might or might not find there, slowly touches eyelids, cheekbones, nostrils, mouth. . . .

But all he encounters is flesh, the plain, ordinary Fausto flesh covering the plain, ordinary Fausto face with the slight ridge on the nose where he'd broken it in a tumble down the stairs; the thin lips his mother insists are a sign of cruelty, a sign of a not fully-developed conscience; the warm eyelids with their tiny yet ever-so-consistent pulse.

He breathes more easily, regaining control, trying to focus attention on his surroundings. A small, beige-coloured room with one door and an opaqued, shatterproof window, its crystals darkened. The room is stifling even though it isn't yet dawn. He realizes the air filtration has been turned off again. His father often does that—to conserve energy, he says. To conserve it for what? Fausto asks. For a better world, his father invariably answers: *We must make sure we leave behind us a better world. It's our one true and necessary duty during our stay on this otherwise cold and miserable planet.* A better world for whom when we might very well be the last? Fausto often feels like asking—but hasn't so far. And what exactly does a better world mean?

Outside, Fausto can hear dull, thudding noises through the walls—the same noises that have awakened him on many previous nights down through the years. Through the window's unbreakable plastic, he can make out vague shadows bobbing up and down. But, without even having to look out, he knows precisely what those noises mean. The festival season is coming up, the one time of the year when the citizens come out to celebrate and invited dignitaries make their up tempo speeches about how bright the future looks and how soon the planet will once more resemble that original paradise so fondly remembered. So fondly sighed after and wished for.

Thus, the vast armies of the homeless (now known as "The Nowhere People") are being herded through the streets again, are being slowly but surely directed to their new destination—the "Safe Habitat Zones" where they will be held (for their own safety, of course) until the celebrations pass and the dignitaries are safely behind blast-proof doors again. While most of the homeless, the veterans of these dislocations, go quietly, some of the younger ones still have some fight in them. They don't take kindly to squads of riot police urging them forward with sophisticated versions of cattle prods—or rather concentrated light beams that form a corral around them, roping them in like old-time dogies on the range.

Screaming in anger and frustration, they take every opportunity to strike at the surrounding buildings and call down curses on the inhabitants, the lucky ones with a well-defined place to sleep thanks to secure corporate positions, business incomes or government-guaranteed pensions. But it's a hopeless anger—for the homes are too well-protected to be damaged by stones or boots, let alone raw fists or foreheads. Even the noise is attenuated so as not to wake the blissful sleepers within.

All except the few like Fausto, of course, who for some reason can hear everything as if it avoids the auditory organs altogether and pierces them straight through the heart. Or rather like a wave movement in the very air itself. And his grandfather, who doesn't sleep at night anyway. Fausto knows. On his own nightly prowls, he has often seen the light glowing beneath his grandfather's door long after his father has done his duty and shut off the air filtration systems.

Fausto shifts uneasily beneath the clammy thinsulate covers, then eases out of bed and sits up, the beads of sweat sliding down to wet the sheets beneath his buttocks. He shivers despite the heat. The nightmare (of the future, perhaps, because in it he has seen himself as a young adult) is still vivid and he wants to know what it might mean before it fades forever. Before morning uncovers its obvious absurdities.

Only one person in the house will—or can—answer that kind of question: his grandfather. For, while the orthodoxy on human behaviour has long since advanced to statistics and the implacable law of large numbers (*pace* Asimov), Fausto's grandfather still believes in what he calls "the psychological and psycho-linguistic basis for individual acts and moral responsibility", as well as such anachronisms as the unconscious along with something known as the id, which Fausto has actually studied in his history class as part of the unit called "Incredulous Past: What We No Longer Believe In & Can't Imagine Anyone Ever Actually Did Believe."

Fausto goes out into the dimly-lit corridor, on tip-toe so as not to make noise. It's just a reflex action on his part. There's little chance his parents will awake, pumped up as they are with the Somna-Lactate solution that drip-drips into their systems all night long: a torrent when they first hook themselves up, a trickle as dawn approaches.

Just as he suspects, the light is on in his grandfather's room—no newfangled laser but rather an old-fashioned table lamp that spills out in uneven yellowish hues from beneath the door and onto the hallway. And that occasionally makes sizzling noises, sputters on and off momentarily, and explodes into darkness. At which point, his grandfather does some groping, some twisting, some swearing, and the light miraculously returns. This time the light is steady in its glow.

Fausto reaches for the handle and eases it open. At the far end of the room, barely visible, his grandfather is sitting as he always sits, with his back to him, hunched over the desk and peering at an oversized manuscript. This is the same manuscript he always studies at this time of night, filled with names, dates and other figures all scrawled out meticulously by hand. And lockets of hair serving as bookmarks.

My past, his grandfather had once told Fausto, brushing flecks of dust from the manuscript's yellowed and brown-stained cover. *It is all here. Or what is left of it. You see: that is where I masturbated once after coming across a sexy photo of your long-gone grandmother; that is where I spilled a mug of coffee in a fit of anger over the news the Italian government was allowing the royal family to return; that is where I cut myself to seal the vow of revenge against our enemy.*

Wrapped around his shoulders and head is the familiar rough woollen shawl, which he claims was made by his own great-grandmother more than a century before, and which had been "knitted straight from the sheep's back." Fausto isn't sure he believes that. He can't imagine anything actually lasting that long. Besides, his grandfather has been known to distort the truth on occasion—or at least to shape it to his own ends, including his involvement in the killing of Mussolini.

Fausto makes his way forward as stealthily as possible, trying to see how far he can advance before his grandfather's sharp ears prick up. Normally, it takes but one or two steps and his familiar voice echoes: *Allore, Signore Faustino, you too are having some trouble to sleep, yes?* And he turns his head in that sly way of his: *Tell your grandfather what the problem is this night. We will solve it together.*

And Fausto speaks to him about the people marching outside and his dreams and the various animals from the Petting Zoo. And his grandfather soothes him and tells him stories of his own youth and how the raging of his hormones and of the war took place at the same time. But not on this occasion. Not even a stirring. Not a twitch. His grandfather must have dozed off at his desk and then lacked the energy to crawl back into bed. Fausto comes up behind him and taps him gently on the shoulder.

Grandpapa, he says. *I've had a strange, strange dream. You wouldn't believe the kind of dream. I saw —*

But Fausto goes no further, can go no further. When his grandfather turns slowly towards him, he sees that it isn't his grandfather at all—not his familiar grandfather at all—but the machine-torturer from his dream. The machine with a skeletal-like see-through face of shiny metal and glass, and pulsing veins beneath it, pulsing red and blue veins beneath it. The machine with the metallic claw that has been probing him, that has been drenching him in acid.

This time he does scream—not so much out of fright but from the feeling that a part of him is in that creature, a part suddenly grown so alien. And then he realizes, still screaming, that it isn't so much a part of himself that has grown alien—it's the sight of it in such unfamiliar surroundings: a face whose inner workings are exposed for all to see and a hand with one finger curled, reeling him back into the nightmare, the corrosive pool.

Scene Two: Just Words

At the snap of a switch and a rapid explosion of lights, Fausto wakes for a second time.

(*Fausto, it's time to wake up,* a familiar voice says, soft and calm as if soothing an infant after a nightmare.)

This time, he knows it isn't a dream.

(*No,* the voice says, *it's definitely not a dream. This is as real as it gets. As real as it'll ever get in here.*)

The voice seems to be telling the truth. Looking up, Fausto sees beyond a bank of floodlights the blue-grey, metallic roof high overhead, ribbed and vaulting and dotted with pinpricks. The familiar pseudo-sky and the pseudo-stars. He sees the cubicle walls with no ceilings and no doors. Through the openings where the doors should be, he sees other cubicles of a similar type: sectioned for easy tearing down and rebuilding. Separated by winding, dead-end corridors as if all part of a maze. He feels the cot around him, warm where the electric pressure points stimulate his naked body and keep the various parts from going numb.

But, wait a minute, he finds himself saying. How do I know all that? How do I know these words and the names of things?

(*Obviously, something—or someone—has been feeding you the information,* the voice says. *Has been providing you with the information all along. After all, it is information that allows us to survive, non e vere?*)

Fausto tries turning his head in the direction from which he feels the voice coming, stretching his neck as far back as it will go. That's when he sees the machinery jutting out from the wall behind him. It's the machine of his dreams—or a variant thereof, its spidery touch all over him and a umbilical cord connection to the top of his head. But it isn't peeling him away layer by layer. Nor is it injecting him with blue acid. Just the brushing of tiny jolts. Like feathers or the waving of wispy, lattice-work fronds deep beneath the ocean.

But I don't know what feathers or lattice-work fronds are like, Fausto says. Or blue acid, for that matter.

(*No need to trouble yourself with that,* the voice says with a chuckle. *The images are created as I think about them—and then project them into your mind. From there, after you've added your input, they come back to me once more.*)

Are you saying you're the one who gave me my dreams?

(*Only the seeds for your dreams. The rest was yours—especially the peeling and the blue acid. An interesting combination of images, don't you think?*)

That's what I was just thinking, Fausto says. Why are you echoing everything I think and say?

(*Not so much echoing. More like sine-waves varying in amplitude. There are times when we're completely in sync and you couldn't tell us apart. But that happens very rarely and only for a split second. The rest of the time, we're either amplifying each other or dampening the effects. Either piggy-backing or trying to buck each other off.*)

Wait a minute, Fausto says. Wait just a minute. I don't know what you're getting at with all this talk of sine waves and amplitudes. There's only one me. One Fausto. And, since I know I am me lying here, you must be an impostor. You must be not-me. Not-Fausto.

(*It's not so simple as that. Not quite so simple. It may have been once but not anymore. You and I, we're connected in —*)

Is that so? Fausto says. Or thinks he says. We'll just see.

And with that, he reaches over his head and yanks out the bundle of wires and tubes that attaches him to the machine— right in the middle of a thought that suggests he do just that.

There, he says, suddenly regaining use of his voice. *That was simple enough, right? First, we're connected—and then we're not. Now, that's what I call simple.* The wires fall to the side, oozing rather than sizzling, dripping something blue. *So much for your sine waves. I think I can think on my own. Thank you very much.*

Despite his bravado, Fausto does feel a twinge of regret, a kind of loneliness at the sudden separation. Like an infant perhaps upon birth. Or the instant you walked out of the cloning tanks and lost contact with the fluids. The all-nourishing fluids that continued to reach out with long, sticky hands. But those were part and parcel of what a person was, something essential, in other words, even if it needed to be discarded at some point. What does this nefarious machinery have to do with it? With him? With me?

Nothing, Fausto says. *Absolutely nothing.*

It's only when Fausto swings around to sit up that he notices another man in the room with him, a man with his hands behind his back and facing the far wall, staring at the wall. No, not at the wall—at one of those store dummies dressed in a tight-fitting blue uniform of some kind, an outfit where all the various muscles and bulges can be seen. Once again, like the voice from the machine, the man is someone who seems familiar, yet Fausto can't quite place him. The lights reflect from his gleaming head and thickly-corded neck. He is wearing a greatcoat with a dapper red collar, the kind used in some countries by high-ranking military men. The moment Fausto's feet touch the floor, he spins around.

Please, please, you mustn't, he says as he comes rushing towards Fausto. *I can't take it any more.*

What are you —

Before Fausto has a chance to finish, the Mussolini (for that's what he is without a doubt) has grasped his hand and knelt down before him, head down.

It's lonely and it's cold, he says, looking from side to side, as if expecting something or someone else. *You can't imagine how lonely and cold it is when you're not here.*

Why shouldn't I be here? Where would I be going?

Fausto tries to pull his hand away.

No, no! You mustn't. He begins to kiss Fausto's hand. *I'll do anything. Anything you ask. Just don't leave again.* He looks up, then furtively behind him. *You can't leave again. I won't make it this time. I'll go with you. I swear to God. I'll . . . I'll. . . .*

He throws himself on the ground, clutching at Fausto's naked leg, pressing his face against Fausto's thigh. Fausto sits on the bed, a terrible weariness upon him.

There, there, he says, patting the Mussolini's head. *I don't know what you're so worried about. But you've nothing to fear. Now, let go of me. We've got to get on with our work. I can't get anything done with you clutching to me.*

But the Mussolini hangs on even tighter.

Oh no, you don't, he says in a whining, irritating voice. *You've pulled that trick before. Yes, you have. The moment I released you, I lost you. You're not going to fool me like that again.*

This is silly, Fausto says. *I can't very well drag you around with me everywhere I go. And I need to get dressed. Sooner or later, you're going to have to release me—even if only to allow me to pull up my trousers.*

You're right, the Mussolini says. *But I've got friends. Allies. They'll be here soon and one of them will take my place. Then, we can dress you. Yes, I've got it all worked out this time. We'll do it in shifts, we'll—*

Let go, dammit, Fausto yells. *I've had enough of this nonsense.*

He slaps the Mussolini across the top of his head. The Mussolini flinches and grits his teeth but he doesn't release his grip on Fausto's leg.

Please, Fausto says. *I don't want to hurt you.*

No, no, the Mussolini says, *go ahead and hurt me. Beat me. Kick me. Shoot me. Anything—if it takes your mind off other things. Use me as your personal punching bag if that'll help. Just don't leave me here again all by myself.*

Fausto sighs and leans back. He's so exhausted he doesn't even have the energy to argue any more—let alone physically force the Mussolini to release him.

Okay, he says, just then noticing what looks like an eye come hovering over the top of the wall.

(*That's a camera,* the voice says. *They've advanced quite a bit since the last time, haven't they?*)

Get out of my head! Fausto yells.

Those voices again, eh? the Mussolini says. *Not a good sign.*

That's how it started the last time, too.

That's how what started? Fausto asks.

Oh no. You're not going to get me to talk about it. My lips are sealed. And, as if to prove it, the Mussolini actually makes a gesture sealing his lips shut.

The camera-eye moves in closer, now floating just above Fausto's head. He can hear the mechanism whirring—and once again knows things he shouldn't. He knows that the data is being transmitted directly to one of the central computer banks where it is stored for future use. For his future use. He knows that this data consists of more than streams of bits and bytes, more than pixels for recreating images in all their three-dimensional glory (or the fake three dimensions of the hologram, in any case). He knows that this is more akin to the primitive belief that someone taking your picture also took a part of your life force. He knows all this even though it makes no sense that he does.

Fausto looks at the mass of wires contained within the still-writhing connector-tube, the tube still searching for someone or something to which it can attach itself. The camera-eye is now a mere few centimetres away from him—so close Fausto can see himself—or a distorted version thereof—in the lens. Without turning away, he reaches behind him for the connector-tube, allowing it to clutch at him. Then, without warning, he swings it viciously at the camera—and sends the camera crashing to the ground.

Bull's eye! he says. *That'll teach you to film someone without asking permission.*

I'm disappointed, the Mussolini says, sighing. *I was hoping for something different this time around. But kids will be kids, I guess.*

The camera-eye tries several times to rise again, managing at one point to come 10 centimetres or so off the ground. But it quickly collapses again and begins emitting the high-pitched wail of a creature in distress.

You've done it now, the Mussolini says, twisting himself as far away from the camera as possible without having to let go of Fausto.

Through the floor emerges one of the Scavengers, looking like a scaly discus on its edge as it rolls towards the camera. Fausto remembers the Scavengers as tiny, insect-like creatures. But this one is at least a metre long when it uncoils, bulbous eyes on thick stalks, razor-sharp, pincer jaw opening and closing compulsively. The camera, as if sensing doom, re-doubles its efforts to get off the ground, to become functional once more.

Come on, little buddy, Fausto says. *You can do it.*

Too late. The camera squeals one last time as it is swallowed and ripples its way through the Scavenger's reticulated body. The Scavenger looks around for a moment, head and first row of waving appendages held high, making sure nothing else needs its services. Then it rolls itself back into a discus, tucks in its legs and immediately vanishes. Literally falls through the solid floor.

Why? the Mussolini says. *Why do you first attack that unfortunate camera and then feel sorry for it? What's the point?*

Because I'm human, I guess, Fausto says. *Or maybe to prove that I am still human.* He shrugs. *Ah, who the hell knows? All I know is that you'd better release me if you don't want the same thing happening to you.*

It has already happened to me, the Mussolini says. *So many times I've lost count.* He shudders. *And I know you're only bluffing. If you feel bad for a camera, just imagine how you'd feel about me.*

Yes, I guess you're right, Fausto says. *Still—*

Suddenly, a man comes rushing into the room, a white-haired old man wearing a coat similar to the Mussolini's, only much rattier and ill-fitting. He's waving a stick above his head. No, not a stick—a cane.

Release him, you motherless fascist pig! he shouts, swinging the cane at the Mussolini. *Release my grandson!*

Before the Mussolini has a chance to react, he takes the brunt of the blow across his shoulders. He's about to take another when he finally lets go of Fausto's leg and rolls away. Fausto quickly stands up.

You're lucky I've lost my pistol, the old man says, slapping at an empty holster. *I would blow you straight back to the hell-hole you've crawled out of.*

You idiot! the Mussolini says, at the same time staying well out of range of the still swinging cane. *He's getting away! And it's all your fault.*

Fausto is walking rapidly down one of the corridors. There's purpose to his step. It's obvious he knows where he is going.

Fausto! Faustino! the old man shouts, running after him. *Ragazzo! Aspettemi. Wait for me. It is your grandfather. Wait.*

Fool, the Mussolini hisses as he takes the uniform off the dummy and slings it over his arm. *All you're good for is cutting off the balls of dead men.*

Get away! the grandfather shouts, swinging his stick. *Or I will do it again. And this time while you are still alive!*

Fausto moves towards the centre of the facility, looking around him as he does so. Things don't seem so makeshift here. Or temporary. The cubicles have doors and ceilings and the blue glow of strip lighting along their sides. Above them are walkways leading to other cubicles—only these are made of glass and are set high above the ground. Like bubble domes. Inside those domes, Fausto sees row upon row of computer monitors. He's too far away to make out the images on the monitors but he can see that they're changing all the time. Changing at speeds almost too rapid for his eyes to follow. Flashing and flickering. Expanding and shrinking. Sometimes all the screens have exactly the same image, duplicated countless times; sometimes all the screens make up one image, each displaying one piece.

Fascinating, Fausto says.

Please, Fausto, the old man says, trying to catch his breath. *Not so fast. I am not as young as I used to be, you know.*

Go away, Fausto says, turning from the screens. *What do you want from me anyway?*

Want? I do not want anything. I am your grandfather. Tuo nonno.

Liar! Fausto says. *My grandfather died a long time ago. I was there. I saw him being taken out in the middle of the night.*

Of course, of course. But then so have you—died, I mean.

What are you talking about?

He means you've done this before, the Mussolini says, standing further back in the corridor.

You stay away from me, too, Fausto says, balling his hands into fists. *I don't need you clutching at me.*

Yes! The old man waves his cane. *You get the hell out of here. This is between me and my grandson—not some petty dictator.*

Okay, okay, the Mussolini says, holding out his hands. *I won't come any closer. Here, though. You might want to put on some clothes. It can get mighty chilly in some of the systems.*

Toss them here, Fausto says. *And no tricks.*

Do not worry, the old man says. *If he dares to try anything, I will crack that skull of his wide open. Swear to God on high, I will.* He chuckles. *I have done it before, you know.*

The Mussolini edges forward until he's almost within range of the cane. Then, he throws the clothes to Fausto.

Now, back off, the old man says. *Let my Faustino do what he has to do.*

Fausto leans against a wall and slips on the blue uniform. It fills and shapes itself until it fits him perfectly, seamless, showing off his taut musculature.

Hmm, he says, touching himself. *I wonder what happens when I'm old and bulging all over.*

He turns and continues walking down the corridor—with the old man and Mussolini behind him, one on either side.

Why don't you like me? the Mussolini asks. *What have I ever done to you?*

The old man starts to sing as loudly as possible: *A la matina, appen'alzata, o Bella Ciao, Bella Ciao, Bella Ciao, Ciao, Ciao! A la matina—*

Sing, old man, sing all you want, the Mussolini says. *It doesn't bother me any more. Not one bit. Bella Ciao, Bella Ciao, Bella Ciao, Ciao, Ciao—see, I can say it, too. And as loudly as you. Le Partigiani, Le Fosse Ardeatine, La Repubblica di Salo—it's all ancient history. As old as the hills. It doesn't mean anything anymore. Doesn't amount to a hill of beans. Like old manure spread over useless fields where nothing will ever grow again. Meaningless!*

Never! the old man says. *It will mean something as long as I am alive. As long as I am there to act as a witness.* He waves the cane in the Mussolini's face. *As long as I can testify and point the accusing finger. As long as there are demagogues running around loose.*

Suit yourself. But right now we've got more urgent things to worry about.

While they've been arguing, Fausto has made his way to the inner circle of the facility, to the edge of the central ring. There, he's confronted by two women who block his path.

Well, well, Fausto says, the voice dispensing more information. *Claretta, the little curly-haired Fascist poetaster, and Rachele, the long-suffering wife and mom. How's your 'invincible Duce' doing now? Looking a bit cowed, I would say.*

It's you I want now, Claretta says in a sultry voice and wiggling suggestively. *You're my hero. That so-called Duce is nothing but a bully. A whipped dog. Come with me. I'll worship you forever. I'll satisfy your every whim. I'll make you feel like you're the king of the world.*

No, take me, Rachele says, actually ripping her blouse to expose her breasts. *I know what a man like you needs. A woman to come home to. Some fair-haired children. Warm bread in the oven.*

Me, me, Claretta says, advancing towards him.

Me, me, Rachele says.

Fausto looks behind him. His grandfather and the Mussolini are approaching. He's trapped between them in the corridor.

This time, you mustn't, the Mussolini says. *You're too important.*

For once, the grandfather says, *that monster is right.*

Stop! All of you! Fausto shouts. *You're wasting your time. I must do this. I have no choice. And no amount of clutching and promises of love and ego-inflation can make a difference—even if that's what I wished from the bottom of my heart.* He holds up his hands to prevent the others from speaking. *Now, I'm going to continue walking down this corridor and I'm going to do what I have to do. You're all welcome to come along—as long as you don't interfere. Is that understood?* He looks from one to the other, waiting for each to nod. The last is Claretta who bows her head and bursts into tears. *Good. Now, make way.*

Let him go, the grandfather says. *If he will not listen to me, it is obvious he will not listen to anyone.*

Fausto brushes by the two women. They fall in behind him as his long strides take him quickly towards the central core of the facility.

This is all your fault, the grandfather says to the Mussolini. *If you would have stayed out of it, maybe this time it might have been different. That should have been me at his bedside. I am his grandfather, after all. I know what is best for him.*

Oh, you mean like the last time, eh? the Mussolini says. *If I remember correctly, you placed your pistol in his hand just before he was about to wake up. I think it was all downhill after that.*

At least it was quick. And merciful.

Fausto stops for a moment at the portal where the corridor meets the central hub. Then, looking back once, he shakes his head and walks through. The camera-eye, which has been discreetly filming, projects a series of holographic images of the grandfather, the Mussolini, Claretta, Rachele and Fausto. The images multiply, receding further and further and becoming smaller and smaller. In each, a Fausto turns and walks through to the central hub. In each, the others wait helplessly.

We must do something, the Racheles are saying, a slight echo reverberating along the corridor.

Come on, the Clarettas are repeating one after the other. *We mustn't let him out of our sight.*

The images, catching up with one another, run towards the central core—and vanish as they reach the limits of the projection. The grandfather, the Mussolini, Claretta and Rachele step inside, not in the least conscious of the fact one day they'll be just one more set of images: the latest, at first, and then gradually shrinking back until they become too small for the human eye to make out—like a buzzing, an eternal buzzing. Images receding to infinity and mistaken for fate. Or flies.

Brrrr, the Mussolini says, shivering as they walk between the cloning tanks, with their iridescent glows and tubular appendages heading skyward. *This place gives me the willies. I'd rather face 50,000 Abissinos anytime.*

There he is! Rachele says.

When they reach him, Fausto is leaning on one of the tanks. No, not just leaning on it. His face is pressed right up against the tank, practically kissing it. Inside the murky green broth, something stirs. Web-like fingers climb up the inside wall, up towards Fausto's face. They push against the glass, desperate for contact. They probe and stick and pulse different shades of green, as if the colours could actually reflect the emotions it is feeling. Fausto snaps his face away.

It told me it's waiting, Fausto says, walking towards the circular stairwell that leads to the top of the tank. *Waiting for me to join it.*

No! Rachele screams.

I've got him, Claretta shouts as she lunges at Fausto and latches onto one of his arms.

Let go of me, you stupid woman, Fausto says. *What do you hope to achieve?*

But before he has a chance to knock her away, Rachele and the Mussolini lunge at him as well—effectively pinning his arms and one leg.

Come on, the Mussolini says to the grandfather. *Get the other leg. We can't let him go this way again. Come on. If we hold him long enough, he might change his mind. Come on!*

But the grandfather is shaking his head, unwilling to take part. Fausto struggles against the three of them. With his free leg, he kicks Claretta and tugs his arm free at the same time. The force of the tug sends him backward against the base of the stairs. He strikes his head and slumps to the ground, a shocked look on his face. Blood begins to pour from his scalp.

Oh my God, Claretta says. *Oh God, no.*

With a slight rumbling sound, a Scavenger surfaces and extends itself. It raises its head in the air as if sniffing around. Then turns towards where Fausto is sitting, still groggy.

Go away, Rachele says, positioning herself in front of Fausto. *Shoo.*

Yes, shoo, Claretta says. *Can't you see he isn't dead?*

But the creature is not to be deterred so easily. It begins to whir and clack, moving its lower jaw up and down. Another appears on the other side, trapping the group between them.

A diversion, the Mussolini says. *We need a diversion.*

It is of no use, the grandfather says. *Once they sense blood, it is all over. We might as well let them take him away and start again.*

No! the Mussolini says. He reaches into his greatcoat and pulls out the grandfather's pistol.

Maniac! the grandfather says, pulling back. *Where did you get that?*

You're always leaving it lying around. I think you wanted me to have it.

Rachele screams as one of the creatures rears up before her.

What now? the grandfather says. *Shooting them will not do any good, you know. I have tried it.*

Them? the Mussolini says. *Who said anything about them?* The Mussolini smiles as he points the pistol at the grandfather. *How many times have you shot me now, old man? Too many to count, eh? Now, it's my turn.*

Shoot if you are going to shoot, the grandfather says, puffing up his chest. *I am not afraid of a filthy, yellow-bellied, whore-sniffing coward like you. Shoot!*

Okay, the Mussolini says—and with that, places the gun in his own mouth and squeezes the trigger.

Rachele screams again; Claretta covers her mouth with her knuckles. A stream of blood spurts out the back of the Mussolini's head and arcs to the ground. The Scavengers halt their advance on Fausto, then turn and race towards the Mussolini, hissing and clicking their beaks furiously. His body is still warm and spasming in its death throes as they methodically cut him up and ingest the pieces.

Come on, Rachele whispers. *We've got to get Fausto out of here.* With help from Claretta, she manages to lift him off the ground. *You, too, old man. Give a hand.*

But the grandfather isn't listening. He just stands there as if in a trance, watching the Mussolini being eaten up.

Hey! Rachele says. *Snap out of it!*

Huh! the grandfather says. *Fausto, yes. Must save Fausto. Yes.*

What are we going to do with him? Claretta says as she and Rachele stand on either side of Fausto to support him.

I know a place, the grandfather says with one last look at the Mussolini—or rather what remains of his severed head. *A place where he will be safe for now.*

Well, come on then, Rachele says. *Before those monsters decide they need another warm body to snack on.*

This way, the grandfather says as he enters one of the tube transportation units.

Rachele and Claretta struggle with Fausto who can barely stand up and has to be dragged. They make it to the tube just in time with several of the Scavengers breathing down on the clear plastic. The grandfather presses a button beneath "Farmland Eco-System" and the tube zooms along, turning everything into a blur. They've gone several hundred metres when the grandfather slaps his fist against the plastic.

Mary Whore Mother Of God! he says. *I have got to go back.*

He stops the tube at the nearest exit and steps out.

What are you doing? Rachele says. *Fausto's still bleeding. Who knows when those Scavengers might come back.*

Just wait here, okay, the grandfather says. *I do not think the Scavengers will hurt you. But if any come near, just get back in the tube and go to the Farmland Eco-System. Otherwise, wait for me here. Do you understand?*

Of course, we understand, Claretta says in a haughty manner. *We're not stupid.*

The grandfather steps into the tube that heads towards the central core area. The tube comes to a stop near the cloning tanks and he walks out, looking around cautiously. There's nothing there. And the floor is gleaming clean where a few moments ago the Mussolini's body had come crashing down.

Damn, he says under his breath. *Whore saints and buggered sheep! Where—*

Then, he sees it, up against the tank stairwell. His pistol. He picks it up, rubs it against his leg and puts it back in the holster.

There, he says, patting the holster. *I feel safer already.* He looks up at the camera-eye whirring overhead. *And you. You tell whoever is in charge here that we are not sitting around anymore.* He pulls the gun out and waves it around. *Do you understand?* He fires in the general direction of the camera. The bullet can be heard reverberating throughout the facility. *You tell him—it—whatever—to come out and face us. Like a man. That is right! Like a man. If he has got any of these.*

And, turning directly towards the camera, he clutches himself between the legs with one hand and jerks forward.

SCENE THREE: CIRCUM LOCUTION

In his delirium, Fausto dreams of dampness and the inability to keep warm. He is constantly shivering, constantly reaching for a blanket that isn't there, constantly trying to curl into a tighter circle. Into a ball with the least possible surface area. And something licks at his face, rough-tongued yet gentle. There's no stripping away of skin this time but rather a replacing, a re-building of the layers. At the same time, he can occasionally make out voices. More voices. But not the voice of his dreams. Not the voice that gave him knowledge he didn't need and instructions he didn't understand, instructions he nevertheless felt compelled to follow. That's gone—one more empty, hollow spot that needs filling.

I'm cold, he says in his damp dream, convulsing into shudders. *I'm really cold. Like ice.*

It's the fever, Rachele says, feeling his forehead. *He's still delirious. My son Romano was like this once. We thought he was going to die. All we could do was keep him warm.*

Maybe we should let him go, the grandfather says. *Who knows what damage has been done. Maybe, he will never recover. Or, if he does, he will be permanently impaired. We do not even have any medicines for him. I say let him go and get ready for a new Fausto.*

No! Claretta says with unusual vehemence. *Our Benito didn't die for nothing.*

<u>*Your*</u> *Benito is already walking around again*, the grandfather says. *And he is getting big and strong and healthy. It is only a matter of time before he becomes the same old blustering fool he always was.*

It's not the same, Claretta says, starting to cry. *It's not—*

Alright, alright, Rachele says, hushing her. *The old man might be right about Fausto. Maybe the blow was too much.*

Finally somebody is starting to make sense.

But, Rachele says, *that doesn't mean we can give up on him. God is still up there watching, I'm certain. Up there somewhere above this godforsaken place. And he wouldn't forgive us if we just sat around and let him die.*

Suit yourselves, the grandfather says. *It is getting stuffy in here. I am going out for some fresh air. As for God, I think he left when we took over playing his role.*

Several days later, the fever breaks and the decision is made for them. Fausto sees the world around him without the ever-present haze of delirium. Judging from the rocky outcroppings overhead, he's in a large cave of some kind, lying on a bed of leaves and straw and covered with a mangy fur pelt. The only light comes from the cave's entrance and two smoky torches burning on the wall. Suddenly, a huge animal comes bounding in and heads straight for him.

No, Fausto says weakly as the animal—he recognizes it as the snow leopard—places its gigantic front paws on his chest and starts to lick his face.

Luna, stop it, a female voice calls out from outside the cave entrance. *You'll hurt poor Fausto.* Claretta rushes in and slaps the snow leopard on the rump. *Off him now!*

The snow leopard reluctantly shifts but, rather than getting off the bed, lies down with a heavy sigh beside Fausto.

Hello, Claretta, Fausto says. *Have you got something to drink?*

Fausto? She peers down at him. *You're awake?*

I think so. Unless I'm dreaming again. Been doing a lot of that lately.

Oh my God! Claretta shouts. *Rachele, come quick. He's awake. Fausto's awake.*

Is it possible? Rachele says as she comes in wiping her hands.

Jeez, Fausto says. *You sound like I've just returned from the dead.*

Rachele looks down at him for a moment. Then, she throws herself into his arms. She sobs into his chest.

Me, too, Claretta says. *Make room.*

She cuddles on the other side. Soon, both are crying.

No more funny stuff, okay, Rachele says, looking up at him.

You mean I can't tell any more jokes?

Silly brute, Claretta says, pounding his chest with her fist. *You know exactly what Rachele means. No more funny stuff means no more funny stuff.*

Well, that makes it all perfectly clear. Right, Luna?

The leopard growls.

Just promise, Rachele says.

Okay, I promise. Whatever it is I'm promising. Now, can I have something to drink, please? I've got an awful thirst.

On your mother's grave, Claretta says.

Sure, whatever, Fausto says. *That's assuming she's dead. I guess she is, eh? Yeah. She would be by now. Whenever now is.*

Stop it, you brute! Claretta says. *You're making my head spin.*

I'm still thirsty, he says.

I'll get a glass of water, Rachele says, throwing him a kiss as she gets up. *Be right back.*

So where's my grandfather? Fausto says, looking around.

Oh, he comes and goes, Claretta says, nuzzling Fausto's ear.

And Benito? Where's that old scoundrel?

You don't remember, do you? Claretta says.

Fausto shakes his head.

And best to keep it that way, Rachele says as she hands him a glass of water. *The new and improved Il Duce should be showing up any day now.*

That's if your grandfather doesn't shoot him first, Claretta says.

I thought he was over that. Fausto takes a sip of water, then leans his head back on the makeshift pillow.

Depends on his mood, Claretta says. *Some days, he pines for someone to talk to, someone he can share his past with.*

Others, Rachele continues, *he's full of the old rage. And he walks around with a black cloud over his head, fuming and making threats.*

Do you know he can still recite the names of the Cave Ardeatine victims—from Agnini, Ferdinando to Zironi, Augusto? Claretta says. *All 335 of them. Sometimes I want to say: 'Enough, already. We get the point.' Although I really don't know what the point is.*

It's like a roll call or a chant, Rachele says. *Like nothing has changed in all these years and decades and. . . .*

She stops.

Centuries, Fausto says. *Is that what you were about to say?*

I get a headache thinking about it, Rachele says. *And all I ever wanted to be was a good wife and mother. Live long enough to see my children become well-established. And have lots of grandchildren. And . . . and then die a happy, peaceful death.*

Give me a hand up, Fausto says. *I want to go outside for a moment.*

The two women look at each other.

What's wrong? Fausto asks.

You're not going to . . . start walking, are you? Claretta asks.

Start walking? Well, of course, I'm going to walk.

Towards the tanks, Rachele says. *She means, walking towards the tanks.*

Why on earth would I want to do that? Fausto asks, scratching his head, and looking back and forth between them. *Have I business there?*

No, no, Claretta says, smiling.

Then, help me up.

The two women lift him to his feet. He staggers forward as he takes his first step but then regains his balance and walks out of the cave on his own. The light blinds him for a moment and he has to shade his eyes until they get used to it.

I remember this, he says. *My grandfather took me here when I was a child. I mean, when I really was a child—the first time.* He scratches his head and laughs. *I guess I was a child at that time— the first time. But who knows, really? Maybe, I was already old and just didn't know it.*

They're standing on the edge of a hilltop, looking out over wheat fields and woods and a stream that sparkles and dances its way through polished boulders. It's a warm day with a yellow sunlamp sending its pulses across the land. There are birds flying overhead. Peregrine falcons, bald eagles, ring-tail pheasants. And animals in the grass. Timber wolves, red foxes, a family of mallards. And silver fish leaping from the water. All the creatures of his Petting Zoo youth. All the miracles of those early days when each

eco-system was like a jack-in-the-box surprise. All the fresh-
ness of the first time.

Imagine, he says, sitting on a rock, *if we could feel like that
again. New and bright and unsoiled. Just once. Not over and over
until it loses its taste. Until the repeating itself becomes all there really
is.*

I know what you mean, Claretta says, dreamily, hugging her
own chest. *It's like when you fall in love for the first time.*

What are you talking about, you hussy? Rachele says in a
mock-angry way. *You fell in love with my husband. You and about
a hundred others.*

I couldn't help it, Claretta says. *I was a foolish young girl at the
time. I fell in love with him the moment I saw him on the balcony of
the Palazzo, bare-chested, shouting and pumping his fist in the air.
It was very arousing. I thought he was the very symbol of the virile
man—all muscle and balls. If he would have asked me, I would have
made love to him right there. Do you know I wrote a poem about him
when I was 14 years old? And I signed it—*

To the invincible Duce from a very small fascist, the grandfather says, finishing for her as he steps out from behind a boul-
der. *Some grand hero you picked. Could not even invade Albania
properly. From the glory that was Rome to the ultimate tragic disaster
that was La Repubblica di Salo!* He glances over at Fausto. *I see
you have finally managed to get out of bed.*

And a warm hello to you, too, grandfather.

We have to talk, the grandfather says. He looks at the two
women then turns back to Fausto. *In private.*

Sure, why not? Fausto says, standing up. *Come on, grandfather. It's a lovely day. Let's you and me go for a walk. Like in the
old days. And I'll lean on you for once.* He turns to Rachele and
Claretta. *Back in a while, ladies. Keep those home fires burning.*

Fausto and his grandfather walk arm in arm down the rut-
ted path that leads to the fields. A slight wind stirs the thigh-
high wheat, sending a ripple of waves through it. Crickets
hop up and down; the buzz of cicadas sets a constant background hum; a viper hisses from the top of a woodpile; the
heat shimmers through rising dust particles.

The wheat needs harvesting, Fausto says, stopping to look around. *Don't you think? That would be something, wouldn't it? To make bread from our very own wheat. I wonder how you do it. Do you know how to do it?*

I used to, the grandfather says. *Although your grandmother would know more about the actual making of the bread. My job was to cut the wheat into sheaves and then thresh the grain. Sometimes to bring it down to the mill to be ground. But the rest—that was the job of your grandmother.*

I never met her, did I?

She died a little after your father was born. Of displacement. Of being displaced. That was a long time ago. So long ago I hardly remember her myself. No, that is not true. I remember her like it was . . . a dream . . . or a vision perhaps. He shakes his head as if to clear it. *Enough of that. The past is long gone here. Doubly and triply gone. It does not even make sense to talk about it.*

Wouldn't you like to bring her back if you could?

I have thought about it, the grandfather says. *Believe me, I have given it a lot of thought. But no. I do not think so. It just would not be the same, now would it? What do they call it: a simulacrum.*

Oh, I don't know. Maybe it would be like a fairy tale. You'd both live forever and ever. In a never-ending paradise. Growing old and then growing young and then growing old again—always together.

More like a horror tale, the grandfather says. *Like those pictures of demons in hell trying to strangle each other out of rage and frustration.*

Maybe you're right, nonno. Maybe you're right.

They resume walking and are soon at the edge of the stream. A small walkway spans the water, although the stream's so shallow at this time of year, you could walk across it by stepping on the exposed stones.

What do you think, nonno? Do you think we could build a little farmhouse up there on the hill? A few sheep? Some cows and pigs? Hens for eggs?

The grandfather takes a pipe out of his pocket, stuffs a pinch of tobacco into the bowl and lights it.

Romantic nonsense, he says, blowing out a puff of white

smoke. *I spend my youth in a place like that. If the stench of the shit does not get you, the miserable hours will. Marx and Engel may have praised the egalitarianism of the hunter-gatherers but they forgot to mention one important fact: no one lived past 30. Besides, what is the point of sticking your hand under the shitty stinking ass of some hen for an egg when the facility provides them free of charge—all cleaned and sterilized and ready to eat?*

Okay, grandfather, Fausto says as they make their way across the bridge. *What's eating you?*

Nothing. I am simply tired, that is all.

That's not all—and you know it. You've got something on your mind. I know you better than that.

It is those women, the grandfather says, using his pipe stem to point back towards the hilltop as if he himself didn't have the time for it.

Rachele and Claretta? What about them?

They are evil, do you not know that? They have consorted with a mass murderer. Someone who led Italy down the path of destruction. Someone who killed his own countrymen. He begins to raise his voice. *And when he was not killing them, he was sending them out to be killed—in Greece and Ethiopia, on the Russian front, in concentration camps. And those women . . . they shared his bed, they—*

Calm yourself, grandfather, Fausto says. *I'm well aware of all that.* He smiles. *After all, I had a great teacher.*

So, why are you now . . . why are you. . . ?

Consorting with them?

Exactly, the grandfather says. *I realize now it is no use killing them. This place keeps recreating them for some unknown reason. Keeps bringing them back like a bad smell. But, we should stay as far away from them as possible. We should avoid them like the malocchio. Like a plague from hell itself.*

They are walking in the woods now, under enormous pine trees whose branches block out the light. The air is cool and heavy with the odour of resin. Fausto stands beneath a tree, passes his hand over its bark. Then he leans over and smells it.

Isn't this simply fantastic? he says, stretching his arms around the tree. *I feel like I'm in the Garden of Eden.*

Well, this Garden has more than one snake in it, the grandfather says. *Anyway, what has got into you? It was not very long ago when the only thing you thought about was killing yourself. Now you are suddenly a bright-eyed little boy again—with his face up against the candy shop window.*

Fausto sits down.

Here. He pats the ground. *Sit beside me for a moment. We'll talk for a moment. Just like we used to.*

The only thing I am interested in talking about, the grandfather says, as he remains standing, *is what you plan on doing about that vigliacco and his two whores. Nothing else is of any importance to me.*

Those two whores, Fausto says, an edge to his voice, *saved my life.* The grandfather is about to say something but Fausto holds up his hand. *And, from what I gather, that vigliacco sacrificed himself for me.*

They have their reasons, the grandfather says matter-of-factly. *I am telling you they know what they are doing. And it has got nothing to do with wanting to help you out. Besides, it is not much of a sacrifice when you know you will be coming back in a brand-new body, now is it? All clean and shiny like a newly-minted coin.*

Okay, then. What are these behind-the-scenes reasons? What are these ulterior motives for nursing me back to life? The grandfather is shaking his head slowly, unable to understand why Fausto can't see his point. *Well, I'm waiting.*

There was a time, the grandfather says, *when you would never think of questioning my judgement. Not even when your own parents tried to turn you against me. There was a time when I could count on your support one hundred percent. And now . . . now you are siding with a misanthrope who would not think twice about feeding you to the pigs if it suited his purposes. And a pair of women who have already shown their true colours in the past and will again when the time comes.*

You asked me before, Fausto says, getting up and brushing off his pants, *why the sudden change of heart—from single-minded suicide one day to bright-eyed child the next. The truth is exactly the opposite. I've gone from being childish and thinking only of myself to understanding something about this place. Something very important. I don't know how it happened. Maybe the blow did it. Maybe the suicide urge has a time limit. Look around.* He turns in a circle, pointing in every direction. *What do you see?*

I see an artificial construct. I see something that is not real.

That's right, Fausto says. *But you're missing one important element. You're forgetting about us. Just these five little humans caught in some pretty massive machinery. And all I know is we've got to rely on one another if we ever want to become masters of our own lives again. And that means all of us—not just you and me—but also that pseudo-Mussolini and his pseudo-women.*

And let's not forget the importance of 'pseudo' in this instance. For one thing, they're not to blame for what the originals did; for another, this constant enmity can only lead to an eternal cycle of death and re-birth—and eventually we're all going to end up lost, not knowing or ever hoping to know who we are. Or were. Or are about to become. That's all I know. As for their motives, I don't know and frankly I don't care. End of speech. He takes his grandfather by the arm. *Come on, nonno. I'm tired now and we'd better be heading back. I need my beauty sleep.*

SCENE FOUR: INSUBORDINATE CLAUSE

Fausto has spent several weeks searching high and low for the Mussolini. He's checked every cubicle in the eighth pod, calling out the Mussolini's name in the dim light. He's also searched the projection room in case a neophyte proto-Mussolini is sitting there waiting for the show to begin. He's left notes and messages on the sticky passage walls, complete with maps of where he and the women can be found. He's inspected the tanks to make sure there hasn't been a foul-up of some sort—though he really doesn't know whether or not he'd be able to tell what a foul-up would look like under the circumstances. But everything seems as it always has in the tanks and the notes and messages go unanswered and the cubicles in the eighth pod are empty and the projection room is gathering dust and Fausto is left scratching his head.

Maybe there are only a certain number of recycles, he says to Claretta as they lie in bed together. *Maybe my grandfather shot so many of them, the genetic imprint has grown tired of trying to reproduce. Figured out the percentages and decided it isn't worth it any longer.* He laughs. *Listen to what I'm saying. As if I know what the hell I'm talking about. Does any of this make any sense to you?*

I have to agree with your grandfather on this, Claretta says, nuzzling his earlobe. *I don't know why you're so anxious to find him. After all, if he's out there, he must know where we are. So, either he's not alive any more or he doesn't want to be found.*

My grandfather wishes you'd disappear, too. What do you say to that?

Oh, is that right, eh? She rolls on top of Fausto and straddles him, rocking back and forth. *There's only one thing disappearing around here.*

She reaches down between his legs and eases herself onto him. Fausto places his hands on her buttocks and, amid squealing noises and grunts, they work their way to climax.

See? Claretta says, catching her breath. *Who needs il Duce when we've got this?*

Could you two keep it down? Rachele says from where she is lying in the corner. *There are people trying to sleep here.*

Oh, stop it, Rachele, Claretta says. *You're just jealous because it's not your turn tonight. You're nothing but a lonely little pussy cat.*

Rachele starts to make little mewling sounds. Then Claretta purrs her lusty satisfaction. Finally, Fausto does his best imitation of strutting male noises. All three burst out laughing at the same time. Fausto lifts the corner of the sheet and Rachele crawls over, slithering up until she's snuggled tight against his side.

I've never been happier in my life, Claretta says.

Not even when il Duce was deflowering you? Fausto says, winking at Rachele.

Brute! Claretta says, slapping him on the chest. *Besides, il Duce didn't deflower me, as you put it. I was married, too, you know. Riccardo Federici. My Ricky Dicky, I liked to call him. A nice guy. Pilot and all. But he just didn't have that . . . that oomph that I needed at the time.*

Oh, you mean he wasn't the leader of a nation? Fausto says.

I was married to the leader of a nation, Rachele says. *And I wished day and night for him to give it all up and go back to being a simple schoolteacher.*

Hey, Fausto says, *it's not too late. You might still get your wish. Maybe this next Mussolini will be the scholarly type. Teach little kids how to share and share alike—like all good socialists should.*

The following day, despite Rachele and Claretta's pleadings not to be left alone, Fausto decides to expand his search beyond the eighth pod. He knows that, in the other seven sections, it's almost impossible to find anyone if they don't want to be found. But he feels it's his duty. Besides, he wants to know what has happened to the Mussolini. He wants to put the entire matter to rest once and for all. So, armed with a knapsack, sleeping bag and food, he begins a trek through the various eco-systems.

Some like the desert and the savannah he hasn't seen since his first visits as a child. He's able to marvel once more at the intricacy of the whole thing, right down to the last grain of sand, the tiniest trapdoor spider, the driest blade of sawgrass, the gnarliest veins on the baobab tree. But no Mussolini. Of course, he could have died and been re-born dozens of times by now and Fausto wouldn't know the difference. The Scavengers would make sure of that. No, wait a minute. He couldn't have died dozens of times: Fausto would have run across the newly-formed proto-Mussolinis in the projection room. Or perhaps not. Perhaps they had finally reached the point where they no longer needed that refresher course.

Fausto moves from the savannah to edge of the ocean. Here, he stands on sheer cliffs watching the waves as they crash far below. The view is the same no matter which way he turns—water on all sides—and he's constantly amazed at the way the facility can create these illusions, how the eco-system seems to extend forever when he knows there's a very definite finite end to it. On the distant rocks, the seals and sea lions splash about; farther out, whales send their spumes into the air.

Fausto breathes in deeply. He has always wanted to be a sailor. Sometimes as a youth, he would imagine his room to be a sailing ship and he would visit faraway places to battle monsters, like all children, he supposes. Or he would sail off into space on that hyper-drive of his own inventing. Perhaps the Mussolini is out there in the mist, edging a one-man sailboat out into the open waters—wherever that might be inside the facility. Perhaps he'll land on some foreign shore—on some tropical island—and declare everything to be his and set up once again a government-in-exile.

Only this time, one based on egalitarian principles, on the principles with which he had started out and which had become twisted for some reason in a mixture of father-hatred and testosterone desire to prove himself a man who couldn't be cowed. Or simply because he knew those socialist principles were doomed to failure given the propensity of human nature to seek the course of least resistance and utmost greed. All for me and me for me. Kiss the ass of those above; kick the ass of those below until yours is the ass everyone must kiss.

But peer out as he might, Fausto can see no sailboat on the waters. Nor any Mussolini anywhere in the vicinity. He turns away, making a mental note that this would be a nice place to end it all if he ever so desires. Again. Another swan dive into a primordial soup—but so much more beautiful and enjoyable than those slimy green tanks.

Perish the thought, he says to himself. I plan on staying alive for . . . for the rest of my unnatural life.

You hear that, he shouts, arms outstretched. *For the rest of my unnatural life! So you'd better watch out.*

He turns back to the water and bursts into laughter. But no matter how loud he laughs, no matter how much lung power he puts out, he's quickly drowned by the waves slamming against the cliff. The lion's roar.

As it should be, he says. *Now and forever more.*

The polar eco-system, Fausto decides, is much like the desert—with grains of snow instead of sand. Even as a child, he thought it was odd that he could stand amid all that snow and not freeze—even if he chose to wear nothing but shorts. One of the quirks of the facility. Individual temperature and climate control. Or maybe just the ability to turn off the pain centres. Several polar bears come bouncing towards him, obviously in a playful mood. He engages in a mock wrestling match, tries to wrap his arms around the chest of one of the bears, feels the enormous bulge of the musculature. One swat and it could toss a seal clear out of the water. Or break Fausto's spine in too many places to count.

Fausto sees an igloo in the middle of the ice-field. He has a quick image of the Mussolini in Inuit clothing, chewing on a piece of blubber. Smoke is rising from the igloo. How is that done without melting the whole thing? he thinks. Very carefully, I guess.

(*Actually,* the voice says, *they make sure first of all that the igloo is perfectly round so that each block of snow is settled on the one below it and the ones to the sides of it. Then, they allow a crust of ice to form on the inside. This crust will continuously form as long as the warm air from the inside meets the cold air from the outside. Did you know that one lit candle can raise the temperature by 40 degrees?*)

Go away, Fausto says. *Nobody asked you.*

(*And yes, they're very careful.*)

He crawls in through the tight opening. Inside, there's a pile of frozen blubber, a tiny lit candle in a metal holder and, oddly enough, what looks at first glance like a book. Fausto thinks this is the first clue he's had as to the Mussolini's whereabouts. But the book turns out to be the cover for a video about a penguin called Pingu and his mischievous adventures. Episode One: How Not To Build An Igloo. Not the sort of thing the Mussolini would carry with him. How Not To Build An Empire or How Not To Get Strung Up While Doing It would be more like it. Fausto spreads out the sleeping bag and crawls into it for the night.

The following morning finds him in the rain forest. Although to his surprise the floor of the rain forest is amazingly clean and tidy, with only a few prehistoric-looking ferns and glowing mushrooms to break the carpet of dead and rotting leaves, it's still the most difficult of the habitats to search effectively. If the Mussolini has chosen to hide in here, there's little chance Fausto will uncover him. His view is limited to the under branches of immense trees that shut out practically all light. From their limbs hang tree boas, two- and three-toed sloths, howler monkeys—all at different levels.

Fausto stops for a moment. The silence slowly gives way to the sound of birds high in the canopy and the croaking of frogs. A giant anaconda slithers by not two metres away. Despite knowing it is harmless, Fausto reacts with a typical human cringe as the creature lifts its snout for a moment to check him out before moving on.

Fausto comes to a clearing, a break where the sunlight can actually reach the forest floor. Here one of the immense trees has collapsed, taking with it a host of smaller trees, liana vines and other vegetation. The area is thick with incredibly-coloured plants: scarlets, blues, yellows. Some velvet to the touch; others prickly and armoured to the hilt. Humming-birds zip from flower to flower, performing their pollination duties; a family of peccaries scurries away; a jaguar suns itself; Heliconius butterflies rise into the air like papier-mâché—and then land again all on the same shrub, hiding it com-pletely.

Fausto stares up into the bright light. High above, barely a speck, a harpy eagle soars on the wind, wings outstretched and unflapping, using the thermal currents. Suddenly a mov-ing rainbow of colours arcs across the clearing and vanishes again in the dense canopy—a flock of macaws, intense ab-stract art that dazzles and hypnotizes Fausto.

(*Hard to imagine that all this is merely a re-creation, isn't it?* the voice says. *That nothing here any longer exists outside the facility: from the silky anteater's 60-centimetre tongue to the giant otter's wolf-like teeth; from the leaf-cutter ant to the Brazilian tapir. Nothing.*)

Fausto shakes his head not quite sure if out of astonish-ment at what the voice is saying or simply trying to knock it out of himself.

After the denseness and suffocating closeness of the rain forest, Fausto is glad to be in the rarified atmosphere of the high mountain eco-system where only the occasional bighorn thunders its hoofs in an otherwise empty landscape. Here, a succession of snow-capped peaks greets him, lined up one behind the other in ever-increasing sizes and casting their im-mense shadows over everything: one part brilliant sunlight; one part deep shadow.

They stand there like stern, old-fashioned fathers with hands on hips, ready to scold at the least perceived fault or misstep. Fausto has the sudden ridiculous urge to yodel. A strangled sound comes out—half-yodel, half-bleat. He thinks then of Thomas Mann for some reason, a not-so-distant writ-er yet from a time that could very well be thousands of years in the past in its attitudes and perceptions.

The words come. They are there because the voice has put them there, has picked them up from some other experiment, some other reproduced brain cells. Fractured. Out of context: *Moments there were, when out of death, and the rebellion of the flesh, there came to thee, as thou tookest stock of thyself, a dream of love. Out of this universal feast of death, out of this extremity of fever, kindling the rain-washed evening sky to a fiery glow, may it be that Love one day shall mount?*

Fausto walks through a windswept pass, overhanging with metres-deep snow that threatens to collapse at any moment. Threatens to bury whoever is standing beneath it. But can it collapse? Can accidents happen? Of course, they can. That's what the Scavengers are for, no? To put things back the way they were before. To erase any traces of "accidents". Fausto comes out the other side. He is standing on the edge of an alpine valley—rocky crags above the tree line, islands of dark green below. Beyond it, more and still more mountains, lined up behind one another, some with their peaks shrouded by clouds, others reflecting glints of gold. There seems no end to them, reaching up to the very sky itself.

For the first time, Fausto becomes consciously aware of the sheer size of the facility, the immensity and vastness of its interior world. But how is it possible? If he remembers correctly from the time as a child when he was still able to come and go, the facility is little more than a few cleverly-concealed buildings on a slag heap, not more than 10,000 square metres in all.

(*Space inside the facility*, the voice reminds him, *isn't the same as space outside the facility. The containment field applies its own laws.*)

Or is it that everything here is an illusion? That the mountains in the distance are merely two-dimensional backdrops? Easily tested, no? Fausto passes his hand over a rock jutting out of the ground. It's definitely three-dimensional: rough, sharp, solid. Real enough, in other words. Perhaps, objects in the facility are two-dimensional—until someone gets close enough to be able to notice the difference. That's crazy, requiring technologies that make cloning full-blown replicas look like child's play.

(*Space inside. . . .*)

Okay, Fausto says. *I heard you the first time.* The important thing is that it makes him realize the practical impossibility of finding the Mussolini in a place like this. In places like these. Sand dunes and ice caps and rain forests and vast oceans and mountain caves. The immense internal spaces. The illusive, elusive twists in the facility's daily reality. Impossible if the Mussolini doesn't want to be found.

It's time to go home.

He turns and heads back through the pass.

SCENE FIVE: TORTURED PHRASES

Despite it being the middle of the night (or the facility's curiously nostalgic semblance of night) when Fausto returns to the hilltop cave, he finds no one there—all except for the snow leopard lying at the entrance, licking first one paw and then the other. That's odd, he says to himself. Claretta and Rachele are afraid of their own shadows. They wouldn't wander off by themselves. Or, if they did, they'd make damn sure to return before nightfall.

Don't you think that's odd? he asks the leopard as he bends down to pet her. She purrs. *I thought you might agree.*

But it's obvious they have gone off. Not only are their clothes and bags missing, there's no sign they were ever there. The only thing left in the cave is his bed with its scraggly furs and straw-stuffed pillow. Oh well, he says, shrugging his shoulders. Guess the country air didn't agree with them. Too bad, I was starting to get used to them.

Fausto lies on his back and stares at the cave ceiling. For all his casual air and glibness, he finds a part of him longing for their company. And it's not just the idea of sharing his bed, although he must admit that's a big part of it—devil-may-care Claretta and motherly Rachele, together or separately. No, they were also just fun to be with. Or maybe it's the fact that, despite the teeming cloning tanks, there are only five distinct humans in the facility. Five ways to split the cloning pie.

Why is that? Will it be that way forever? Is there any way to increase the numbers? Not without more genetic material, I suppose. Not even the facility can create something out of nothing, right? And will this, too, come to an end one day? Will this, too, be the victim of entropy? A shadow looms over him—Luna, preparing to take her place by his side. He falls asleep to her soft purring, a silly thought bubbling up from the depths: I wonder what my parents would say if they saw me now, in a cave with a snow leopard at my side. The mom: *Fausto. Be polite, speak when you're spoken to and don't shake the paw of any strange leopards.* The dad: *Leopards are a distinct liability. They eat a lot, have to be exercised all the time and you can't even claim them as a deduction on your income tax.*

Ah, my lovely parents, Fausto says out loud, watching the shadow of the fire flickering on the cave roof. *Little more than ghosts now floating in the ether, their bodies dust particles scattered from one end of the galaxy to the other.*

In the morning, his grandfather is waiting outside the cave for him, sitting on a rock and smoking his pipe as if nothing has happened. Before him is a tray with a pot of coffee, milk, sugar, croissants and various jams and jellies.

Ah, the grandfather says, *the seeker returns. I gather your search did not bear any fruit.*

I wouldn't go that far, Fausto says. He pours himself some coffee and sips on it as he walks out to the edge of the hilltop. *I got a chance to check out parts of the facility I hadn't seen in years. I also had some time to think about our situation.*

Thinking, his grandfather says, joining him in a cup of coffee. *That is always good. What was your thinking about?*

The universe. The facility. Me and you. He looks over at his grandfather. *Why Claretta and Rachele weren't here when I got back.*

They got bored, I guess, his grandfather says, spreading jelly on a croissant. *You know how women like these are. Easily bored. Looking for their next thrill.*

I guess you're right, Fausto says. *Oh well. We've got more important work, isn't that so?*

Of course, we do! his grandfather says. He looks at Fausto. *And what might that be?*

Escape. We've got to find a way to get out of this place. Get back to the real world. Pick up our lives where we left off. Right?

Ah yes. Of course. Pick up where we left off.

So, come on. Drink up and let's get the day started. I want to go down to the central hub area. I've got some theories. I think I've been approaching this all wrong. Come on, come on, slow poke.

Whoa, there, take it easy, his grandfather says. *What has got into you all of a sudden anyway? Let us just relax for a while. Sip our coffee and talk. About the good old days.*

No time to talk, Fausto says, taking his grandfather by the arm. *As you used to say: Andiamo, ragazzo. We've got work to do!*

Okay. But do not be surprised if things do not turn out the way you want them to. Besides, I for one am not so keen on putting my life back the way it used to be.

And why not?

I am supposed to be dead, remember?

So am I, nonno. So am I. All it means is that we've got nothing to lose. Right? Nothing to lose and everything to gain.

They come to the end of the Farmland Eco-System.

Tube or a brisk walk? Fausto asks.

Let's walk, the grandfather says.

Fausto takes his grandfather and marches him arm in arm down the corridor to the central hub, singing *Bella Ciao* at the top of his lungs.

Me and you, again, his grandfather says, stopping to catch his breath at a spot where the corridor branches off. *Just the way it was meant to be. Without that nauseating little man coming between us.*

Yes, the nauseating little man, Fausto says. *So, what did you do to him? You can tell me. It'll be a secret between me and these walls.*

Do? I did not do anything to him. What are you talking about?

Oh, come on, now, Fausto says smiling. *You couldn't have killed him because then a new one would come out and you'd be back to square one.* He wags his finger at his grandfather. *Oh you naughty man, you. You've got him locked up somewhere, right? That must be it. Locked up with a supply of food and water so he doesn't die. That's why he hasn't tried to find us. It's the only logical explanation.*

Fausto, the last time I saw the Mussolini was the last time you saw him. Being chopped to bits by the Scavengers.

Liar! Fausto says, suddenly grabbing his grandfather by

the throat and pushing him up against the wall. *Now, where have you got him stashed away?*

You are choking me, his grandfather says. *Please. I can not . . . I can not breathe.*

That's the object of the exercise, Fausto says. He uses his other hand to remove the grandfather's gun from its holster. *I squeeze tighter and tighter until there's no more air and you turn blue and then grey. And then the Scavengers come for you.* He lets his grandfather go, stuffing the gun into his belt. *But not right now. Right now, we're going to find a way out of here.* He takes his grandfather's arm again and leads the stunned man down the corridor. *And one other thing. From now on, if you dare pull any of your stunts like shooting people just because you feel like it or making them disappear because it suits your purposes, you'll answer to me. Is that understood?* His grandfather nods, looking straight ahead. There are tears in his eyes.

Good. And don't think that being family will protect you either. There's no such thing in here—as you well know. You might think I'm Fausto your grandson. The person named after you. But I'm not. I might look like him. Might even act like him on occasion. But I'm not him. I'm a creature that came out of those cloning tanks. Just like you. There's no automatic respect here because you're Fausto The Elder. You have to earn it just like everybody else. The sooner you understand that, the better off you'll be. Right?

Yes, his grandfather says weakly, rubbing his throat.

Good, Fausto says, as he hugs his grandfather's shoulder and gives him a kiss on the cheek. *I'm glad we cleared the air on that. Wouldn't want any more misunderstandings.* He releases his grandfather's arm. *And I forgive you for what you've done with Claretta and Rachele. I forgive you for all that.* He lifts his grandfather's chin. *You did do away with them, didn't you? Come on, you can tell me. No more secrets.*

I . . . no. . . .

No lies now. I don't like liars.

Yes, his grandfather says, barely above a hoarse whisper. *Yes. But I did not—*

Stop! Fausto holds up his hand. *Don't say another word. I don't want to get angry at you again. That wouldn't be very nice. What's done is done. Che sera, sera, as the old song goes. Let's just say you did it out of love for me, yes?* His grandfather nods eagerly. *Now, get along. Can't afford to stand around all day chatting. I've got work to do.*

His grandfather stands for a moment, as if rooted to the spot by the shock of it all. As if still not believing what has just happened to him. Then, he staggers away along the adjoining corridor, barely able to stand up without supporting himself against the wall. He seems to be sagging with each step, getting smaller and smaller.

Adio, nonno, Fausto says, waving his arm in a papal salute. *Keep in touch, eh?*

He turns and continues down the corridor towards the central hub, whistling *Bella Ciao* in a jaunty, devil-may-care manner—as if he doesn't have a worry or a thought in the world. He has gone some 30 metres when he suddenly stops and clutches his head with both hands.

Oh my God, he says, *what have I done? What have I just done? I just attacked my own grandfather. No, it isn't possible. I just—. Oh Jesus—*

He begins to hit his forehead against the corridor wall, slowly, methodically.

No, I didn't do that. No, it can't be.

As he continues to strike his head against the wall, there are rumblings along the floor. It swells as if being pushed by waves. Several Scavengers emerge, tightly rolled up at first but then stretching to their full lengths. Fausto stops abruptly and turns towards them.

What do you want, eh? You think I'm going to do myself in, right? You'd like that, wouldn't you? Well, fuck you!

He kicks out at one of the Scavengers but it easily avoids the blow.

I'm not going to do you the favour of killing myself, Fausto shouts. *Do you understand? Not again. Never again.* He waves as if giving them the brush off. *You're wasting your time. Go back where you came from.*

The two Scavengers weave back and forth for a moment, as if trying to decide what to do. Then, they roll up into a ball and vanish, leaving only telltale ripples in the floor.

Good riddance. And don't come back!

Fausto runs off in the direction his grandfather took, calling out his name. It shouldn't take long to catch up to him. But the old man isn't there and there's the sound of the tube swishing along the wall.

Nonno, Fausto shouts, trying to run alongside the tube. *Forgive me. I . . . I don't know what came over me.* He stops as the tube picks up speed. *You must forgive me. I wasn't myself.* He slides down to the floor. *It's just another dream,* he says, holding his head with his hands. *I'll wake up and none of it will have happened.* He shouts after his grandfather: *Nonno, it didn't happen, right? I never . . . I . . .* He can't bring himself to say it. He shouts again: *You must forgive me, nonno. You must!*

He is still shouting when two scrawny, naked figures, dripping from the cloning tanks, come around the corner. They stop in their tracks the moment they see him. Then start to back away from him.

Claretta? Rachele? Fausto says, holding his arms out to them. *Is that really you? Oh my God, am I ever glad to see you.*

The two let out horrendous shrieks and run down the corridor in the direction from which they've come. Back towards the central pod, leaving wet gooey footprints in their wake.

No, wait! Fausto says. *Claretta! Rachele! Please. Don't leave me here. Please. Let me explain.*

He gets up and tries to follow them. But they quickly vanish in the dim, localized light of the corridors. He comes to where the passageway to the central pod is bisected by another of the rings. Now, he really doesn't know which way to go as they could have headed in any of three possible directions. Or even more if they've continued down to the next set of rings. No, strike that, Fausto says to himself. Stop and think a moment. It doesn't make sense that they would go back to the central pod. There's nothing there but the cloning tanks—at least at this level. And, from the looks of it, they've just come from there.

So it's either to the left or to the right. To the right as he faces the central pod, the nearest eco-system is the polar wasteland. Followed by the rain forest. Not very likely. To the left, on the other hand, is the shortest way to the eighth eco-system—the cubicles. Just a quick tube ride. He places his ear against the wall. Yes, he can hear the vibration of the transport system.

Fausto decides not to take the tube himself as that would alert Claretta and Rachele to his presence. He turns left and heads down the ring, his breathing laboured and sounding very loud in the narrow tunnel-like passage. For the first time ever, he feels claustrophobic, hemmed in. Aware of the low ceiling and tight walls. He thinks of sudden floods. The word "wadi" flashes by. Or the release of poison gases from the vents that stud the walls. Or even an encounter with some freak just emerged from the cloning tanks, with just enough residual energy to make it to the corridors—and to slash and rip at anything in its path until it expires in a pool of green vomit.

That only makes Fausto's breathing more difficult. And the more he tries not to think about it, the worse it gets. By the time he comes out of the ring into the eighth enclosure, it's all he can do to catch his breath. This is crazy, he says to himself. I've been going in and out of those rings for as long as I can remember. It's the fastest way to get around in here. Otherwise, it'll mean going down the more expansive corridors to the central pod each time I want to go to any of the other enclosures. No way. When the time comes, I'll just have to force myself.

He shakes his head and looks around. The eighth eco-system is as dark, sparse and haunted-looking as ever with its row upon row of identical grey cubicles. Some are stacked on top of each other, with metallic doors that slide open with a hiss; others, scattered around the periphery, are in a constant state of being torn down and re-built, like giant children's blocks. It was in one of these, Fausto recalls, that he experienced his most disturbing dreams, the hand-like machine clawing at his face. He shudders, then stands very still—to the point of holding his breath. A moment later, he's rewarded by the sound of bare feet slapping, scurrying across the metal grates.

Come out, Fausto calls. *I'm not going to hurt you. I just want to talk.* The words echo back at him. *Claretta, Rachele. I know you're in here. Come on. It's only me, Fausto. I'm going to sit right here, okay? I'm not going to move. Here, right where you can see that I'm not dangerous.*

Fausto sits on the edge of the open elevator leading to the upper-level cubicles. A few moments later, he hears footsteps and looks up. Claretta and Rachele are leaning over a railing three stories above him. They're still naked and Fausto can see their gleaming bodies in the dark, their breasts like white moons that gravity is trying to pull earthwards.

What do you want? Claretta says.

Want? Fausto says. *I don't want anything. I was worried about you, that's all.* He steps into the elevator. *I'm so glad that I've found you again. Wait for me. I'll be right up.*

No! Rachele says. *Stay right where you are.*

Rachele, it's me, Fausto. Remember? A warm cave? An even warmer bed? I've come to take you back.

No! Claretta says. *We don't want to go back. We know what happened last time. We know. You can't fool us anymore. And that crazy grandfather of yours. He shot us in cold blood.*

While we were sleeping, Rachele says.

Yes, while we were sleeping, Claretta repeats. *The rotten old coward couldn't even look us in the eye.*

I'm sorry, Fausto says, holding out his hands. *It won't happen again. You have my word on it.*

Your word? Rachele says. *What good is that? You left us all alone and went off on a wild goose chase. You left us with that crazy old man. And those awful creatures. They couldn't even wait for us to die properly.*

Fausto presses the elevator button and it begins to rise.

Stop! Claretta says, placing one leg over the rail. *Stop— or you'll never see us again. I swear—we'll jump. And we'll jump again. Each time!*

Okay, okay, Fausto says, stopping on the second level. *I shouldn't have left you. I just didn't know my grandfather would do something like that. What can I do to make it up to you? I want us to be friends again.*

Go away, then, Rachele says. *Leave us in peace for a while. Maybe later when we're not feeling so hurt. . . .*

Yes, Fausto says. *Maybe you're right. Maybe I should leave you alone for now. Yes, maybe I'll do that.* He smiles weakly up at them. *I'm still so glad to see you both. Bye, for now. If you change your minds, I'll be waiting for you in the cave.*

He lowers the elevator shaft back to the ground floor. Rachele and Claretta watch him walking towards the ring passageway, shoulders drooping, head down. Fausto takes a breath and vanishes into the tunnel. But the moment he's out of their sight, he stops and presses himself against the wall. From there, he sees the naked forms of Rachele and Claretta call up the elevator, step into it and take it to the ground level.

He ducks back as they take one last look around before heading off towards the peripheral cubicles. Fausto follows at a safe distance, thankful this once for the shadows that pervade the eighth pod and give it the look of a film noir set. After walking furtively for several minutes, Rachele and Claretta stop, look to the left and right, and then enter one of the cubicles on the edge of the pod. Fausto waits a few moments more, then peeks in.

Claretta and Rachele are kneeling before the Mussolini, almost as if in prayer. He too is naked, lying on what seems the same bed that once held the dreaming Fausto.

Please, Claretta is saying. *Don't do this.*

I must, the Mussolini says. *I must find an answer. Now, stand back.*

Claretta and Rachele move aside. Fausto can now see a bundle of wires leading from Mussolini's head to the familiar machine above him; another bundle, surrounded by a clear plastic tube, is connected to his penis. His penis? Fausto doesn't remember a similar tube connected to his own penis. Perhaps it isn't the same cot and machinery, after all. Perhaps one more variation. Perhaps even the machines aren't allowed to expire peacefully without some form of re-birth.

The tubing snakes around as if it were alive. The Mussolini's thick, mottled torso is jerking up and down, like some oversized frog being subjected to electric shock treatment. Claretta and Rachele pin his legs in an attempt to hold him still, afraid perhaps he is going to tear himself to pieces. But he's too strong for them. His motions become more and more frenzied until he arches up and ejaculates into the plastic tube. But it isn't semen that's quickly sucked up the tube and into the guts of the machine. No, it's blood, gurgling as it makes its way through the tubing to vanish into the second level of the pod.

The Mussolini lies back exhausted and drenched in sweat. Rachele mops his forehead while Claretta gently detaches the wires and pulls the tube from his penis—to reveal a retractable needle inserted into the urinary tract. She wipes away a remaining dribble of blood and rubs him with cream.

Again, the Mussolini says weakly, lifting his head for a moment before falling back. *I was very close that time. This close!* He indicates how close by holding his thumb and forefinger a centimetre apart. *Oh so very close.* He lies very still, moving only his eyes. *Voices in my head. Voices. Trying to tell me what to do.*

Please, my brave, noble Duce, Rachele says. *You must stop now. Before something goes terribly, terribly wrong.*

She's right, Claretta says. *This isn't getting you anywhere.*

I must know, the Mussolini says. *I must discover the secrets of this place. The voices. It's our only hope, don't you see? Our only way out.* His tone and timbre change abruptly, become harsher and authoritarian: *Now, do as I say. Or leave me and I'll manage on my own. Do you understand?*

Rachele stands back. Claretta lets out a deep sigh and is about to re-attach the wires when Fausto comes rushing out of the shadows.

Stop right there, he says as he stands over the Mussolini. *That's my machine. You have no right to use my machine.*

You tricked us, Claretta says.

Yes, Rachele says, *you promised.*

But Fausto isn't listening. He's too busy pushing at the Mussolini, trying to get him off the cot.

Get up! he says. *That machine wasn't meant for you.*

Can't you see he's too weak? Claretta says. *Leave him rest for a while.*

No! Fausto says petulantly. *This is my machine. Do you understand? I want him out of here—now!*

The Mussolini struggles to get up. He stumbles, falls to his knees. His large, fleshy body quivers and seems about to melt away. Claretta and Rachele come to his aid, helping him back up. The three of them begin to walk out of the cubicle, the Mussolini supporting himseif on their shoulders. He stops near the exit and turns his head back towards Fausto.

Good luck, he says.

What do you mean by that?

I'm wishing you luck. Nothing more; nothing less.

Well, I don't need your luck. Fausto busies himself with preparations for placing himself under the machine. *What I needed once was your support. But you made yourself scarce. I searched high and low for you.*

I didn't want to get between you and your grandfather. He shrugs and continues to walk away. *Sorry if I've offended you.*

How the mighty have fallen. From absolute dictator to absolute coward.

Why are you being so cruel? Rachele says, wiping away tears. *What is it you want from him? From us?*

Nothing, Fausto says, waving them away. *What could I possibly want from the likes of you? From the likes of tired, useless creations?* He sits on the bed. *Now get out and let me be. And if you happen to see that old rundown idiot who thinks he's my grandfather, tell him to stay away from me, too. Far, far away. The last thing I need right now is his gibberish.*

Rachele, Claretta and the Mussolini stagger out and disappear into the shadows. The shuffling of feet can be heard for a few moments more, echoing amid the cubicles—but then there's absolute silence. Fausto tilts his head so that he's looking up at the machinery—like the underbelly of an insect's carapace. It's definitely not the same machine. Aside from the extra tube, this one's larger, with a thicker complex of wires to his head—and even more ominous-looking spidery, reticulated claws.

I must, Fausto says aloud as he gingerly touches one of the needle-sharp fingers, passes his hand over what he's come to call the "penis borer". *The Mussolini was right about one thing. It might be my one chance of getting out of this place.* He removes his clothing and it rolls itself up on the floor. He sits down and looks around the cubicle one last time.

I know you're out there, somewhere, he shouts. His words echo back at him. *Wish me luck. Or go to hell!*

As he lies back on the cot, the machinery hums into action. The insect's carapace is directly above him, a mere half-metre above him. The various sections click and clack, cold clinical sounds to undo even the bravest soul. The thick bundle of wires spirals forward and clamps down on his skull. The needles search for the right points of entry.

I can't die, Fausto says, as he watches a reflection of the wires against the machine's shiny surface. *Dying is an impossibility. Therefore, I have nothing to fear. Nothing to fear. It only stands to reason.* He begins to sing: *A la matina, apena alzatta, o Bella Ciao, Bella Ciao, Bella Ciao Ciao Ciao . . . a la matina. . . .*

The first needle finds the right spot and goes in, displacing bone as if it were putty. Fausto tenses and braces himself. But there is no pain—and soon no more anxiety. Just a letting go. Fausto smiles. *Or is it the first needle smiling?* he asks himself. It doesn't matter. Soon, the others have all been inserted. Fausto feels detached, in a state of connected disconnection, floating serenely above the flesh and blood creature on the cot. One last whir as the "penis borer" eases into position. Fausto watches with bemusement as the needle attaches itself not to his penis but rather to his belly button.

Of course, the Fausto floating overhead says as the machine becomes part of the vital circuit for his counterpart. *Umbilical re-connection. Going back to dear old mom. Dear old mechanical mom. That silly Mussolini and his one-track macho ways. One of these days he'll get something right. One of these days, he'll—*

Before he can complete the thought, the Fausto floating overhead is pulled back down and re-united with the one under the machinery. The distinction is lost. Their phases and amplitudes become one again, as the voice might have said. But the voice is inexplicably silent. Nowhere to be heard. Fausto expects it to pipe up at any moment though, to remind him he is no longer alone. Or to taunt him with its logical conundrums.

He shuts his eyes and holds his breath. Nothing. The only sound is that of Fausto's blood being pumped out through the tube and then back again into his head . . . out through the tube and back into his head . . . He re-opens his eyes. He can see the blood pulsing through the clear tube, heading off on its journey. A meaningless journey from where Fausto is lying.

Come out, come out, wherever you are, Fausto says. *I know you're out there. You can't fool me with your silent ways.*

More whirring above him. The clickity clack of spidery fingers. A needle. A long, thin needle. Coming sideways. A long, thin needle being inserted directly into his brain. And then being withdrawn again.

No! he screams.

Or thinks he screams.

No!

He's dissolving. Bit by bit, he's dissolving. Liquefying. Parts of him are turning to liquid. To jelly. Puddling at the base of the contraption like hot fat melting off a roast. This is it again, he thinks. This is where I die again, one more experiment gone fatally wrong. And a fresh me comes out of the tanks, bright-eyed and bushy-tailed. Bright-eyed and bushy-tailed?

What the hell does that mean? Squirrels? Monkeys? Bush babies?

Everything is starting to swirl above him. Water down a drain, swirling and being thrown out again by the centrifugal force. Or a black hole's event horizon. He sees his feet slide in first, twisted in a psychedelic image, squeezed like a mop, forced to give up their liquid. Then his legs, his chest, his arms, his neck, all torqued and stretched and scrunched into impossible shapes before slipping down the drain. He tries to fight back, to pull himself back but it's no use. The forces are too powerful, suction forces imploding into the vacuum of space, pulling him along for the ride—and erasing him at the same time.

The fact that he knows he'll be back, that he can't really be erased, doesn't help much at that moment. Doesn't ease the fear of non-existence. Fausto lets out one final scream as his mouth twists and his head bursts like a red flower and, drop by drop, vanishes down the drain. Into the black hole. Out in space. In a place where contact lasts forever, where a universal circuit is completed and you're spread so thin you can feel the individual molecules struggling to keep in touch with each other.

SCENE SIX: SPLIT INFINITIES

The first surprise when Fausto comes to again is that he isn't emerging wet and naked from a cloning tank and he isn't walking awkwardly and in a state of disorientation down a dark, narrow corridor with slimy walls and he isn't experiencing the feeling of having all that self-knowledge come zooming back into his head with the force of a sledgehammer. Instead, he's sitting in some sort of high-backed swivel seat, like a captain or pilot chair, in a dome-shaped room. He's sitting in this plush chair, surrounded on all sides by computer consoles and wall-sized monitors on which ever-changing scenes are being played out.

The second surprise is that Fausto is familiar yet unfamiliar with this room. Or this area. And that's hardly possible as he's been over every part of the facility during his many lifetimes here, been over it with, as he likes to put it, a fine tooth-comb. A room like this, an area this size, would have been difficult to overlook. Impossible. Unless, of course . . . A hidden room within a hidden facility. Doubly hidden. If they could create the latter, why not the former? But no. That's not it at all.

He finally realizes where he is—it's just the perspective that's off. Before this, he'd only seen the room from the outside, from a cherry picker. Or from beneath. The control room. He looks down beneath his feet. The floor is made of clear plastic. He can see right through to the cloning tanks below. For a moment, he panics, feels as if he's about to fall through. As if the floor were about to become porous. And then a part of it actually does, creating a hole large enough for a man to plunge through. Wavelets from the cloning tanks become fingers reaching up to him, inviting him in. Fausto pulls his legs up to his chin, assuming a fetal position on the chair. The fingers dissolve; the hole closes again.

Just another of the facility's tricks, he says. *I'm onto you.*

But he stays on the chair, feet safely off the ground for the time being. Just to be sure.

Yes, I'm onto you.

The monitor directly in front of him now shows a familiar scene: the mountain top cave where the snow leopard lives and which he shared with Claretta and Rachele. There's his grandfather sitting oh so forlornly. Head bowed as if it were the end of the world. Sitting on a rocky outcropping next to the leopard.

Tell me, dear Giacomo, he says, stroking the great cat, *where is the honour in all this? Humans were not meant to live like this, I agree. We were meant to suffer, to commit acts of greatness and meanness. To live and to die. Happy or miserable or a bit of both. But to live and to die nevertheless: O patria mia, vedo le mura e gli archi/ e le colonne e i simulacri e l'erme/ torri degli avi nostri,/ ma la gloria non vedo,/ non vedo il lauro e il ferro ond'eran carchi/ i nostri padri antichi. Or fatta inerme,/ nuda la fronte e nudo il petto mostri.*

He bows his head again. *What have I done to deserve this?*

The leopard yawns and licks its paws.

Nonno, Fausto shouts at the monitor. *Cheer up! It's only a game after all. We can't all be winners, you know.*

He swivels to face another monitor. The Mussolini, Claretta and Rachele are wandering about in the area where he had last seen them, poking their heads into one grey-walled enclosure after another as they are constantly being built and re-built.

Bah, Claretta is saying, *I've had enough of this. We're not going to find anything around here. This place gives me the willies. Let's go.*

Yes, Benito, Rachele says, *time to stop this nonsense, don't you think? We're all getting hungry and tired.*

No, no, the Mussolini says, shaking his head. *It's around here somewhere. I know it is. You two go on back. I'll catch up with you later. Go, go.*

No way, Claretta says, latching tightly onto his arm. *Not with that creep lurking around. We're sticking together.*

Creep? Fausto says. *Is that any way to talk about your benefactor? Your best and only friend in the whole wide world?*

He scans the rest of the monitors. The scenes are constantly shifting, images flickering on and off: at one moment blank, the next showing bits and pieces of the various ecosystems, jumping from place to place and from time to time. There's Fausto walking through the rain forest; there he is inside a polar igloo; there he is again on ocean-side hill top. And now as he tutors the newly-formed Mussolinis. And there beneath the machine, still coupled with the fluid pulsing out one end and in the other.

Just like I thought, he says wearily. *One more glorified projection room. Nothing I haven't seen before. Nothing I haven't done before. Over and over till stagnation do us part. Not even the peace of collapsing to dust.*

He jumps up out of the chair and shouts: *Come on! Show me something different! This is me in the here and now. Not some past Fausto you're dissecting to create some future Fausto. Show me something new!*

What would you like to see? a voice echoes in the room as the monitors all go blank at the same time.

Not a voice. Not any voice. The voice. The voice from Fausto's nightmares. And not coming from inside his head this time. Definitely outside. Definitely from somewhere within the room itself.

Who . . . who. . . .

Who am I? Is that what you wish to ask?

Yes, Fausto says, turning slowly on the spot in the hope of pinpointing the source of the voice. *That's exactly what—*

Unimportant, believe me, the voice says, not unkindly. *Just like it's not really all that important that your statement about being in the here and now is not strictly true. The there and then would probably be more accurate. But seeing how much humans value identity, the so-called individualness of each corporeal unit, I suppose you won't feel comfortable until I tell you who I am.*

You're right, Fausto says, still unable to zero in, for no matter which way he turns, the voice is coming directly at him. From the walls maybe.

I am the voice.

Well, duh, Fausto says. *I kind of figured that out for myself. I want to know who you are—and I'm not fond of ventriloquists.*

Glad to see you haven't lost your sense of humour, the voice says with a chuckle. *It's one of the more endearing things about the human animal.*

Look, Fausto says. *If you're nothing but a talking computer program, I'm not really all that impressed.*

Oh no, the voice says. *I wouldn't blame you if that's what I was. I'm not crazy about them myself. A little too self-assured, for my liking.*

So, what are you then?

I am—

And don't say 'the voice' or I might start smashing things.

I am—and here there should be some trumpet fanfare, no doubt— the facility. Congratulations for finally finding your way in. Even if it took you a few tries. Let me see . . . a baker's dozen to be exact.

What are you talking about? I've been trapped here—

Confidentially, the voice says, assuming an almost whispering, don't-let-the-others-hear-me air, *I'm glad it was you and not that Mussolini fellow. That would have been a disaster. Let me tell you, a real disaster. I don't know what I would have done if—*

Stop! Fausto shouts. *Stop right there.*

Yes?

Back up, Fausto says, sitting back on the chair.

Oh, I'm sorry. Guess I was going a little fast, wasn't I? Assuming a little too much, eh? To which point would you like me to return?

To the point where you said who you are.

The voice laughs what could be described as a belly laugh. A guffaw.

I see, it says. *The statement 'I am the facility' is a little too simple for you. Almost beneath notice. Like a single-celled amoeba. You want more complex explanations, well-balanced equations on both sides of the equal sign. Genetic code variations on a grand scale leading to individual beasts.*

No, I just want to know who you are. And when you're going to come out of your little hiding place—probably from behind one of those panels. Like The Wizard or something.

Sorry to disappoint you, Fausto Contadino the 13th—I guess that should be the 14th if one counts the original model—but what you see is what you get. Or what you don't see is what you get.

Enough of this crap! Fausto shouts, slapping the sides of the chair. *Show yourself. Or I start pulling wires.*

Tell you what, the voice says as calmly as ever. *They say a picture is worth a thousand words, right? Although now I guess it's three-D holograms or something, isn't it?*

You're really starting to piss me off.

Humour me, the voice says. *Lean back in that chair. Let your head settle back and place your arms on the rests. Get comfortable, in other words.*

Now what? Fausto says. *Psychoanalysis? Are you going to turn out to be my Freudian slip of a subconscious?*

Look, the voice says with a sudden edge to it. *If you really insist on being difficult, I'll just open up another hole, zip you back from whence you came and start all over with No. 14. Or 15 or whatever number you are. I don't care, really. I've got all the time in the world.*

Okay, okay, Fausto says, leaning his head back and settling his arms on the rests. As he does so, he feels a tightening, as if the chair is squeezing him. And a slightly cold feeling against the back of his head. Not an altogether unpleasant sensation but he still starts forward. Jerks his head forward.

Don't be alarmed, the voice says. *We must make good, firm contact. That's the key. So just relax. You're the captain of your own fate.*

Very funny, Fausto says.

Now, shut your eyes, the voice says. *Not too tightly. Just so you can concentrate better. Now, I want you to think of the most beautiful animal in the world. No, let's try that again. I want you to remember what you thought was the most beautiful animal when you were a child. A very young child. When the possible and the impossible were still one and the same. When there was no wall between the actual and the potential.*

Fausto tries to think back, tries to picture what he felt was the most beautiful creature in the world when he was a child. At first, he finds it hard because he's trying to be logical about it, trying to eliminate the candidates one at a time. Like an old-fashioned police line up: lion, bird of paradise, giraffe, whale . . . except that the only place Fausto had ever seen any of these creatures was in the education modules . . . elephant, eagle, penguin, tiger. . . .

No, the voice says. *You must let yourself go. Don't think only of the possible.*

Fausto tries to blank out his mind. Allows himself to float away. Thoughtless. Uncaring. And then it comes to him, out of an early childhood book. A picture book. It comes to him like a vivid image of innocence. The crude yet magical rainbow colours of a childhood picture book. The impossible straining to become actual.

Excellent, the voice says. *Most excellent. See what miracles you can accomplish with a little effort. You can open your eyes now.*

Fausto opens his eyes. There, below him, below his feet, is the outline of the creature from that picture book. Amorphous at first but slowly becoming more and more defined. White. A white figure. Shimmering green-tinged. A white horse. A white horse emerging from the cloning tank. A white horse shaking the liquid from its sleek back. A white horse pawing the ground, clopping the metal floor and neighing. A white horse looking up at him. A white horse with large silver eyes. With large glittering silver eyes. A white horse with a long white mane and a single white horn spiralling from its forehead.

PART THREE

ON HIS FATE:
CONVERSATIONS WITH THE GOD

> All is far off, there is no way back,
> the dead are not dead,
> the living are not alive

Scene One: Over-Taking Control

Time passes. Doesn't it, your honour? From second to second, minute to minute, hour to hour, day to day . . . you get the point. You get the fucking point. Time passes. And yet more time passes. In an understated, barely defined room, a leg slides imperceptibly off a bed, naked foot coming to rest on the floor. On the cold cold floor. A hand moves achingly slowly towards an exposed breast. Lavishly white in the barely defined room. Ever closer until finger and nipple, until finger and chocolate bud nipple are only a fraction of a millimetre apart. Only a synaptic spark apart. While a sonorous voice drones on: *A minute passes. And another minute passes. And yet another minute passes.*

I must be thinking of an old comedy skit. An ancient, mouldy and by now completely forgotten comedy skit. Or the two hoboes under a long-dead, makeshift tree in *Waiting For Godot,* the not-so-subtle distillation of 20th century angst and doubt. If nobody made us, then who made us? I wouldn't have known how to ask that the first time around. In fact, I don't think I would have known who or what *Waiting For Godot* was. But I do now—and it makes all the difference in the world. Not!

I'm thinking of all the creatures that have come and gone—and gone and come—since I first arrived here. I'm thinking of the lure of immortality within all of us. The urge to live forever. The desire to always be here. The standing still at last of time. Or, at the very least, the regulation of time within a standard framework that rests outside the boundaries where death lurks in all its wild unpredictability. Now, isn't that a mouthful?

You're twenty and then twenty-five and then thirty and

then forty and then sixty and then ninety and then twenty again. Just by thinking it. Just by a simple submersion. Simple painless submersion. Wouldn't that be wonderful? Wouldn't that be simply marvellous? Wouldn't that be loverly. . . ? Wouldn't it now?

Time passes, doesn't it, your honour, while it stands still? Passes ever so slowly while it stands ever so still? I'm thinking of all the times I learned to play the guitar flawlessly. Repetition upon repetition of the same notes. The same chords. The same fingering. Until those fingers bled. Until I got it right. Until it couldn't be any more perfect. Until the emptiness swallowed me up again in its perfection. I played the guitar flawlessly and without the least feeling. Without giving one sweet fuck about it.

Nothing but numbness. A numbness that started at the centre and eventually spread out to my fingers, forcing them to cease as well their useless perfection. I'm thinking of all the times I learned to box, to swim, to dance, to sing, to manage great companies, to run entire countries, to perform feats of prestidigitation, to hold my breath forever, to conduct lab tests over and over again, to commit the perfect crime, to achieve useless perfection. Over and over without end. Amen.

And here I am again, back in the control room high above the tanks. As if nothing's happened. No, I no longer need to attach myself to that infernal machine to get up here. Thank goodness for that (although I'm willing to bet the Mussolini is still at it and Lord knows what orifices he's using now). The door panel is wide open before me and there's a normal staircase, a normal spiral staircase made of a bright, shiny metallic substance leading from the lower floor. I simply walk up, clanking all the way, and here I am. Lord and master of all I survey.

If I press against the chair so that the back of my head touches, I activate the cloning computers, all those lovely monitors and buttons and CPUs performing their DNA crunching at impossible speeds, all the possible combinations and permutations of the 30,000 active genetic bits that supposedly make up a human being. The typical human being. Yep. And I can create whatever I feel like, whatever my imagination dreams up, twist those double helixes into whatever shape I desire.

But I won't do that again. Not that I'm not tempted, mind you. The offer of being a god with what seem unlimited powers is always difficult to turn down. Just ask Yahweh. Well into his dotage but he still won't give it up. But I've learned my lesson on that. Of the permutations and combinations spinning out on those screens, churning away within those processors, only a very few are actually possible—and only a very few of those viable. I've learned my lesson the hard way. I wonder if God has.

Just as I was getting used to the idea, just as I had stopped rubbing my eyes for the wonder of it all, my fabulous creature left me. Abandoned me. Almost as quickly as it had appeared. As if, after holding on for as long as possible, it could no more withstand the forces of gravity, the tug of the earth. As if it didn't have the skeleton or musculature or strength of character. As if it . . . Whatever.

One moment, sunshine above and below, hand clutching its mane, I was riding through a vast field of wheat, heavy with golden tassels, like a proud warrior from some other time; the next, the creature was collapsing in a heap beneath me. Literally melting away and sending me skidding to the ground. I pleaded with it to get up again, to give it one more try, to not let me down that way. It's only been a few days, I said with the illogic of desperation. Surely you can do better than that?

But it looked at me like I imagine a pained and agonizing dying child would look at his parents ("Let me go, please, let me go") and then slowly shut its huge eyes. Lowered its head and began to melt. And the Scavengers burst out of the ground, clacking their mandibles in eager anticipation. In my rage, in my impotence, in my denial, I prepared to fight them with fists and feet, with clumps of earth, with sticks and stones.

Yes, I knew even then that such a fight was hopeless, that I couldn't drive them all away, that sooner or later they'd close in and swallow up the remains. And yes, I knew they were just remains, a heap of rotting, stinking flesh lacking all grace and shape with, in the end, only the horn left to taunt me before it too was cleaned up. I knew all that even then. After all, why should it have been any different for my creation? Like everything else—monster, mere mongrel or incredible sight to behold—that had come crawling out of the tanks without the proper DNA credentials, my creature had paid the price.

But I couldn't help myself. I couldn't believe the creature had simply melted away on its own. That such beauty could vanish as quickly as it had been created. I needed someone or something to blame. Or to vent my rage against. As the ultimate representatives of the facility, the Scavengers would do nicely, thank you very much.

It was thus I managed to keep them at bay until well into the night, managed to keep them from the rapidly diminishing pile with curses and screams and threats. And even then I knew that, sooner or later, I'd fall asleep and besides my creature was nothing but this stinking heap of flesh and the Scavengers were simply doing their job. You want to know the funniest thing about it? I also knew that the Scavengers were, in some way, respecting my wishes. I had seen them in action before and, believe me, there was no stopping them when they smelled death. Or rather, the coming cessation of this particular life.

I had always thought it was an automatic reaction of theirs—like the brain firing off a signal to a muscle to do its bidding. The muscle can't help itself; the Scavengers couldn't help themselves. Or so I'd always assumed. But there they were, encircling me yet keeping their distance as the heap became smaller and smaller, as everything vanished but the horn, its ivory-spiralled grooves like a stab to the heart. And, just before I fell asleep in that unending field of golden wheat, curled up next to the horn, my arms wrapped around that horn, I had this strange sensation that they were watching me or commiserating with me or even feeling my pain.

Yes, that these ugly, vicious, reticulated, unnatural, unthinking machines were feeling sorry for <u>me</u>, a human being endowed with everything they lacked—from sentiment and passion to free will and the ability to choose my own destiny. Imagine the gall. For that, they deserved a few more "Fuck right offs!" screamed into the well-regulated night air. Not too hot and not too cold. Adjusted to make sleeping as pleasant as possible. *Fuck right off,* I muttered, shaking my fist at the moon. At the mountains. At the owls. At those perfect, swivel-headed, traditionally-wise owls that I always assume are really spies for the facility, sending back digital data to be parsed and digested by the masters of the place.

In the morning, I awoke in that field—the sun hovering overhead just for me, warming me up; the wind ever-so-gently caressing the tops of the wheat; the song birds chirping merrily away. Merely another day in the facility like the one before and a preview of what tomorrow would bring. Time passes, your honour; time stands still. You learn to kill; you learn to play the guitar; you learn to change sex; you learn to be sexless.

I stayed curled up for another few minutes, hoping it had all been a terrible nightmare and that my creature had simply gone down to the nearby stream to quench its thirst and that it would at any moment snort in my ear or try to wake me with a gentle nuzzle or prod me with its unique horn. Nothing. And nothing left. Not even the hole into which my creature had vanished.

I sat there staring at the earth, the rich seed-bearing earth, full of warmth and nourishment. Another lesson taught, right? The stupidity of emotional attachment, right? But what good are these lessons if there's no going forward? Or is it the trying again that counts? And, if so, what sort of trying? Killing myself over and over again? Accepting my fate like the Mussolinis and Racheles and Clarettas? Constantly railing against it like my grandfather? What? What is it I'm supposed to do? What is it I'm supposed to learn?

I looked up and found myself surrounded by animals of all kinds, from the smallest to the largest, from the rarest to the most common, from every eco-system in the facility, as far as the eye could see. I was at the centre of this vast circling—or living helix or whatever, spiralling out, receding into the distance. And they all seemed to be looking at me, staring at me with unblinking eyes. Wherever I turned, there were eyes on me. But they weren't hostile. Rather it was as if they were trying to tell me something, to burn something into me that they couldn't communicate by language.

At first, the urge was to shoo them all away, to tell them to mind their own business: *Mind your own fucking business! I'm the only human here! You just don't know!* But I knew somehow that wouldn't do any good, that they wouldn't listen. As I also knew that what they were trying to tell me was important. After all, why would they leave their comfortable nooks and crannies to form this circle around me? It certainly wasn't to console me for the loss of my childhood fantasy creature. These animals had no room for fantasies. They lived at the heart of things—and that's what they wanted me to do: to forget about fantasy and to finally get to that heart of things.

Okay, okay, I said. *I get the point.* It's funny how we sometimes use animals to express certain emotions: "I feel sheepish" or "bullish" or "coltish" or "wolfish" or "cowed" or "making a jackass of myself" or "doggedly pursuing my dreams". And we never stop to think what exactly those expressions mean. Or whether or not the actual animals appreciate the stereotyping. But, at that moment, with all those eyes staring at me, I had to admit that what I had been doing up to then was something completely human—I had been pitying myself, a frenzy of self-pity and loathing. And I had been using that self-pity and loathing as a shell to protect myself from the truth.

No animal would ever stoop so low. They faced the truth in their own way every moment they were alive—directly, with nothing between them and the outside. And it came out in their eyes—trusting, sober, intelligent eyes. No, not trusting, sober, intelligent. Those were human words. But all words are human words. So there was no way to describe those eyes. Or to put them in context. They were just there. Just like the animals were just there. Just like my grandfather and Mussolini and Rachele and Claretta were just there. And just like I was just there.

I knew then what it felt like to be separated from your essence, from the thing that you think makes you what you think you are. And to just be. And I didn't like it. Not one bit. It's like standing naked, shivering, in the cold, impenetrable dark, not knowing what is up or down. Floating. Not touching anything. Reaching out into the cold, impenetrable dark and meeting no resistance.

And suddenly giant spotlights are shining on you from every direction, while all around you echo the murmurs and whispers and laughter of people you can't see because you're blinded and you're trying to cover up. And you find yourself thinking: Is this what Adam and Eve felt like when their creator shone his all-knowing spotlight on them? When he separated their existence from their essence? Or is it exactly the reverse? Is this what it feels like to have the two yoked together so that you're constantly thinking about your nakedness? Constantly aware of your relationship to the rest of the universe?

The facility was supposed to do away with that, with at least that. With that at the very least. Well, wasn't it? I mean, what's the point of living forever if all you do is continue to accumulate guilt? And doubt? And shame? And self-pity? And loathing? What's the point if all the problems and headaches of being mortal remain? *Tell me, huh,* I said to the animals around me. *Tell me what's the point?*

Ah, but I was being oh so human again and the animals soon lost interest. Besides, since when had they been beset by "guilt" or "doubt" or "shame" or "self-pity" or "loathing"? When's the last time you saw a donkey sitting raptly in a theatre, watching Vladimir and Estragon go through their contortions beneath that scraggly, limbless tree? Or a dog speculating on Oedipus at that crossroad?

One by one, heads lowered, they turned from me and left, indicating in no uncertain terms that the show was over, that whatever message they'd tried to impart had gone unheeded. That, as usual, in my attempt to verbalize, I had lost whatever real significance their gathering had. Or perhaps it had signified nothing at all—simply the herd instinct coming to the fore, attracted by the odour of my loss. Of my heart aching and pounding in my chest.

Naturally, being human, the first thing I tried to do once I made it back to the control tower, as I like to call it, was to bring my creature back to life. This time, it lasted all of a few minutes, barely making it out of the cloning tanks before it collapsed and was gobbled up, leaving a momentary phosphorescent glow behind. Essence of phosphorescence. Glistening of unlistening. Okay, I said. If you're not going to let me create light, then I'd better stick to darkness.

I dredged up every one of my childhood nightmares—slobbering, blind, green-slimed horrors from the centre of the earth; alien methane super terrors from Jupiter; quasi-human monstrosities from hell itself—and hurled them at the facility. Day after day, I brought them forth, searching for the one that would defeat the place, that would cut through the force field and let the outside world in once more.

On occasion, I heard screams, the crunching of bone, the smacking of lips. But having a few animals devoured was a small price to pay for the opportunity to break free. One of the creatures—a lizard-like concoction with razor claws and clacking beak and looking almost two-dimensional—managed to make it up the stairs, crawling the last few steps in a puddle of acidic ooze. It looked at me with malevolent intelligence, as if it knew what I was trying to do—and then lunged. Fortunately, it fell short, collapsing at my feet, claws still cutting the air in scissored frenzy. Or perhaps not so fortunately. Or perhaps it was neither fortunate nor unfortunate. It just was.

That was this morning. And that was my last attempt at creating "monsters". Be they nightmare or wish fulfillment.

Merely fanciful or truly hideous. Or even straightforward-looking on the outside. What is a monster? A monster is anything that doesn't have a piece of genetic material bubbling away amid the broth of the cloning tanks, waiting to be actualized by the computers.

I must face facts. The animals now in the facility are the only ones that can be re-created with the hope of carrying on a "normal" existence. No silver-eyed unicorns and no fire-breathing dragons—as enticing as these might be. And so far, we five are the only human beings who can last more than a couple of days. Others—be they simple flukes of nature or aberrations from my fevered brain or even perfect replicas from the court of Louis XV—march straight from the cloning tanks into the maws of the Scavengers.

The Scavengers! Of course. They're real. They must have a piece of their genetic imprint in the cloning computers. Why hadn't I thought of it before? Simply reproduce enough Scavengers to cause an overload. Simply flood the facility with them so that the place would eventually self-destruct, eventually devour itself. It's so obvious. I sit in the chair, playing perfectly my guitar, fiddling perfectly my fiddle, and set out to create as many Scavengers as possible. It isn't long before they're rolling out of the tanks one after the other, wave after wave, phalanxes in perfect formation, armoured shells clanging in unison.

What are you doing? the Mussolini asks, the only one with the courage to visit me up in my pilot's house. *The last thing we need is more of those accursed creatures.*

Any time now, I say, feeling very self-satisfied. *Any time now, they'll turn on each other and bring the facility to a grinding halt.*

Turn on each other? What if they turn on us?

That's okay, too, I say, watching my grandfather, Claretta and Rachele huddling beneath the stairs. *I've got no problem with that. Do you? One way or another, we'll be free of this place. Wouldn't you like that?*

I have spoken too soon. Fifty metres from the tanks, the perfect formations start to fall apart; fifty metres further and they begin to trip over each other; fifty metres still further and the real Scavengers rise up, so obviously different when placed side by side with the pseudos. So obviously real.

Your plan seems not to be working very well, the Mussolini says, gloating. *Thank goodness for that.*

You shut up, I say. *This shouldn't be happening. I did everything right this time. I used the actual genetic material . . . I. . . .*

Yes, I have done everything right. And yet it seems I've made one little mistake: I've assumed that the Scavengers are like the rest of us, reproducible with the right DNA imprint. Obviously, that isn't the case. Obviously, they and not us are the unique ones, the ones created in the likeness of their god, a constant and permanent presence.

Here, I say to the Mussolini as I stand up. *Sit in the chair. Let's see what you can do. Let's see what you can come up with.*

Seriously?

Of course.

No tricks, he says, swaying, caught between the urge to flee and the inability to resist the offer. *You're not going to trick me?*

I'm all out of tricks, I say, making an exaggerated motion towards the seat. *Do your best.*

He leans back in the chair, shuts his eyes and concentrates. The computer screens churn and seemingly process but nothing happens. Nothing appears.

See, he says, pointing, *you're holding something back. The machine. The key is the machine, isn't it? I'm convinced it's the machine.*

Whatever you say.

I'm going back there. I'm going to get it right.

You do that, I say, sitting in the chair and strumming on the arm-rests. *And good luck.*

My grandfather, Rachele and Claretta refuse to come up here. My grandfather is in a permanent funk, barely talking to me, resentful of the fact our relationship has done a complete 360 degree turn somewhere along the way. He sulks and skulks, lets out these long, deep sighs and shakes his head knowingly. Rachele and Claretta cling to one another, like a pair of schoolgirls in a horror movie. They've never recovered from their traumatic last deaths. Every noise, every shadow makes them rigid with fear.

The Mussolini returns from another bout with the machine, each time more beaten and shattered than the previous. Despite the fact I've shown him the proper way to hook himself up, he's still unable to make the link with the cloning computers. I've concluded it's programmed to respond only to me. Why? Who knows. Perhaps because I was the last one into the facility—the last "real" human, that is. Or perhaps because I was the first one to discover the control tower. Or perhaps for no reason at all—just another one of the creators' whims.

You're keeping something from me, the Mussolini says. *I can smell it.* Here he taps the side of his nose—just like my grandfather had oh those so many aeons ago. *And I don't blame you. I'd do the same myself if I were in your shoes.*

I'm tired, I say. *I need to get some sleep. You're welcome to it.*

I walk out of the control room and down the spiral stairs.

One of these days, the Mussolini shouts behind me. *One of these days, I'm going to uncover your little secret. Then I won't be your puppet any more. No sirree. Then you'll be my puppet. I'll string you along.*

I laugh and then continue down the stairs as if dangling from strings. At the bottom, my grandfather awaits, sullen as usual.

Nonno! I say, as cheerfully as possible. *How about going for a walk? I haven't seen the polar bears in a while.*

You go ahead, he says in a whiny, irritating voice. *I do not have the energy anymore.*

Ha! You're as strong as an ox. Fit as a bull. Healthy as a horse. I remember the animals that had surrounded me. They flash before me. *Come on. I bet Luna is desperate for some company. We'll share some strong cheese and bread. Some provolone and homemade. Just like in the old days. What do you say?*

The old days are gone, he says, shaking his head. *Long dead and gone. And we are long dead and gone, too. What you see is nothing but an empty shell. The husk after the kernel is no longer there. Walking, talking husks. Empty . . . broken. . . .*

Okay, okay, I say, waving him off. *I get the point. I understand.*
Do you? he says. *Do you really?*

I look closely at my grandfather. He hasn't changed much
physically from the days when he first brought me here. Of
course, whenever he wears out, the facility simply re-incar-
nates him, turns him into a newer, fresher model—of about
the same age as when he last came to the facility. But each re-
birth also makes him less like my grandfather and more like
a sourpuss old man with bitterness and failure etched deep in
his heart. It accumulates around him.

Whoever said we grow wiser with age and thus infinitely
wiser with infinite age didn't know what the fuck he was talking about. More penny-ante knowledge crammed into our
heads; more useless details about the world around us, more
blind groping for non-existent answers . . . But wisdom? Not
likely. I watch him slink away, dusty, defeated, dead in every
way but one.

See you, Nonno, I yell out, waving and putting on a happy
face. *If you feel like talking, you know where to find me.*

I turn and am about to step into the tube that'll take me to
what I like to call my home—the cave on the hillside so much
like the faded pictures of the farmland surrounding my
grandfather's village. And why shouldn't I call it my home
now? I've probably lived there longer than anywhere else,
right?

It occurs to me that, with my control of the cloning computers, I could create just about any kind of home I like.
There aren't the same restrictions on non-living objects: a
castle, a mansion, an orbiter—anything's possible. And I
could create some fancy modes of transportation, too—even
teleportation, I bet, if I put my mind to it. Ha, ha. Some way
to send the essential DNA through computers and out the
other side. And robots and androids to serve me. At my beck
and call. Like an all-powerful lord striding across the land.

But I like my cave and I like doing things for myself and
the tube is fast enough for me when I'm too tired to walk.
So there. Besides, I've been there and done that. Built

myself servants of every stripe. Experimented with both sexes—at the same time. In one android body. There's a wildness to it—at first. And then an everlasting boredom. An emptiness. No, better to keep things simple.

I step into the tube.

Can I come, too? the Mussolini meekly calls out behind me as I'm about to press the button. I hesitate, not looking back. *Please.*

Sure, I say. *But no more bullshit. Is that understood? No more talk about hooking up to the machine and how I'm holding something back. You mention it once and you're out. I need your word on that.*

I promise, he says, walking briskly towards me. *On my sainted mother's grave.*

And us? Rachele and Claretta say in unison, their faces peering out from the edge of the corridor, from as close as they'll get to the central cloning area.

Aren't you going to take us? Rachele says.

You can't leave us here, Claretta says, shivering as she looks around.

No, I guess I can't, I say, stepping out of the tube. *Come on. The more, the merrier.*

Just like the good old days, eh? Rachele says, linking my arm with hers.

Just like the good old days, I say.

I hold out my other arm. Claretta takes it.

Come on, Rachele says, beckoning the Mussolini to join us.

In that case, why not walk? I say.

And the four of us skip down the corridor as if we don't have a care in the world. As if we're off to see the wizard or something.

Just like the good old days.

SCENE TWO: ATAVISTIC URGES

Well, not quite.

Even in a place where you can repeat your mistakes as many times as you want or try to work them through until you've dissected each and every one, until you get the sequence of events exactly right, the good old days are the good old days—when they actually weren't the good old days but rather one more struggle to work through. A prism of remembrance to help create those wonderful selective memories all surrounded by the golden halo of youth and sweet innocence. A purging of the unpleasant, expunging of the excremental. And thank God for it. Total recall is the one thing we don't need around here.

Don't get me wrong. I enjoy Rachele and Claretta's company. A lot. They keep my spirits up and make me laugh and occasionally allow me to forget who and where I am. We play games and chase each other around and roll in the wheat fields. Like unruly children. We sit around a fire in the evening and talk and talk and talk and sing songs and then lie back and watch the embers rise into the sky. Which we sometimes pretend not to remember is a fake one and has a sun that gives off no heat.

Occasionally, the two of them will burst inexplicably into tears and huddle together sobbing, arms wrapped around one another in a convulsive hug. Questions, caresses, signs of sympathy do no good at such times. I've learned to leave them be, to completely ignore them. Sometimes they go for hours that way and sometimes even days. But they eventually come out of it to re-join me at the campfire or at the breakfast table or in my bed.

I've even learned to appreciate the Mussolini and, just like my grandfather and I used to do "in the good old days," we often take trips together to some of the other eco-systems. And I confide in him. Let him in on some of my darkest secrets and wishes. Why not? I believe everyone should have their own personal father confessor. Just because mine happens to look like a petty yet ruthless dictator . . . Besides, despite his rhetoric, he's completely loyal to me. (Perhaps it's simply because I'm the only one who can make the cloning computers work but I don't care about his motives). And he did save my life—or one of my lives, didn't he?

Speaking of monsters, I say to him late one evening as we huddle inside my favourite igloo, readying for a night's sleepover, *bet you can't guess who I brought up from the control tower during one of my fits of rage. During one of the times I wanted to destroy everything and everyone.*

Medusa? I shake my head. *The Gorgon? A horror from beneath the sea? The Thing? The Creature From The Black Lagoon? The 50-Foot Woman? The 43rd President of the United States?*

Nope. Not even close.

Not fair, he says pouting. *The list of potential monsters is so long we could be here for weeks before I guessed right. I need something more to go on.*

Okay, okay, I say, lighting the candle that'll keep us warm, *I'll give you a hint. The first time around, this monster is reputed to have devoured millions.*

Godzilla! the Mussolini exclaims, clapping his hands. *He scooped them up by the handful as if they were breakfast cereal.*

Sorry, you're not getting any closer.

Leviathan? The Creature From The Sixteenth Dimension? The Killer Tomato That Ate Cincinnati?

Nope, nope and nope. You're forgetting one kind of monster.

One kind of monster? Give me another hint. One more hint.

Okay, I'll make it easy for you. In fact, I'll give it away. This particular monster was once a contemporary of yours. More than a contemporary. A buddy, really.

What! he says—and then stops. He looks at me wide-eyed. *You didn't?*

Yep. I had to, you know. I had to see what would happen.

And?

And nothing. Like all the other monsters, he walked naked and dripping out of the cloning tanks, made his way as far as the first circle of tunnels and then simply dissolved after a few minutes. And, like all the others, he was promptly taken away by our very clean and conscientious Scavengers.

That's it? The blubber candle flickered. *Did you get a chance to speak to him? Did he say or do anything out of the ordinary?*

Out of the ordinary? Hmm. He might have looked up at me for a moment but that was about it.

So, he looked up at you. What were his eyes like? They say his eyes had the fires of hell burning in them.

Fear and pain. That's what I saw in them. And plenty of confusion. It reminded me of the first time I saw you. Do you remember that?

All too clearly. Your grandfather was—is—a tough old bird. Boy, he really had it in for me, didn't he? He touches his skull. *I can still feel that bullet ripping through me and my grey matter exploding out the back of my head.* He laughs. *I don't think your grandfather's been the same since he stopped doing that.*

You might be onto something there, I say. *Hey, here's an idea. Why don't you let him start over? It might get his spirits up again if he can kill you on a regular basis.* I place my fingers against his head in the shape of a gun and pull the trigger. *Pow, pow, pilgrim.*

Thank you but no thank you. Besides, now that Bella Ciao no longer causes that old Il Duce fascist to come out in me, I don't think it'll be quite the same.

You're right, of course, I say, blowing imaginary smoke away from the tip of my index finger. *Never quite the same as the good old days.*

The igloo is filled with black smoke from the whale blubber candle, swirling towards the air hole at the top. I rub my eyes and yawn. Across from me, the Mussolini stretches out on his layers of seal skin and fur, his pillow a rolled-up sleeping bag.

Tell me about yourself, he says.

What do you want to know? I ask, plumping up my own sleeping-bag pillow. *What can I tell you that you don't already know?*

Everything. Absolutely everything. I want to know all about you. As if this is the first time we meet.

I don't know, I say. *I might bore you to death.*

You owe me one, the Mussolini says. *You played your game. Now, it's my turn. Pretend this is a game.*

Okay, you asked for it.

I begin by describing what the world was like in the first half of the 21st century—all the old familiar certainties already eroding under the onslaught of technologies gone berserk, technologies increasing ten-fold by the minute—and then ten-fold by the second, technologies that no single human being any longer had any control over. And yet at the same time, a world with plenty of both old and new deadliness, inequalities and abrupt quantum leaps—such as the sudden disappearance of most of the animals.

I tell him all about my life before I entered the facility: my childhood, my parents, the fiancée I'd left behind. I tell him about my dreams and nightmares and try to put into words what on earth possessed me to abandon said family and fiancée to see that my grandfather's wishes were fulfilled.

Everything about my parents was staid and uneventful, I say. *All except for my grandfather. He was different. Exotic. A call to adventure.*

So you did it on a whim?

On a whim? That's one way of putting it, yes.

Just like your grandfather dredging me up—and you—

And me dredging up dear old Adolf.

Only one difference. I'm still here.

Hmm, I wonder, I say. *I wonder what he would have been like if he'd been allowed to live.* I laugh. *Probably would have become a great painter or artist or something. What do you think? Maybe a diplomat. Or a doctor who cures cancer. Or a scientific genius. Maybe he would have created a place just like this. What do you think?*

The Mussolini looks at me with a slow shake of his head.

I think it's time we go to sleep, he says.

I think you're right, I say.

Besides, he says with his back turned to me, *you could always bring him back—and then, before he melts, ask him what he wants to do with his life.*

How about peasant farmer? School teacher?

Good night, Fausto. Sweet dreams.

Tinker, tailor, soldier, sailor, lawyer, baker, candlestick maker?

Are you done?

No, no. I got it, I say, clapping my hands. *Just the right occupation for him. The perfect way to atone for all his past sins. Can you guess what it is? Come on.*

Rabbi, the Mussolini says.

Precisely, I say. *One of those obsessed, scholarly-type rabbis that spend their lives trying to decipher one word, one syllable, from the Talmud. Never eating, never washing. Not even caring if anything— life, love, liberty—exists outside that one word.*

I want this to last forever. Really, I do. I want to end my days like this. I want to cruise through the cloning wars in a permanent state of forgetful bliss. A forgetful spate of permanent hiss. I want to believe in God. Really, I do. I want the rays of the sunflower plant to scatter its petals on me. Over and over again. I want my friends to love me unconditionally. Without mercy or pity or hard feelings. I want to believe. Really, I do. I want to be denied any choice in the matter.

I want to be told that I'll die one day just like everyone else. That I'll be lowered into the cold, cold ground. That the willows will bow their heads and weep for my negation. That the crisp, cool autumn leaves will tumble haphazard on my gravesite. That someone will bring flowers, leaving behind wet footprints reflecting moonlight. That the slight pressure of kneeling and memory will be felt all the way down to my bones. That the worms will look up for a moment before resuming their collective chomping. That I'll be dust again and the winds will peel me off and parts of me will lodge in parts of others and I'll return in a state of pertinent flux. Permanent lux.

And only perhaps ten thousand, ten million, ten million

million years down the road, those winds will bring me to myself again (minus, of course, a few molecules here and there). And someone can take a newspaper photo of me with the customary caption: "Miracles do happen. A human being just like this human being existed once. Hard to believe, yes. But true."

I want to believe. Really, I do. And Rachele, Claretta and the Mussolini do their best. In fact, I think I'm starting to get the hang of it when my grandfather shows up early one morning. So early, I'm still in bed, Rachele and Claretta on either side of me; the Mussolini asleep in front of the altar he's set up for the pantheon of gods he recently uncovered in the facility's holo-library.

There must be something to genetics, I tell him. *Your original wanted to bring Italy back to the glory that was imperial Rome. You want to bring back their gods.*

No, the Mussolini says, *not their gods. The Greek gods. The Romans didn't have any gods of their own to speak of. Well, they did . . . Penates and Lares mostly. Kind of like household gods. Vague little things with no personality and character, no human traits. But they stole all the real gods from the Greeks. I can admit it now, although I probably would have shot on sight anyone who dared say such a thing when I was il Duce.*

Now, little holographic images fill the area above his altar—Zeus, Hera, Ares, Aphrodite and the rest. On occasion, they perform for us, excerpts from the well-worn tales of gods interacting with humans. Nothing mysterious about it. Nothing like it would become later on with the "one God" thing. Just sex and action adventures and jealousy and revenge and monsters and trickery. A lot of trickery. Especially on the part of the humans. And who can blame them? They had to find some way to level the playing field.

Those gods might have been powerful and radiant and full of magic but they definitely come across as being none too smart. Or possessing even basic knowledge of human psychology and motivation. Our favourite tale is that of Demeter, goddess of the corn, and her daughter Persephone. The tears flow as Persephone is dragged back to Hades for her four-month winter stay and we all rejoice when she rises again in the spring, bringing with her flowering meadows and tiny grain stalks.

Our second most favourite tale is of the life, death and resurrection of Dionysus, god of the vine. We watch in horror as his body is cut away, trimmed just like a vine before winter comes, chopped until only a gnarled stump remains. Then, as the new buds burst through once more, like a green miracle against what looks totally brown and dead, we celebrate by drinking ourselves into a stupor and then trying to imitate some of the bacchanalian feats performed by his followers.

My grandfather, of course, doesn't participate in any of this. In fact, he keeps to himself—even though I've invited him several times to join us. He says he prefers to live alone, deep in the heart of the eighth eco-system. Truth is, I don't think he's ever forgiven me for befriending the Mussolini. Or maybe he still holds the time I attacked him against me. So, I'm pleasantly surprised when he shows up this morning at the door of the cave. Even though my head still throbs from the previous evening's celebrations and there are clothes strewn everywhere and the Mussolini is snoring loudly in his corner beneath the altar.

Nonno! I exclaim, in my excitement jumping out of bed with no clothes on. *You've changed your mind. That's wonderful!*

I do not want to bother you, my grandfather says in his stiff formal way, trying to avoid having to stare at my naked body.

No, no, I say, looking around for something to cover myself. *It's no bother.* I finally wrap a towel around my waist. *No bother at all.* I turn to Rachele and Claretta who are yawning and stretching beneath the sheets. *Isn't that great, girls? Now all five of us can live together. One big happy family.*

I have come for the trunk, my grandfather says.

Trunk? I say. *What trunk?*

My trunk, he says, stepping by me towards the back of the cave. *Just give me back my trunk and I will leave again.*

Your trunk? I block his path. *You gave me that trunk when you died. It was in your will. Now, I believe it belongs to me. Don't you think?*

As you can see, he says, *I am no longer dead. Therefore, the will is no longer valid. Therefore, the trunk belongs to me.*

He's got a point there, a sleepy Mussolini says from his corner. *This is the kind of case that could keep lawyers going for centuries. Your honour, I contend the property doth revert to me upon my re-birth. My previous incarnation was not of sound mind.*

Nonno Fausto, I say. *I'm very sorry but I can't let you have that trunk. If you want, if you really insist, we'll go down to the control tower and I'll duplicate one for you. Then, we can both have one.*

Get out of my way, Faustino, or I will—

You'll what? I place my hands on my hips. *What will you do? Come on. Speak up. I would really like to know.*

Fine, he says, turning around. *Have it your way.* He looks at the Mussolini and then Rachele and Claretta. *After all, you have not honoured my wishes since the day you entered this accursed place. Why start now, eh? Why be respectful now?*

What's so important about that trunk, anyway? I ask as he starts to walk away. *There's nothing but a lot of old junk in it.*

You would not understand, he says, stopping for a moment at the entrance to the cave. *Not in a million years.*

Try me, I shout. *Come over here and explain it to me. Come on. I'm willing to listen. We've got all the time in the world. Probably even more than a million years.* But he simply continues out without turning back. *Bah,* I say, dropping the towel and crawling back into bed, *I think he's going senile.*

Tithonus, the Mussolini says.

Who?

A handsome mortal that Aurora, goddess of the Dawn, fell in love with, he says in his singsong, storytelling voice. *She had him given immortality but forgot to ask for eternal youth. So he grew older and older and more and more weak and tinier and tinier until all you could hear was his tiny little voice squeaking away in protest. Eventually, she got tired of him and turned him into a grasshopper.*

Oh, that's cruel, Claretta says, snuggling up on one side of me.

Gods are always cruel, Rachele says, snuggling up on the other.

But why? Claretta says.

Because they can be, both the Mussolini and I say at the same time—and burst into laughter.

My grandfather doesn't give up on the trunk so easily. Several days later, we return from a day trip to the beach to discover the cave has been thoroughly ransacked in our absence.

My altar! the Mussolini cries out. *Look what he's done to my altar.*

The hologram machine has been smashed to pieces; the pedestals overturned and the flower vases holding the Mussolini's offerings to the gods hurled against the walls. The rest of the cave is in no better shape: my bedsheets torn to shreds; clothes ripped up; food scattered and splattered.

Nonno, I say, tut-tutting and shaking my head, *now, you're being a bad boy. Now, you're starting to piss me off.*

Replacing what my grandfather has destroyed is easily done. One trip to the control tower and we've got a bunch of shiny new toys, bigger and better than ever. In fact, the only hard work is hauling it all back from the edge of the Farmland Eco-System where the tube stops to the cave. While up in the control tower, I let the Mussolini try his hand at cloning something again. But it still doesn't work.

I'm sorry, I say. *Looks like you're stuck with me as cloning master around here.*

One of these days, he says, wagging his finger towards the sky.

As for the trunk, well . . . my grandfather never did find it. After his first visit, I took the precaution of removing it from the cave and hiding it beneath a pile of hay. I uncover it now, curious as to why my grandfather would suddenly want it so badly. I find the same old dusty stuff in it, stuff I haven't looked at in who knows how long: my grandfather's initial gun; the Mason jar; the photograph showing a group of men in ragged military outfits standing over the original Mussolini's mutilated body; the newspaper ad for volunteers for genetic experiments; the envelope and letter explaining it all to me; the leather-bound Bible with the lockets of hair in it; my fiancée's love letters; and the small cigar box with the eyeball, plastic card and piece of paper that has *Bella Ciao* written on it.

I don't get it, I say, sifting through the material. *There's nothing here of any real value. Unless he thinks the eyeball and the ID still work. No, he knows they don't. He saw me trying to use them to get out again.*

Then maybe you should give the trunk back to him, the Mussolini says. *A goodwill gesture and peace offering on your part.*

Maybe you're right, I say. *I'll take it down to him in the morning. We'll have a nice chat and be friends again. One big happy family again. Just like in the good old days. Yes! That's what I'll do.*

In the middle of the night, after a series of my usual dreams, one of which involves my sitting in front of the trunk and pulling out all sorts of hideous creatures, I sit up in bed, snap into an upright position and begin punching the air before me.

Sonovabitch! I say. *Of course!*

What? Claretta says, sleepily from beside me. *What is it?*

There is something valuable in that trunk, I say, jumping out of bed. *Christ, how could I have missed it? How could I have been so stupid?*

What are you talking about? Rachele says as she rolls over. *Come back to bed.*

Something very valuable, I say. I begin to pace back and forth. *The most valuable thing in this place. The only thing that's worth anything. And I almost handed it over to him. So that he could destroy it, I bet. That's why he wanted it. To destroy it.*

Of course! the Mussolini says. *DNA.*

Exactly, I say. *DNA. Fresh DNA. Untouched, unused, unadulterated DNA. The stuff of life ever after.*

SCENE THREE: BALANCING EQUATIONS

My mother emerges first. I feel like a child again. Or the way I imagine a child should feel. I feel as if my heart is going to burst. Ready to explode.

Nakedness is commonplace around here. One gets used to it over the decades. Yet, the moment she rises out of the tank, still blind, stunned and stumbling, I rush over to wrap her in a thermal blanket, embarrassed at seeing her un-clothed. In fact, I've ordered everyone else to stay away.

She sits on the floor, shivering. I squat down beside her, then reach over and wipe the film from her eyes. She looks at me—or in my direction. I can't really tell if she sees me or not. No, I know she can't. What I mean to say is that I can't really tell if she senses me or not.

Hello, mother, I say. I've rehearsed this moment for days on end, trying to come up with something significant or impor-tant to say. *Hello, mother* is the best I can do. For the moment. *It's me. It's Fausto. Your son. Remember?*

But, of course, she doesn't know me. How could she? She barely knows herself. She opens her mouth and greenish guck dribbles out from the corners, explodes out of her nose and ears. And then she begins to wail, like a new-born child which, in a way, she is. I try to comfort her but she continues to howl, continues to sit there huddled beneath the blanket and wailing. A long, continuous mewling like a cat in distress . . . or something.

Mother, I say, not really sure what to do to make her feel better. *Don't be afraid. You're not alone. I'm going to help you. I'm here to help. Don't be frightened.*

There's a splashing sound behind me. Someone else emerging from the tanks. At the top step and now descending.

It's my father—also naked, also blind and groping.

I've programmed both of them with pretty much the phys-ical appearance they had when I left. Except they still look different. At the time, I thought they were so old. So out of it. So uncool. Now, I can see they're barely into middle age—55 perhaps, at the most, for my father, and early-50s or so for my mother. And they're in very good shape. Well, okay, so maybe I enhanced their physiques a little bit. Just a little, though. Just so they'd fit into the facility more easily. Wouldn't want any untoward bulges and droops, now would we? Not with these form-fitting outfits.

Nice and trim, I say to myself. *Cosmetic corrections are the easi-est.*

My father stumbles away from the cloning tanks, arms held out before him for fear of crashing into something. I step in front of him, steadying him.

Welcome back, father, I say, wrapping him in a blanket as well. *You probably don't appreciate it yet but I'm about to give you a second chance. Not too many get that second chance. No sir. Not too many.*

He makes a gurgling sound before plopping down next to my mother. The film falls from his eyes; the green guck comes gushing out of his mouth; he, too, begins to wail, high-pitched, guaranteed to get the parent's attention. My mother responds in kind. Both rock back and forth, rhythmically, but not quite in unison. They never could dance together very well.

It'll be alright, I say, sitting between them and squeezing their shoulders. *You'll see. Everything will be just fine. You bet! We'll be one big happy family again. In no time at all. You'll see.* I call out: *Okay, it's safe to come out now.*

The Mussolini emerges from the corridor. Behind him, I can see Rachele and Claretta as nervous as ever about this area.

My, what a handsome couple, the Mussolini says. *Mr. and Mrs. Contadino. Or should I call them Joe and Rosa? I'm jealous, Fausto. Really jealous. I want a set of parents, too. Why are you the only one with parents around here? Why—*

Okay, okay, I say. *Enough. Now come over here and give me a hand. We've got to get them to the projection room as quickly as possible.*

With the Mussolini's help, I manage to lead my parents into the projection room and get them seated.

How long will this take? the Mussolini asks.

Hopefully, no more than a week or so, I say, strapping them in and placing electrode leads against their skulls. *I've programmed the computer so that their memories are only dormant instead of non-existent.*

Unlike me, you mean?

Yep. But the next time you . . . pass away . . . it'll be the same. You won't have to go through all those months of re-training.

That's a relief, he says. *Going around with blanks where your memories should be is no fun. No fun at all.*

Tell me about it.

My mother and father sit passively as I activate the holograms. The scenes are recreations of our house, room by room. In the first ones, I'm a young child sitting at the breakfast table. I watch to see if there's any reaction when my hologram mother pours me a glass of Simul-Lactate. Or when my hologram dad kisses my hologram mom before leaving for work. Nothing. Well, perhaps, a slight twitch from my mother. But that could be anything including a surge in the electrical input. They stare impassively.

We've got to speed this up, I say, pacing before them. *I can't leave them helpless this way. Who knows what might happen.*

Uh, not a good idea, Fausto, the Mussolini says. *You're already pushing it. If you're worried about your grandfather . . . This door locks from the inside, right?*

You can override the code so that no one gets in without your palm print.

Most excellent, he says. *We'll take turns standing guard on your parents. How's that? At least one person with them at all times.*

I don't—

No, I insist! And I'll go first. He begins to march back and forth. *Hup one two three; hup one two three.* He grins. *See, I remember I was a soldier once. A long time ago. I even fought in some war*

*somewhere. It's like riding a bike. Once you've been in the trenches,
you never forget. Especially if the enemy is firing canisters of foul gas
at you.*

Okay, okay, I say laughing. *You go first. I'll relieve you in 12
hours.*

Hup one two three, the Mussolini says, resuming his marching. Then he stops and calls out: *Salo.*

Salo?

The password, he says. And spells it out: *S-A-L-O. As in Kingdom of the damned! The last doorway before hell itself.*

As I step outside, the door seals shut behind me. Using
my palm print, I try to open it just to be sure. Nothing. Maybe I'm overreacting but my grandfather did go a little weird
when I told him a few days ago I was bringing my parents
back. Almost too calm in his reaction. As if he had something
up his sleeve.

You have gone mad, he said in a tight, clipped voice. *Completely mad. The power has gone to your head. What is it you hope to
achieve? What do you hope to gain?*

They're my parents, nonno, I said.

And your father is my son. What does that prove?

I want to see them again. I want us to be a family.

Impossible, he said. *And you know it.*

*I know no such thing. I know only that I miss them terribly and
that I want them to be alive again. What's so wrong with that?*

What is so wrong with that? he said, raising his voice. *It is a
mockery. A travesty of what it means to be human. Look at us. Bad
enough that we must live like this—if you wish to call it living. Why
do you want to force your parents to do the same?*

He put his hand on my arm, the first time he'd touched
me in months. *Listen to me, Fausto. Destroy those pieces of hair.
Burn them. Drop them in acid. Let the dead be.*

Too late, I said. *I've already inserted them into the cloning tanks.
They're part of the computer's program.*

Then be prepared to accept the consequences.

Consequences? What consequences? I took a breath and tried
to control myself. *Is that a threat?* He started to walk away from

me. *Come back here.* He stopped, and slowly turned towards me. *Are you threatening me?*

I threaten you? he said laughing. *I am nothing but an old man. A tired, weak old man. What power do I have to threaten you?*

And if you can't see fit to welcome mom and dad to the facility then just stay out of their way. If you dare hurt—

I repeat, he said. *I have no power to hurt anyone. Nor do I have the intention. You, on the other hand. . . .*

Me? Now, you're starting to go senile, old man. Why would I want to hurt my own parents? I'm the one who's trying to bring them back, remember?

He shrugged and walked away. I haven't seen him since but I know where I can find him most days—in the eighth eco-system, in one of those boxes where he first introduced me to the Mussolini. He sits there, in a trance, listening to his antiquated music all day long. Or simply staring off into space. Or tinkering with ancient toys and machinery. In the evenings, he takes a stroll through the system, occasionally looking up and tipping his cap at the camera that follows him everywhere.

But, despite the fact he's under constant surveillance, I can't get over the feeling he's planning something. That he's looking for some way to disrupt my plans. But what? He knows that killing me or my parents wouldn't solve anything. He knows that the cloning computer would simply recreate us.

And the Mussolini? Can I trust him? He sacrificed his life for me once, didn't he? But he knew he'd be back so it wasn't really that hard a sacrifice. I have no choice. I've got to trust someone. Yes, in a perfect world, I'd prefer it to be my grandfather. That would be much more natural. Blood and all that. I mean, who would you choose if given the choice: your natural grandfather or the clone of a ruthless dictator? But he's not allowing me to do it. It's the Mussolini or no one.

Rachele and Claretta are sweet and tender and warmhearted—to a fault. The most human of us all, really. But they just haven't adjusted to the facility. They still think of it as alien. A place of dreams and nightmares and things they can't explain. Besides, they've got each other. That's where their devotion and trust truly lies.

No, it's the Mussolini. And to be cynical about it, what if he does betray me? What if he somehow subverts the training process? Turns my parents into what they aren't? I'll just start all over again, that's all. No problem. They can be brought back at any time. Once their DNA is in the cloning tanks and their genetic program in the computer, there's no turning back. They're immortal now. You hear that, mom and dad. You're immortal now—just like the Mussolini's gods. You can't die—not as long as I'm in charge here.

I relieve the Mussolini after 12 hours. Already, that look of being completely lost is gone from my parents' eyes. Now, they simply look confused. They still can't speak so I can't ask them about what it is that puzzles them so much. And I can't even rely on my own experiences here. Once you "awake" to your own identity, it's like being born all over again. You can't remember anything that went on before that—except in the same way some people claim to be able to remember their time in the womb.

They're coming along wonderfully, the Mussolini says, rubbing his hands together. *I'm really excited. This means a new era in the facility, I'm sure of it.*

I hope so, I say. *Sometimes, listening to my grandfather, this seems like the biggest mistake I've ever made.*

Sure, it could be a mistake. But where would we be if we were afraid of making mistakes, eh? Probably still living in caves like those Neanderthals.

We look at each other and burst into laughter.

Okay, okay, he says. *But we're living there by choice. Not because we don't know any better.*

And I won't be living there for much longer, I say, adjusting the electrodes leading to my mother.

A brand new house, a brand new family. I do hope you'll let us visit once in a while. The girls and me.

The doors—

Suddenly, the alarms go off: *Warning, warning! Danger! Please evacuate the cloning area immediately! Repeat: evacuate the cloning area immediately.*

What the— I turn to the Mussolini. *Stay here! Close the door behind me and let no one in without the password. Understood?*

He nods. I run out of the projection room towards the central hub. The alarms are still being sounded: *Warning! Warning! Danger of detonation. Evacuate immediately.* I look up at the surveillance cameras. There, on every screen, is my grandfather. He is sitting in the control room chair.

Grandfather! I shout. *What are you doing in there? Get out of there before it explodes. Can't you hear the alarms?*

Of course, he can hear the alarms. He's responsible for them. All out of breath, I stop at the foot of the stairs leading up to the control room: *Danger. One minute to detonation. Evacuate the area immediately.*

My grandfather is clearly visible now—as is the crude home-made device he's strapped to himself.

You would not listen to me, he says. *Well, I am going to make sure you cannot do it again. You had better leave now if you do not want to get blown apart, too.* He laughs. *Who says those wartime skills are of no use once it is over.*

This is crazy, I say, shaking my head. *And a waste of time. You can't*—

Warning. Thirty seconds. Control tower and cloning tanks targeted. Evacuate immediately.

Down with the fascists! my grandfather shouts, pumping a fist into the air. *Down with all dictators and those who want to play god!*

He begins to sing *Bella Ciao* at the top of his voice. I turn and walk quickly away from the central hub area. I know now there's no reasoning with my grandfather. He's in a state of war again and nothing will convince him otherwise. Once I'm safely away deep within the corridors, I watch on one of the screens as the control tower and the cloning tanks are ripped apart by powerful explosions: the control tower reduced to bits of glass and metal, with the occasional piece of bloody flesh just to add some colour; the cloning tanks splintered and shattered with liquid and unfinished DNA accretions surging out in all directions.

You can't do anything to hurt the facility, I now say, finishing the thought I had started before the explosion. *I'm sorry, nonno. It really is all in vain. Nothing you can do can harm this place. And I mean nothing. Believe me, I've tried.*

I watch as wave after wave of Scavengers rises to start the clean up, devouring everything in their path, cutting through tangles of solid metal as easily as human flesh. Within minutes, there's no sign of the destruction left—and only a clean empty space where the control tower and cloning tanks had been.

And then the real miracle—a new control tower and cloning tanks appearing out of what seems thin air, shimmering as if looking for the exact location where they can materialize, the exact spot where they can solidify. Identical to the previous ones and just as functional. I'd like to be surprised at what's happening but that's not possible. I've seen this all before. Nothing new here.

I wait for a few moments as the Scavengers finish their clean up and then make my way to the control room. There, I sit in my chair and prevent the cloning computer from creating a new grandfather, inhibiting his DNA so that it isn't actuated. It hurts to do so but I think it's for the best. At least for the time being.

Besides, it's not like I've erased him completely. It's not like I can erase him completely. Once in the cloning computer, there's no turning back. And the inhibiting process can always be reversed later on. Yes, after my parents are fully formed and are able to fend for themselves. Of course, I could have simply allowed my grandfather to re-emerge with absolutely no memory of his previous actions. But that would mean having to go through the re-training process with him. No, this is cleaner and easier.

In fact, when it comes time to re-incarnate him, I might bring my parents into the decision-making process: Mom and dad, how do you feel about bringing nonno back? The four of us one big happy family again? Oh, come on now. He had his good points. Plenty of good points. After all, if it weren't for him, none of this would have happened. We'd all be long dead and buried. We'd all be long forgotten. It's always better to be alive, isn't it? No matter what. Sure, it is. Anyway, I need you to help me decide. Like a pair of trusted advisors.

Hey, maybe that's what it really means to be a God—not the Eternal Clone Maker but the one deciding who or what not to pull out from that bank of infinite possibilities. Who or what to keep from cluttering up an already densely packed universe. Who or what can really make a difference.

Scene Four: Parental Guidance

Faustino, what is this place? my mother says to me one day as I sit beside her in the projection room. As I sit beside her one more time. As I have sat beside her for many days before, holding her hand, staring into her unseeing eyes.

The facility, I say without even thinking.

And a moment later, it hits me: those are the first words my mother has uttered. That's the first thing she's said since she emerged out of the tanks. What has it been now? A month?

Mom! I exclaim, jumping up. *You're talking. You're—*

Of course, she's talking. She always talked up a storm, so why shouldn't she be talking now?

Dad!

What is this place? my mother asks again. *Is this heaven?* She looks around. *It doesn't look like any heaven I've ever imagined.*

No, mom, I say, laughing. *This is home.*

It doesn't look much like home, either, my dad says.

And you..., my mother says. *We thought you were... you were....*

Dead, my dad says. *Mom always had trouble with that word.*

We waited so long for you to come back, my mother says. *We waited years and years and years. And then your dad... your dad ... died ... and then ... and then I.... She clutches her head. Oh my God! My head hurts. This isn't heaven! This is hell! This is where we'll be tormented forever for our sins.*

No, it's not hell either, I say, alarmed at the turn the conversation is taking. *Wait a minute! How do you know all that? How do you know about me going away and the two of you dying? You couldn't possibly know any of that.*

Whoa, there, son, my dad says. *If we don't know about it, who would? It happened to us, didn't it? We're the ones it happened to, aren't we?*

Y. . . yes, I say.

Of course, my dad says.

I sit back. There's only one explanation: the Mussolini must have made it part of the training program. He must have used some of my conjectures and stories, some of the things I told him. I turn to my dad.

How did you die?

Why I. . . .Why, I guess . . . Of course, I . . . He stands there, scratching his head. *Funny. I can't remember. It's there. I know it is. But I can't remember at this moment. Isn't that funny? That is really strange.*

And you, mom? I ask. *Did you live a long time after dad died?*

I . . . I suppose so. She looks around the projection room, passes her fingers along the back of the chair. *Don't women nearly always live longer than their spouses? Something to do with job stress, doesn't it? I was reading about that somewhere. Or maybe I saw it on the television.*

Okay, I say, *so tell me: how exactly did you die? Swiftly? Slowly and painfully? Accidentally? Naturally?*

Oh dear, my mother says, looking around helplessly, her hands fluttering before her. *I can't remember either.*

That's because neither of you died. I mean, how could you when you're both here, alive and healthy? Besides, I'm going to make sure you stay that way for a long, long time. So no more talk of death or heaven and hell. Right? They both nod. *What's important is that we're a family again. Isn't that so?*

That's right, my mom says, taking my arm. *A family.*

Our strong point, my dad says, always pushing the issue beyond where it could reasonably go. *It was as a family that we managed to survive those horrible times. And now . . . we're going to do it again.*

Come on, then, I say, opening the door to the projection room. *It's time I showed you your . . . our . . . new home.*

Waiting for us outside are the Mussolini, Claretta and Rachele. The moment we step out, they begin clapping.

And who are these people? my mother asks.

Friends of mine, I say.

Don't I know you from somewhere? my father asks, peering closely at the Mussolini. *You look very familiar.*

Benito Mussolini, he says, bowing. *Il Duce to his friends. At your service.*

Nope, my father says. *The name doesn't ring a bell. But glad to meet you anyway. Any friend of Fausto's is—*

You're . . . you're. . . , my mother says. *Oh where have I seen you before?*

Probably on posters, the Mussolini says, instinctively puffing himself up. *Or maybe in an old newsreel. Of course, I had a uniform then.*

A uniform? my father says. *What kind—*

He's the man in the room with you when I wasn't there, I say. *That's how you know him. Unless, of course,*—I give the Mussolini a sideways glance—*he's been feeding you other things you wouldn't otherwise know about.*

Me? the Mussolini says, all grinning and innocent.

This is Rachele, I say. *Mrs. Mussolini.*

A pleasure, Rachele says.

And this is Claretta. She's . . . she's. . . .

A friend, Claretta says, taking both my mother's hands in hers, and then kissing her on either cheek. *Welcome from all of us. We've all been looking forward to this day.*

Yes, the Mussolini says, *this calls for a celebration. It's not every day that one of us has his parents—*

Some other time, I say, cutting him off. *My parents are very tired after their long journey.*

Yes, yes, of course, the Mussolini says.

Come along now, I say, leading my parents away.

Nice to meet you, my mother says. *We'll have to have you all for dinner one of these evenings.*

Lasagna, the Mussolini says, rubbing his stomach. *You'll have to make us one of your famous lasagnas.*

How did he know about my lasagna? my mother asks as we continue to walk away.

I told them everything about you, I say. *There are very few secrets in this place.*

Where are we again? my father asks, looking around and passing his hand along one of the corridor walls.

I don't know its official name, I say. *I just call it 'The Facility'.*

Oh yes, my mother says. *This is the place your grandfather used to take you as a child, isn't it?*

That's right, I say. *He used to call it The Petting Zoo.*

The last time we saw you, you were coming here, weren't you? my father says. *I remember it clearly now. Waving good-bye. Your mother wouldn't come out. She stood by the window crying. Funny, that's the last thing I do remember clearly. Everything else is like a fog in my head.*

Yes, my mother says. *It's almost as if my life stopped at that moment. At the moment you went out of my sight. Isn't that strange?*

Don't worry, mom and dad, I say, trying to change the subject. *It'll all come back in time. I'm sure of it. In the meantime, enjoy the scenery.*

It doesn't hurt to tell a little lie once in a while. That's what the Mussolini always says. Just a little white lie. For the greater good. Or the lesser evil. Or to avoid unnecessary confusion. Or further explanation. It's either that or fill their heads with fake memories from the time they last saw me to the moment they died. Whenever that was.

Come on, I say, stepping into the tube. *We'll take a fast ride.*

They follow me in. I press the button for the eighth eco-system. It takes less than a minute and allows me to avoid the actual corridor which still brings feelings of claustrophobia.

Here we are, I say. *Home sweet home.*

Until recently, the eighth eco-system consisted of row on row of grey box-like rooms, stacked one on top of the other. Now, this section of the system is as perfect a replica as memory can create of the house in which I lived as a child, complete with cross-streets, the façades of other buildings nearby and a sky where a sickly sun tries constantly to burn its way through steel-grey smog.

Yes, I know this isn't anyone's idea of paradise and that I could have had the computer create just about anything—from a tile-roofed hacienda on a Caribbean beach to a white-stoned villa in the Tuscany hills. But my parents have had enough displacement and I want them to feel at home—at least for a little while. Later, with their input, we might re-arrange things a little. Beach, hills or even one of those deluxe orbiters they were always talking about as their retirement fantasy. Just a little trip to the control room—and presto.

It's lovely, my mother says.

Yes, isn't it?

I reach to open the door.

Wait, my dad says. *Shouldn't you de-activate the alarm first?*

No need for that around here, I say, as the door slides open. *See, no locks and no alarm systems. Just go right in.*

Oh my, my father says as we step inside and a blast of cool air hits us. *Looks like someone forgot to turn off the air filtration unit. That'll cost us a pretty penny. Not to mention the utilities people knocking at the door.*

You can keep the unit on 24 hours a day, I say. *Everything is free—compliments of The Facility.*

Well, we wouldn't want to take advantage, my father says. He reaches over and turns off the air filtration unit. *You know what they say. The oldest habits are the hardest to break. Waste not, want not.*

But—

Your father's right, my mother says. *We've lived frugally all our lives. Not showing off in front of others less fortunate. We can't just change our spots now.*

Well, okay, I say. *But I'm keeping the air unit on all the time in my room. I don't mind splurging a little bit.*

Look at the big shot, my father says, laughing. *A little schooling and all of a sudden he's a big shot.*

Is anybody hungry? I ask.

Oh dear, my mother says. *I forgot to do the shopping. Hmm, I wonder if the butcher shop is still open. That's if he'll even let me back in after what Father did.*

No need, I say, throwing open the fridge door. *Everything you'll ever want is in here.*

My father lets out a low whistle; my mother claps her hands together. The fridge is packed with row upon row of every food imaginable. There's literally no end to it, attached as it is directly to a replicator.

Take something out, I say, demonstrating with a gold-coloured pear, *and another replaces it.*

Oh my, my mother says. *This is heaven.*

No, I say, taking a bite out of the pear. *Just the miracle of cloning. And not just the food either. Anything you want, anything you need—just let me know and I'll get it for you. New furniture, computers, clothes pins—though I'm not sure what you'd need those for as you can simply discard your clothes when they get dirty.*

My parents sit down at the kitchen table—just like they used to those many years, decades and perhaps centuries ago. I sit opposite them. I can see in their eyes that they're having trouble grasping the concept. I reach across and take hold of their hands, squeezing gently.

I know it's a bit confusing, I say. *But you'll get the hang of it. You see, this is all for you. It's all here to make you happy. The Facility has no other purpose but to cater to our needs. To make sure we're not lacking anything.*

I guess I understand that, my father says, looking at my mother. *But I don't know. We're just not used to—*

Don't worry, dear, my mother says. *You'll feel better when you go to work, when you get a good day's work in you. You were always happiest at the end of a solid day's work. Then you could put your feet up and relax.*

Well. . . , I start to say. Then stop. I don't want to tell him there's no work here. That no one works because all the work is done for you. And The Facility definitely doesn't need tax accountants seeing as no one pays any taxes. Besides, even if tax accountants were needed, it has thousands of sophisticated computers to do the job. But I don't tell him any of that.

Yes, my father says, *I guess I do like my work.* He looks at me. *It's that feeling of accomplishment. Every man has to be proud of something, doesn't he? Otherwise, what's the point? You might as well be a mutant rat-beetle beneath the subway.*

You're absolutely right, dad, I say, making a mental note to have The Facility create some type of tax office building—

whatever that looks like. *But right now, take advantage of this little holiday of yours. There's plenty to see around here. Why there are some animals that haven't existed for decades. For centuries. Go out and explore. Or if you'd like, I can come with you. I know this place like the back of my hand. You, too, mom. Clean air. No more smog or killer pollution. Fields and forests and rivers and marshlands, mountains and oceans and deserts and snow—it's a completely different world here. You'll see.*

That's kind of you, dear, my mother says. *But you know I've never been much for going outside. Just give me a well-equipped kitchen and I'm happy. Speaking of which, when do you want to invite your friends over?*

Give the word, mom, and I'll have them here before you can say Lasagne Verdi Con Agnello e Peperoni.

Before going to sleep—in my own room, in my own bed, imagine—I take a tour of the house, familiarizing myself with it once more. I half-expect my grandfather to be sitting in his chair, finger poised over some cobwebbed tome, about to point out some obscure historical inaccuracy. Or perhaps blowing the dust off one of his ancient records, almost obsolete even at the turn of the century.

He isn't there, of course. I know that beforehand. But I don't feel bad about it. I don't feel bad because I know I can bring him into the picture any time I want. It's not like he's been lost forever. Or that he'll ever again be in danger of dying in a hospital somewhere. No, he's safe now, safely out of harm's way. And, of course, my parents don't ask about where he is because they think he's dead. They <u>know</u> he's dead, having witnessed his body being wheeled out in the middle of the night. Well, not quite witnessed. Just carefully implanted memories of my witnessing their witnessing.

As I lie in bed, crisp white sheets almost crackling, I have this feeling of pure contentment. I can honestly say I've never been happier. And for the first time, I have nothing but praise for The Facility. As well as remorse for my previous attempts to sabotage it. There might not be any God up there, any so-called Supreme Being pulling the strings while sipping on some golden nectar and fondling a Marilyn Monroe looka-like. But who needs Him? Her? It?

For the first time, I feel there's a purpose to stopping the cycle, to halting the wheel that's supposed to crush and grind us all into the dust. And soon there'll be even more of a rea-son for it all, a most wonderful reason for it all. But it's a complete surprise. Even the Mussolini doesn't know about it. I roll over, sigh and hug the pillow. I'm a child again. We're all children again. And at last I see The Facility for what it is: a fantastic, gigantic, never-ending playground. Filled with the most marvellous toys and incredible magic acts. A place to have fun, in other words. After all, once you've removed the threat of mortality, is there any reason to be serious again? You might as well spend your time playing games. Taking chances. Exploring the limits.

SCENE FIVE: FAMILIAR URGES

My parents are already up when I arise. I can smell fresh coffee and pancakes and I can hear the sound of toast popping. My mother is humming tunelessly, barely above the whirr of my father's depilatory. I stand at the foot of the stairs unnoticed for a few moments, simply watching them as they go about their familiar business.

Isn't this ever so strange? my mother says, reaching into the fridge. *I take an egg out of the tray and another appears. I don't know if I'll ever get used to that.*

Modern technology, my father says. *The new wonders of the world. I pressed all kinds of buttons on the computer before I realized all you have to do is talk to it—like you would a child. And it talks back, too.*

Morning, everyone, I say, stepping into the kitchen.

Ah, there you are, sleepy head, my mother says. She hugs me. *Did you have pleasant dreams?*

Slept like a log. And you?

Well, we had a little trouble there, to tell you the truth, my father says. *Until I turned off the air filtration.*

Oh you and your air filtration, my mother says, winking at me. *Your dad always has to have something to gripe about, doesn't he?*

It's not griping, my father says. *It's making sure things are done right. If there's anything the tax department has taught me, it's to make sure of the details. Get the details right and the rest will take care of itself. Right, Fausto?*

Absolutely, dad, I say.

And I say it's love, my mother says. *Love makes sure things go right. You can make all the mistakes you want as long as you have love in your heart.*

Boy oh boy, my father says. *That would go over big down at the office. Imagine if I told my supervisor I made a huge error that cost taxpayers a few million. But not to worry. I did it with love in my heart.*

Oh. . . , my mother begins—and pauses, as if something's slipped her mind. *You're always exaggerating.* She turns to me. *I only meant. . . .*

I know what you meant, mother, I say. *And so does dad. He's just trying to give you a hard time.*

Such a kidder, my mother says, slapping him gently on the forearm. *He's always been a great kidder. I think that's why I fell in love with him in the first place.*

And here I thought it was because of my big muscles.

Big muscles, hah! Remember the time you tried lifting the sofa so Fausto could get his toy from underneath it? Mr. Big Muscles was on his back for a week.

Details again, my father says. *A bad back isn't the same as big muscles. Isn't that right, Fausto?*

I've got to go out for a while, I say. *Some things to take care of. Who'd like to come along? Get to see some of the other parts of the facility?*

You two go ahead, dear, my mother says. *I'll stay here and clean up a bit. This place needs a good vacuuming.*

Mom, this place is self-cleaning.

Well, then I'll . . . I'll just sit and watch some television. There must be some awfully nice TV programs these days. And then, before you know it, it'll be time to start preparing dinner. You'll bring your friends over tonight, right?

A good idea, mom. I'll bring my friends over. In fact, that's perfect. I've got an important announcement to make.

There's already less grey in the sky when my father and I step outside. Already more sun coming through. And less smog. And tiny trees are sprouting where once there was nothing but cracked cement and the effects of acid rain. And even the house is starting to look brighter, no longer so prison-like.

What's that smell? my father asks, sniffing the air. *It's familiar but I can't place it. Can't quite place it.*

Lilac, I say, not because I recognize the smell of lilac but because I ordered the facility to reproduce some for my father's sake.

Of course! he exclaims, taking a deep sniff. *I remember it from when I was a young man. We had lilac bushes around our house. All around them. Your grandfather used to take care of them.* He takes another sniff while I marvel at the thoroughness of the training program. *That's lovely. I had forgotten what it smelled like. Just those first few weeks in spring—and then it was gone again.*

Our first visit is to the cave where Luna comes bounding out towards us, causing my father to cringe and cover his head before realizing all she wants to do is lick him.

Friendly wild animals, he says, shaking his head while holding out his hand. *I don't know if I'll ever get used to it.*

Then it's Rachele and Claretta who come running up to me, calling out my name and hugging and kissing me.

And even friendlier humans, my father says, after they do the same to him. *That might be even harder to get used to.*

Welcome to our humble abode, Mr. Contadino, the Mussolini says, standing in front of the cave. *May I call you Joe?*

Joe? my father says.

That's your name, dad, I say with a laugh.

Of course, of course, my father says, scratching his head. *The mind plays tricks sometimes. Mine suddenly went blank.*

That's alright, the Mussolini says. *So, what do you think, Joe?*

My father lets out a low whistle as he slowly scans the countryside, a vista of wheat fields stretching for what seems miles in every direction, evergreen forests in the distance, mountains behind them, peaks capped in white.

And the facility, as you call it, does all this?

Shivery, isn't it? Claretta says.

I don't even like to think about it, Rachele says.

Come on now, the Mussolini says. *It's only as mysterious as the rest of world. I mean, have we ever solved that mystery? Just a lot of scientific mumbo-jumbo but are we nearer the truth?*

I suppose you're right, my father says.

Anyway, I say, *we didn't come here to talk about the mysteries of the world. We're here to invite the three of you to supper tonight.*

Oh goody! Claretta says, clapping her hands. *A proper dinner party.*

What can we bring? Rachele asks.

Just yourselves, I say. *And get ready for another surprise. Or a surprise announcement at any rate.*

More surprises? the Mussolini says. *You've been full of them lately, haven't you? A veritable surprise machine.*

I like to keep you on your toes. I turn to my father. *Come along now. There's plenty more I want to show you.*

We wave good-bye to Claretta, Rachele and the Mussolini and head off down the path that cuts through the nearest wheat field. I try to give my father the grand tour of the various eco-systems—or as many as we can get to in a day. As I watch my father "ooh" and "ah" over the various creatures, some of which he's never seen before and others only the implanted memories of his youth, I find myself amazed at my own lack of amazement, of how surely humans adapt, at how we quickly start to take for granted what once was so alien and awe-inspiring.

It's like the old biblical Noah's Ark, my father says, patting the side of a huge water buffalo as we stand in the midst of a wild rice field.

Except he only collected the animals two by two. Here, we can actually create them. Or re-create them.

So it's true, my father says. *I'd been hearing stories about such things where I worked. But I never really believed it.*

Come on. I'll show you.

I take him to the control room above the cloning tanks. As he stands looking at the computer monitors with their genetic information whizzing by too fast for the eye to follow, I sit in the chair and activate the cloning process.

What are you doing? he asks.

A surprise, I say. *A pleasant surprise.*

So that's where the animals actually come from? my father says, turning towards the tanks.

Yes, I say, trying to decide whether or not to tell him about his own recent birth. *The supercomputers keep things balanced. Not too few and not too many. When the computers decide more are needed, they send the appropriate cloning signals to the tanks.*

Any animals at all?

As we walk back down the stairs, I explain to him about the kinds of animals that don't last too long. And about The Scavengers.

I'm glad to hear there are limits, he says. *But it's still kind of frightening. And there's a feeling about it not being quite right. Coming out of a tank like that instead of a mother's womb.* He shakes his head. *Do you see what I'm saying? Somehow, it doesn't feel natural.*

You'll get used to it, I say—and decide at the last moment against telling him. Plenty of time for him to find out on his own. If he hasn't figured it out already. After all, it has been a long long time since humans made genetic distinctions between themselves and the so-called "lower" animals. *Everyone does. Sooner or later.*

I suppose you're right, he says. *I will get used to it. I got used to no trees and no animals; I'll get used to this.*

That's the spirit!

By the time we get back to the house, the sky has brightened even more, the lilac bushes are everywhere and the brickwork has lost its scorched acid rain look. There are even cats and dogs running about the streets—like something out of a child's story book. I'd thought about including human androids—new parents pushing baby carriages, milkmen, delivery people—but decided against it as too much for the time being. Too much input for my parents to handle right now. Besides, I can always introduce them later.

Inside, the house smells of herbs and spices and lasagna baking in the oven. My mother has placed a vase of cut lilacs on the table and plates, silverware and crystal glasses for six—as if for a formal dinner. My father goes into the kitchen and begins to tell my mother all that we've seen. Their voices are like those of excited children, rapid fire and undisciplined, jumping from one subject to another with little logic. The kitchen fills with squeals and high-pitched laughter.

I feel a surge of nostalgia so strong my legs buckle and I have to lean against a wall for a moment. Nostalgia? But things weren't like that when I was a child. The world was dark and gloomy and laughter was a very scarce commodity—especially around our household. This is something entirely new and entirely wonderful. I look around me to make sure it's real and not one of my terrible dreams in reverse. And I realize there is no way for me to tell, really.

Fausto, is it true? my mother calls out from the kitchen. *All those animals? And you can make them out of nothing?*

Well, not quite out of nothing, I say, joining them. *Their DNA has to exist in the cloning tanks. If you'd like, I can get you one as a pet.*

A pet? my mother and father both say.

Just tell me what you want and I'll get it for you.

I don't know, Fausto, my father says. *We've never had pets. At least not since I was very young. Isn't it against the law or something?*

Around here, I'm the law, I say, making a fist against my chest for emphasis. *So, what kind would you like? Regular like a dog or cat? Or exotic—snake, dodo bird, crocodile?*

Oh no, oh no, my mother says, shivering. *Those make me afraid. I don't know if I could sleep knowing one of those was wandering around the house. Or, God forbid, under my bed.*

Your mother's right, my dad says. *That would be a bit much.*

Okay, then, I say. *Regular pet, it is.* I already have a particular one in mind. *Just a cuddly bundle who'll lick you to death if you'll let her.*

For the first time, I regret not having set up any way to communicate with the Mussolini and the others at the cave. We've never needed one before, I guess, so no one thought of it. But now that the community is expanding. . . . A simple task for the computers to create a linked terminal to the cave. Our own intranet. Or maybe image projection might be better. Appear as a holographic image in the middle of the cave and vice versa. I'm sure the facility would have no trouble with that.

Scene Six: A View to Normal

This time around, though, none of that is needed. When I open the door to let the Mussolini, Rachele and Claretta in, I see Luna stretched out on the sidewalk behind them. As if she's read my mind. And why not? Stranger things have happened.

We tried to shoo her away a couple of times, the Mussolini says. *But she wouldn't listen. She'd go back a few steps and then slink towards us again.*

It's like she wanted to come and see you, Rachele says. *Like she's missed you.*

That's okay, I say, holding out my hand so that Luna can lick it. *To tell you the truth, I was thinking of her as a pet for my parents. If it's okay with you, of course.*

Okay with us? the Mussolini says. *Of course, it's okay with us. She's your pet, after all.*

Wow! Rachele says. *What is that delicious smell?*

Come in, come in, I say. *You too, Luna. Come on.*

My mother gasps and takes a step backward as Luna strides lumbering into the house.

Don't worry, dear, my father says, nervously holding out his hand for Luna to lick. *She's friendly . . . I think.*

What . . . ?

It's a snow leopard, I say. *Her name is Luna. Just let her give you the once over.*

My mother stands very still as Luna circles around her, sniffs once or twice, then turns and plunks herself down right in front of the door.

Already making herself at home, the Mussolini says. *I think she's going to like it here.*

You bet, Rachele says, squatting down to stroke Luna.

I beg your pardon? my father says.

Your new pet, I say. *It was going to be a surprise but I guess she couldn't wait to get to her new home. So, what do you think?*

I . . . I don't know, my mother says. *I'm afraid—*

Nonsense, Claretta says, as she too leans down to stroke the leopard's fur. *Luna's as gentle as a lamb.*

As cuddly as a koala, Rachele says.

As harmless as a . . . a . . . The Mussolini scratches his head. *I can't think of a harmless animal starting with haitch. Hyena? Guess not, eh?*

That's okay, my father says. *I think we get the point.*

Tell you what, I say. *Let's give it a try. If you're still nervous in a couple of days, we'll think of something else. Okay?* My mother nods reluctantly, all the while keeping her eye on Luna. *Great! Now, let's eat.*

The meal starts quietly but soon becomes more and more boisterous as several bottles of wine are emptied, bottles from an endless supply. My mother sits at the head of the table, basking in the glory of the food; my father is in a state I've never seen before—pleasantly drunk. And deep into a discussion with the Mussolini.

So, my father says, *I could keep pulling bottles of wine out forever and I'd never run out. But how is that possible? What about the . . . the law . . . of supply and demand? What about the conversation . . . I mean . . . conservation of matter and energy?*

Precisely! the Mussolini says. *I agree with you entirely. The whole thing is impossible. Absurd. Utterly ridiculous. Ergo, we are not here. Ergo, I'll have another glass of non-wine.*

Why is it, Claretta says, her foot rubbing against mine, *that every time men get drunk, they think they become better at discussing the deep mysteries of life?*

Beats me, I say. *Probably a protective mechanism.*

Or they suddenly become better lovers, Rachele says. She leans over and whispers in my ear: *Benito can't get it up any more without guzzling a few first.*

Sorry to hear that, I say.

Men are afraid, my mother says suddenly.

Afraid? all the men including me say at the same time.

Oh dear, did I really say that? my mother says, covering her mouth and giggling. *I really meant to say. . . .*

You meant exactly that, Claretta says. *Men are afraid.*

Of what, my dear? the Mussolini asks.

Of taking a chance, Claretta says, looking at me. *Of admitting they care for someone enough to share a life.*

In here? the Mussolini says. *That's absurd. Right, Fausto? Tell them how silly it is to think they can lead a normal life in here.*

I, for one, am not afraid, I say. *In fact, this is as good a time as any.* I re-fill my wine glass and stand up. *As we're all gathered here tonight—all except for grandpapa who's in abeyance, I want to make an announcement. An important announcement.*

Oh my, says Rachele. *I wonder what it could be.*

Commitment, Claretta says, smiling at me. *It has to do with commitment.*

Yes, it does, I say. *I want you all to know that . . . and I've been thinking about this for a very long time . . . that I'm planning on get-ting married.* As I say this everyone tries to speak at once. *And hopefully starting a family. The old way!*

Congratulations, son, my father says. *And who's the lucky one—as if we didn't already know?*

The choices are few, the Mussolini says.

She'll make a wonderful wife, my mother says, patting Clar-etta on the hand.

Best man, the Mussolini says. *As the only non-family male here, the honour naturally falls on me. Fear not. I'll do you proud.*

Sounds good to me, I say.

I want to be the bridesmaid, Rachele says. *Even if I am already married.*

Sure, I say. *Both you and Claretta can be bridesmaids.*

Claretta? my mother says. *But I thought. . . .*

I'm not sure what you thought, mother, I say, taking another sip of wine. *But I'm going to marry Evelyn.*

Evelyn? the Mussolini asks. *Who—*

His fiancée, my father says, slowly twirling the glass of wine in his hand and inspecting it as if he's found something extraordinarily fascinating in it. Or unappetizing. *The fiancée he left behind all those years ago.*

But . . . but. . . , my mother says. *She's . . . not here . . . she's. . . .*

I'm so happy for you, Claretta says before she knocks her chair back, bursts into tears and rushes out of the room, standing at the open door with her back to us.

Thank you, I say, not quite sure what has just happened.

Pig! Rachele says under her breath as she follows Claretta out.

Women become so emotional about these things, says the Mussolini. *Tears of joy. Tears of joy. I guess it's all part of their charm.* He holds out his hand to me. *I guess congratulations are in order, yes?*

Fausto, my mother says. *I don't understand. I thought Claretta was. . . .*

We're just friends, mother, I say as Claretta's sobbing grows louder in the background. *We're just good friends.*

Until this very moment, I sincerely believed that. Just friends who liked to share a bed once in a while. Innocent fun.

And Evelyn—, my mother says. *Isn't she . . . no longer with us?*

He's going to bring her back, my father says glumly. He turns towards me. *Isn't that right? You're going to bring her back from the dead? Just like you brought us back.* He takes a swig of wine. *You did bring us back, didn't you?*

The process has already been started, I say, watching Claretta being hustled out the door by Rachele. I look at the Mussolini still seated at the dinner table. He shrugs. *Excuse me. I'll be right back.*

I follow them out.

Rachele, Claretta, I call out. *Wait!*

Claretta stops and turns back.

Leave her be, Rachele says. *Haven't you done enough harm already?*

What do you want? Claretta says, wiping her eyes.

I'm sorry about the misunderstanding, I say. *I didn't know—*

Forget it, Claretta says. *I was the foolish one for believing it possible. Serves me right for being so silly.* She tries to laugh bravely. *I hope you and your Evelyn have a wonderful life together.*

Claretta turns and walks off into the night.

Rachele, I say. *I don't want this to get in the way of our friendship. I still want us to be friends, right?*

Whatever you say, Fausto. After all, you're the boss around here. You give the orders.

What are you talking about? I say. *Have I ever given you any orders?*

You don't have to, Fausto. We all know who's in command. We all know who we shouldn't upset.

This is ridiculous, I say. *I don't want to be anybody's boss. I don't want to order you around. I just want a normal life. That's all I've wanted all along. And I thought that's what you wanted too.*

Good-bye, Fausto. If you want to keep deluding yourself about a normal life, go right ahead. Just don't expect the rest of us to go along anymore. We all know you're in control. You proved that with your parents and you proved it again tonight.

She, too, turns and walks away, then stops.

By the way, she says, without turning around, *whatever happened to your grandfather? Did he get in the way of your normal life?*

My grandfather? What does he have—

Just that it's a little ridiculous talking about a normal life when you can shut us down anytime you want, isn't it now? When we're at your mercy.

I would never—

Never is a long, long time, she says—and disappears into the darkness.

This is all about jealousy, isn't it? I shout. *You're jealous of Evelyn. How petty can you get? My grandfather was right after all. Ah, to hell with you!*

I walk back into the house. My parents and the Mussolini are still seated around the kitchen table, looking every which way but at me.

I suppose you all think this is a bad idea, too, I say, sitting down.

Fausto, the Mussolini says, *feel free to do as you please. And to bring back whomever you can. No one can stop you anyway, can they?*

Is that what this is about? I can operate the cloning computers and you can't?

Well. . . .

I just want you to be happy, my mother says. *If Evelyn makes you happy, that's fine.*

And you, dad, I say, *what do you have to say?*

I go along with your mother.

I'm glad, I say. *You never met Evelyn, did you?*

No, my mother says. *But you did send us a picture of her. I think.* She turns to my father. *Didn't he, Joe?*

Yes. A lovely girl. A bright, lovely girl.

Well, the Mussolini says, getting up, *I'd better get back. Check up on those wild and crazy girls of my own.*

I'll see you to the door.

The Mussolini and I stand outside the door. Hands in his pocket, he looks up at my parents' house.

You don't have to live in that cave any more, you know, I say. *Just let me know what you want and I'll have the facility build it for you.*

Anything? the Mussolini says.

Anything at all.

Well, that's very kind of you, he says. *But I think the girls have gotten comfortable in the cave. Mighty comfortable. And, you know, I have my altar there . . . it's kind of cozy . . . if you know what I mean. Like home, you know. Maybe one day we'll get tired of it. But right now. . . .*

Sure, sure, I say. *But if you change your mind, just let me know, okay? And anything else you need, let me know that, too.*

Great, the Mussolini says. *That's great to know. Be seeing you. Bye.*

He starts to walk away, then stops.

One thing, he says. *One thing I was going to ask you before . . . you know . . . things got a little out of hand.*

What?

I was just wondering. You said that you can't create anything without the DNA already being present. . . .

Her thumbprint, I say. *She cut her finger while sealing one of her love letters to me. There were traces of her blood on the envelope.*

You're not serious?

Yep.

Now that's what I call fate.

No more than the presence of Rachele and Claretta.

Touché, he says. *Sometimes I forget.*

He waves, then turns and walks away. I'm about to go back into the house when Luna goes past me.

Hey, I say, *where do you think you're going?*

Luna yawns, stretches, sharpens her claws on the sidewalk and then continues out into the darkness, following the Mussolini home.

Oh well, I say, *guess there's nothing like familiar surroundings. Even for a snow leopard.* I call out: *Come back and visit, you hear. Anytime you want. You'll always be welcome. The door will always be open.*

I turn and stand watching the yellow glow from inside the house, the moonlight overhead. The air still smells of lilac—and of the kind of excitement I haven't felt in a long, long time. Too bad the others aren't as appreciative.

SCENE SEVEN: THE GOD ANSWERS

I'm sitting in the projection room and the entrance is sealed—from the inside. I've been sitting here for several days, all by myself. I've even changed the "Salo" code so that the Mussolini can't get in—and I know he desperately wants to get in, knocking on the door each morning insisting I open up. I don't want to see him—or anyone else—right now. And I tell him that. I tell him I need time to myself, time to think things through.

It's nice and comfortable in here—and well it should be. This is the place where I first learned about myself, the place that holds both my past and my present. And perhaps the future as well. It's also a place filled with lots of memories for me—some fond and some not so pleasant. I remember the first Mussolini all those years . . . decades? . . . centuries? . . . ago . . . when I still had to "train" each one . . . all my own rebirths . . . the slow, whittling away of my inability to accept what had happened to me, of the unique fate that awaited me.

Here also are stored the painful memories of my grandfather, made even more difficult by the superimposition of images of our early times together with those of his last days as a wild-eyed partisan saboteur bent on destroying the facility, the blast that scattered him to the winds. I wonder if somewhere in the cloning tank his various genetic components aren't saying "I told you so" right at this very moment.

And what I don't remember I can easily conjure up. All I have to do is give the order and the computer retrieves it for instant viewing. Dusty and mouldy archives—metaphorically speaking, of course—coming alive once again in the space before me; perfectly-recreated records unable to help themselves, unable to turn themselves off even as they contemplate, Hamlet-like, their own existence.

But this morning I'm not interested in the far past, in the dim mists of time swirling about my ankles like the swamps of pre-history. Or the mid-21st century, for that matter. It's the much more recent past I want to mull over. The past of the last few months. In the desperate hope that it'll dull the ache, ease the pain, clear the air, cleanse my soul. Or, at the very least, it'll cause me to wake up to the knowledge this is just another of my nightmares and I'll come to once more in that room with the Mussolini beside me, begging me not to do something rash.

Right now, though, I'm watching my parents desperately trying to make things work but unable to shake the lethargy that has fallen over them since the evening I announced Evelyn's re-birth. Unable to re-establish any kind of link to the natural world.

We don't belong here, my mother is saying as the four of us sit at the breakfast table. *We're dead. This is going against God and all His wishes. We should be in the ground. We should have rotted away.*

Nonsense! I say. *That's absolute nonsense. You should be exactly where you are. No place else but where you are this moment.*

Your mother's right, my father says. *This is unnatural. It goes against our destiny as human beings.*

But that's just it, I say. *We make our own destiny here. We're no longer at the mercy of unpredictable natural forces. Of death and decay. This is the dream of every human being who ever lived. We can finally live happily ever after without having to worry about something going wrong. Can't you see how wonderful that is?* I turn towards Evelyn who has been staring off, her blue eyes unblinking. *Tell them I'm right. Make them understand.*

She sighs, gets up and begins to walk towards the front entrance.

Evelyn! I say. *What's wrong with you?*

Nothing, she says as she steps out, not bothering to look back. *Everything is fine.*

But, of course, nothing is fine. When I first brought her back to the house after the training period, I attributed her condition to the fact she still had to get used to the idea of being alive again. Just like my parents, I thought, she needed time to adjust. To re-adjust. The stunned look on her face was just that, a temporary reaction to the shock. We'd all been through it and I, for one, definitely understood. Or thought I did. Three weeks later, the stunned look had been replaced by a blank one. She walked around the house as if she were a ghost. As if the walls, sofas, tables and other objects around her didn't really exist. Or as if she considered herself non-existent and everything else too dense to penetrate.

I love you, I said the first night as we lay in bed together, moonlight streaming in through the window so that I could clearly see her body next to mine.

Why? she asked.

Why? Because I do. I've always loved you. Ever since the first time I caught a glimpse of you in that macro-economics class. I reached over and placed a hand on her breast—cool and uncomplicated, flesh formed into the perfect object of desire. *And you? When did you realize you were in love with me?*

Rather than answering, she rolled over onto me and straddled me, reaching down to slip my penis into her. At the time, I thought this was answer enough, a direct way of showing her love without wasting words trying to describe her feelings. Abrupt and to the point. Now that I replay the scene as a hologram before me, I'm not so sure. Perhaps it's because I can see her face more clearly from this angle. It's hard and cold and determined. Not at all the face of someone in love but rather of someone who wants to get something over with as quickly and efficiently as possible. And with the least fuss.

You don't love me, do you? I say to her image. *You may have loved me once—I'm not even sure of that anymore—but you definitely don't love me now.*

Sometimes, I would catch her touching herself—while watching television or standing in the kitchen, for example. Not in a sexual way or in an effort at arousal but more out of awe and disbelief. Out of a sense she was dream-walking. Or expected to suddenly vanish without any explanation.

I devoted all my time to her, to making her feel welcome. While at university, we'd often talked about having children, about the pros and cons and bringing them into a world where little was certain except that things would get worse. Now, I felt, would be the right time to start a family—in a place that was completely safe and predictable.

Wouldn't that be wonderful? I said as we picnicked in a field of wildflowers. *A little boy and girl to call our own. One of each. We could watch them grow up. . . .*

And then watch them grow up again, she said in a deadened voice. *And again.* She paused. *And again.*

That's right, I said. *A never ending family with no fear of what the future might bring. Like living in the Garden of Eden. An eternal family.*

I don't think so, she said, offering me one of the breaded veal sandwiches my mother had made. *I don't think I'm in the mood for children.*

What do you mean not in the mood? I don't understand.

What's there to understand? she said, her voice taking on a hard edge. *Or not understand? I don't want children right now. Is that clear enough for you?*

Okay, I said, mouth full of sandwich. *Maybe later. Maybe when you're a little more used to your new life.*

I pushed her. I prodded her. I joked about having children. Then, she began to stay away from the house. At first only for a few hours at a time. Then for longer and longer periods. She'd leave early in the morning, sometimes even before I'd risen, and only return late in the evening. When I asked her where she'd been, she say: *Oh, around.* Or: *Just went for a walk.*

Of course, as she was being captured on video the whole time, I could have easily tapped into the nearest computer screen and discovered exactly where she was or where she'd been. But, for the longest time, I didn't do that, thinking it some violation of our trust as lovers. Something not done. Finally, several days ago, fearing the worst, I gave in. I found her in the cave, of all places, bawling her eyes out with Rachele, Claretta and the Mussolini trying to comfort her.

There, there, Rachele said. *Who knows? Maybe having a child or two might be the best thing for you. I know it helped keep my marriage together—for a while anyway.*

But I told you, Evelyn said, wiping her eyes. *I don't love him. I don't know how to tell him but I don't love him. How can I love him when I don't even know him?*

When she said that, it was as if someone had stuck a lance into my heart. It was as if all my dreams had been deflated and I was a burst balloon sputtering through the air with no way to control myself. I immediately switched off the monitor, not interested in hearing anything else she might say. The pain was great enough already. I had held out hope that her lethargy was simply a passing phase, that she'd get over it eventually and then the two of us would work towards starting a family of our own. Now, I realized that was all part of my own self-delusion, the fantasy world I had created around myself.

I spent the rest of the day wandering aimlessly around the facility, alternating lengthy periods of silence and conversations with myself: How stupid could I be? How utterly imbecilic of me to think I could simply conjure up an Evelyn from the tanks and assume she'd be the same Evelyn who had fallen in love with me. Everyone tried to tell me as much, circling round the question without ever actually asking it. But it should have been asked. You should have warned me. A simple 'How do you know she'll love you?' would have been enough. Or would it?

Perhaps my blinders wouldn't have allowed me to see it. Perhaps I would have lashed out at the person daring to ask such a question, the person daring to put such doubts into my head. Isn't it funny? We eliminate all uncertainty from our lives, even the uncertainty of death, and think that's all there is to it. That from that moment on everything will be pre-programmed to make us happy. And we forget the basic dilemma of what it is to be human.

I love Evelyn. Are you sure you love her? Well, let's say I love the idea of her, her perfect body, her boyish haircut, her acute mind and sense of humour. What else is there? I love her—period. End of discussion. But she doesn't love you, does she? Something failed to click when she came out of those tanks, something that couldn't be turned on by filling her mind with the details of Evelyn.

Perhaps the same thing happened to everyone else. Perhaps my parents don't really consider themselves my parents but the parents of someone they lost decades ago. Perhaps the Mussolini and Rachele are only play-acting at loving one another—or, miracle of miracles, they fell in love all over again once they were resurrected. Or their relationship was forged once again thanks to the tortures my grandfather put them through. And Claretta. Poor Claretta. Claretta is the one who loves me. Or loved me anyway before I slapped her awake with a born-again Evelyn. Is Claretta the one I love? Do I know what the word means in the stretch of eternity? Does it matter? I've got decisions to make. Important decisions to make. Yes! Time to get to it.

When I looked up, I found myself in front of the house. Another perfect late afternoon. The sun was shining and the air pleasantly warm; the lilac bushes were flowering again; soothing music floated up from hidden speakers; the new neighbourhood fountain shot sprays of multi-coloured water into the air, giving a rainbow effect.

Mom, dad, I called out as I entered, anxious to tell them about my first decision: to give Evelyn freedom to do as she wanted. To cut her loose. Set her free.

There was no answer. But, of course. Their customary afternoon naps. Old habits are hard to break. I went into the kitchen to get something to drink. There was a note on the table, along with two half-empty glasses. Odd, I thought, my mother is normally obsessive about not leaving glasses and dishes around. I picked up the note:

Fausto, your mother and I love you very much. It's a very fast-acting poison. By the time you read this, we'll both be dead. Please, don't bring us back again. Please. We beg you. Don't make us go through this again. If you love us.

No! I yelled, looking about wildly. *No! You can't do this!*

I dropped the note and rushed to their bedroom, praying I'd find them still alive and not yet food for the Scavengers. But it was too late. The room was empty. My first thought was to get to the control tower and re-create them. As quickly as possible. Surely life must be more pleasant than eternal emptiness, perpetual non-existence. Surely, it couldn't be that bad here. Surely, they had made a mistake and would now want me to correct it. Surely, it was simply temporary insanity. Surely. I changed my mind, however, after I played back the video of their last few moments together. Holding hands, they faced directly into the camera.

We're so sorry, my mother said. *But we can't live this way. Please forgive us for what we're about to do. We're so sorry.*

Your mother and I have decided this is for the best, my father said. *We've tried and tried to fit in. We've tried to pretend that things are normal. But it doesn't work. The harder we try, the worse it gets.*

We're simple people, my mother said. *We don't understand any of this. We don't understand television programs where you get to watch everything you did that day—over and over again. We don't want any of that. We want to go back where we came from. That way you'll at least have memories of us. Memories of your mother and father. Good-bye. We both love you very much.*

Good-bye, my father said. *Thank you for trying so hard to make life normal for us. Thank you for the lilac trees. Especially for the lilac trees.* He smiled. *Good-bye.*

They both smiled and waved. Tiny little waves.

Good-bye, I say, giving back a tiny little wave.

And they swallowed the poison, crumpling to the floor in one another's arms, bodies shuddering and twisted.

I've watched this half a dozen times, each time stopping as the ominous shadows hover above them. I've watched it over and over in the hope, perhaps, that there might eventually be a different outcome. But I finally weary of my own delusion and let the video continue forward. The Scavengers seem reluctant at first, something I've noticed more and more lately. An almost human hesitancy. But they soon warm to the task and my parents are no more.

And there I am, walking in to find only the note and the half-empty glasses on the kitchen table.

You're not going to bring them back, are you? Evelyn pleaded with me that evening. *They were so unhappy. So desperately unhappy. That's all they talked about. How miserable and unhappy they were.*

So why didn't they tell me? I might have been able to help. Maybe find them a place of their own. Send them off on a holiday.

You still don't get it, do you? Evelyn said. *There was nothing you could do to make them happy. Except turn them into nothing again.*

And you?

I don't know, she said, shrugging. *I also don't know if I have the courage to do what they did. In some ways, it's good to be alive.*

I leave it up to you, I said. *I know you don't care for me so I'm not going to force you to stay with me. And, if you decide to follow my parents, I won't stop you.*

I'd like to go away for a while and think it over, she said.

Sure, I said, almost nonchalantly, all the while trying to keep my legs from collapsing beneath me, my world from sinking into a vast sea of despond.

She packed that same evening—a knapsack with a change of clothing. It's the last time I saw her face to face. I wanted to find some way to convince her to stay. I wanted her to suddenly change her mind, declare undying love for me and take her place by my side. But what could I tell her that I hadn't already told her? I had already shown her the love letters we'd exchanged and they had made her burst into tears, saying what a lucky woman the original Evelyn must have been to feel such passion.

Both of you were lucky, she said. *Or it felt like you were lucky.*

So why did I leave her, right? Why did I abandon her the first time?

Yes, I would ask that question, she said. *In my heart, I would definitely ask that question.*

All I had left was to make promises I couldn't keep. Yes, I could promise her that I would give up my ability to control the DNA computers. That I would program the computers not to bring us back once we died. That I would re-introduce fate, luck, chance, accidents, tomorrow's uncertainty into our lives.

But I didn't even know if those were things I could actually do. I suspect there are some over-riding controls that not even I can get to. Some pre-set mechanisms deep in the heart of the "real" facility. Besides, there's always the problem of putting all those goodies back into the box. Stuffing the monster back in. In the end, I just told her I loved her and if she ever changed her mind . . . she knew where to find me.

There's that pounding on the door again. I switch on the camera hovering above the entrance, seeing the Mussolini's fish-eyed face.

Open up, Fausto, the Mussolini says, looking up at the camera. *Come on. I just want to talk to you. You can't stay in there forever.*

I can see Rachele and Claretta in the background. They wave meekly while holding onto one another.

Go away, I shout over the intercom system. *I'll come out when I'm good and ready. Now, stop bothering me.*

I switch off the camera and lean back in my chair. In my hand, I hold the tiny disc on which has been imprinted Evelyn's journey once she left me—more than three days' worth, hour by hour and minute by minute. I have deliberately avoided looking at it until now, deliberately put it off, promising I'd destroy it if she returned in the meantime. Back into my loving arms. Now, hands trembling, I slip it into the holographic imaging machine. I can't wait any longer. I have to know.

You hear that, I say, shouting. *I have to know.*

I have to know, the monitors spread around the projection room echo. Mocking or concerned? No, simply mechanical.

Her image appears. Early on, while still within sight of the house, she stops several times and seems on the verge of turning back. Once, she even takes a few steps before changing her mind again. The camera follows her out past the eighth enclosure and into the corridor leading to the other eco-systems. At this point, I play a little game with myself, trying to guess where she's going to go next. Already, as I watch her image, she feels like someone else. Like someone I really don't know. Like someone I'm simply curious about. At the same time, another part of me is screaming: *What are you doing? Go after her, you fool! You can't let her get away like this. You can't allow her to drop out of your life like this without a trace.*

And I'm at the entrance to the projection room before realizing it's too late to go after her. That what I'm watching. . . .

The cave, I say. *You're headed for the cave. Right?*

Wrong. She goes nowhere near the cave. Nowhere near the other still surviving humans. Instead, she re-traces some of my own journeys through the various eco-systems, journeys she probably watched right in this room: the marsh, the rain forest, the polar cap, the mountains. . . . Wherever she goes, I brace myself for the worst. I grip the sides of my chair and await the moment when she'll do herself in, followed quickly by the Scavenger feast.

I have absolutely no doubt this is her intention—even if she doesn't quite consciously know it. After all, what other purpose would she have for leaving here? What other reason for her behaviour to this point? I know because I did it myself. Because it took several re-incarnations to wean myself off the urge to simply vanish again. Before I no longer succumbed.

So, when she stands on the edge of the cliffs that surround the facility ocean, I have trouble looking at the hologram. And I catch my breath. When she holds out her arms to the elements and leans forward to embrace the wind, I cry out and rush to try to pull her back—and fall through her and flat on my face instead. I breathe a sigh of relief when she turns away from the water and begins a slow descent to the shore. But even when she's safely at sea level I'm wary. Perhaps, she'll simply walk into the water and drown herself. Or allow herself to be crushed by the momentous waves as the tide rises and they slam against the sharp rocks.

Slowly, she removes her clothing and folds it neatly in a pile. Then sits on the rough sand, back to the camera. As I reach out and pass my hand along her fleshy hourglass, up and down her spinal cord, I swear I can feel the warmth beneath my fingertips, the electric pulse, the spell of the brief period we spent together. She sits this way unmoving for an hour or so, with the water slowly rising until it reaches her waist, until it covers the sand.

That's it, I say to myself. She's going to drown herself. She's going to let the water rise and rise until she can no longer keep her head above it. But no. When the water is at the level of her breasts, she suddenly stands up, almost like a jack-in-the-box, takes a deep breath and brushes herself off.

Now this is really it, I say. *This is where it all ends. Into the depths.*

One more surprise. Rather than walking towards the water, she turns and heads back towards the bottom of the cliffs, towards the innumerable caves. The water is rising higher and higher. Soon, only her head will be visible. She disappears into a cave and I lose sight of her.

No! I yell. *You'll be trapped in there.*

But, you fool, that's exactly what she wants to do. That way she won't have a choice. Won't be able to change her mind at the last moment when her natural instinct for self-preservation takes over. Even if she floats to the top, it's only a matter of time before those tiny air spaces are also filled with water. Only a matter of time before the air runs out. I've just about resigned myself to her fate when she comes floating out of the cave in a small boat, a skiff of some sort.

What the. . . .

She begins to row out towards the open water, struggling against the waves which have calmed down considerably at high tide. Once far enough from shore, she rigs up a small sail. Only then does it hit me. Only then do I understand what she's trying to do. What she's really doing.

You bitch! I scream, lashing out at her image, slashing away to deform her digital image for a moment before it re-builds itself. *You can't do this to me. This is my facility. I control it. And*

I'll reproduce you if I want. You can't run away and hide. Sooner or later, you'll have to return. I'll have you then again. I'll control your comings and goings again—even if I have to kill you to do it. Do you understand? You can't escape me.

But they're just words. I have no idea where she's gone or what's out there. The camera follows the boat out as far as possible but then it too must stop—or risk running out of energy. I watch with helpless rage as Evelyn and the boat become smaller and smaller. I watch with clenched fists as the boat becomes first a speck on the horizon and then vanishes completely between grey water and grey sky. I watch for the next several hours in the hope she'll change her mind and turn around. Or at least do me the favour of plunging into the watery depths. No such luck. I fast forward the hologram, collapsing three days into a few minutes. No return trip. Just swirling water and sky.

You bitch! I repeat more quietly, sitting on the floor. *You fucking cold-hearted ungrateful bitch!*

I hold the tiny chip in my hand, the chip that contains Evelyn's last journey. Practically indestructible, playable in reverse for my edification, accessible at any point and for any stretch of time, a three-D mockery. I start to blubber, unable to hold it back. Then I laugh. Then, flopping onto on the floor, I laugh and cry at the same time. Now I know what it's like to be a powerless God. Damned if you do and damned if you don't. *Damned*—now there's an interesting choice of words for a God.

I lower my head so that it touches my chest. Like a pouting baby. Like a crybaby. I look up at the ceiling, at the projection room's marvellous ceiling with its myriad machines ready to play back every single incident that has ever taken place within the facility. Another mockery. For wouldn't it take a lifetime to view all that? And what about what took place while you were viewing what had previously taken place? And . . . and what purpose does it serve? What the fuck good does it do me? I need to be a true God. I need for everything to be happening at once. Right before me—from start to finish.

I need for time and space to stand still while I sort through them. Make my way through the detritus. The dustbins of history.

No. I need for time and space to stand still while I re-arrange them, twist them around, mould them to my liking. I need to be able to reach in and do some tweaking. I need to be able to throw a monkey wrench into the works, to bring it to a complete standstill, if necessary. I need to reverse the flow . . . step into the stream and reverse it . . . I need to reach in and yank out my own heart . . . excise those feelings that keep me from becoming a true god . . . that keep me chained down forever human . . . I need. . . .

Go after her, you fool, the old familiar voice hums. *Never mind this god bullshit! Prove that you're still a man. Go after her and bring her back. Drag her back, if you must. Drag her back by the hair, if need be. Stomp her into submission. Then kill her if she insists on resisting you. Make sure she can't escape to a place where you can't touch her and where the ache in your heart goes on forever. After all, what else does love mean? Kill her over and over again, if you must. If that's the only way to keep her beside you. Kill her with the best of intentions. Kill her with a loving look in your eye.*

PART FOUR

BEYOND CHOOSING

I have no name and no face, I am here,
cast at my feet, looking at myself
looking to see myself seen.

SCENE ONE: FIRST ENDINGS

Claretta, Rachele, the Mussolini and a brand-new grandfather stand on the shoreline. The first three are waving Fausto good-bye; the grandfather is standing slightly to one side, shuffling and looking at his feet. They've just helped push Fausto's boat out to sea and are now standing there helpless with the water lapping at their ankles, the tide receding one more time.

Fausto could have had the facility build him any kind of boat he wanted, any kind the technology would allow. Some sort of flying machine, perhaps, so that he could speed along and skim above the surface for rapid survey. Or even some form of detection equipment that would do all the work of finding Evelyn for him, mapping out the quadrants so methodically nothing would escape their signals. He might have even been able to go immediately to her position. But he would have none of it. He wanted a boat identical to the one used by Evelyn for her outward journey. Down to the tattered sail. And he used the holographic images to have the facility recreate it. Down to the tattered sail.

We won't see you again, will we? Claretta had wailed. *You're leaving us for good, aren't you?*

That's nonsense, the Mussolini had said with a semblance of his usual bluster and a puffing out of his chest. *Of course, we'll see him again. He'll return the moment he finds his true love. Won't you? He'll rescue her. Won't you?*

Yes, he'll come back to us, Rachele had said, comforting Claretta. *We're his friends. He knows we love him very much. That we care for him like a brother. He knows we'll be waiting for him with open arms.*

Why did you bring me back to life? the grandfather had said, ignoring everyone else. *Just to watch you leave again? To punish me? And why are you wasting your time on this . . . this nonsense? This wild goose chase? Why not just wait for her to die and then have the facility recreate her?*

Here, Fausto had said, turning his back on the others so they couldn't see him and handing his grandfather a holo-gram disc. *This will explain everything. You can do what you want with it. Show it to the others or don't. It's up to you.*

Now the talking is over. Now Fausto waves at them, watch-ing them grow smaller and smaller on the shoreline. And they wave at him, watching him grow smaller and smaller on the horizon. For a while, they can still see him as the boat bobs up on the crests, rising like a toy on the crests. But then he's gone and the only way they can keep track of him is through the surveillance camera that follows him out as far as it can. Before it too must turn back, severing the tie that has held them so far. They climb to the top of the cliffs in the hope of catching one last glimpse of him. Too late. The ever-shifting clouds and water play tricks on their eyes, never standing still long enough to allow them a fix.

Bye, Claretta shouts into the wind.

Come, the Mussolini says. *Let's go home. Perhaps I can make an offering to the gods of the seas for him and his safe return.*

The Mussolini, Claretta and Rachele turn away. The grand-father remains on the cliff, looking out.

You're more than welcome to come with us, the Mussolini says. *Plenty of room and good company.*

Meet me in the projection room, the grandfather says after a moment of silence.

What? the Mussolini says. *What on earth for?*

Just do as I say, damn you! the grandfather shouts. *Before I change my mind and you can all go to hell! Straight to hell!*

The grandfather turns to face the ocean again. The Mus-solini, Claretta and Rachele watch him for a few moments, then look at one another and continue to walk away.

Fausto, caught between sky and sea and having lost all vi-sual contact with land, is soon struggling to keep up his cour-age. Surrounded by mist and clouds, the spray of countless waves, the knowledge that this ocean is indeed as vast and expansive as it looked from shore (or so it seems once in its midst), he's starting to have some doubts as to the feasibility of what he's doing. Perhaps the task is futile, perhaps the searching for another boat under these conditions is a foolish fancy on his part. A limp needle in a watery haystack.

After all, his grandfather is right about one thing. Evelyns, like everything else in the facility, are a dime a dozen. But something keeps telling him that the only version of Evelyn he wants is the one now in existence, the one wandering through the same soup that has him befuddled and confused. The rest, even the most perfect ones, would be flawed copies in his eyes.

No, he says, shaking his head, *I'm not going to give up now. I'm going to find you or die trying.* He laughs. *Or try dying.*

The darkness descends and with it a calming of the waves. The clouds clear away, revealing thousands of stars, each twinkling to its own rhythm. The miracles of random programming, the pinpricks punching holes in the fabric. Fausto huddles in the bottom of the gently rocking boat, curls up and tries to get some sleep. He tries not to think of the decision he's made. The decisions he's made. And those he will soon be making.

There's no going back now, he says. *Definitely no going back now. Even if I turned around and headed back to shore.* He looks around—water in all directions. *Whichever way that might be. Going back is not an option.*

The Mussolini, Claretta and Rachele have gathered in the projection room. The Mussolini marches back and forth; Claretta and Rachele huddle together on one chair.

I wonder what that wicked old man wants, Claretta says. Then she giggles. *Maybe he's going to shoot us all again. That's what he does best.*

Oh you're bad, Claretta, Rachele says. *Very bad.*

Could you two keep it down? the Mussolini says. *I'm trying to think.*

Think? Claretta says. *About what?*

A plan, he says, still pacing. *We've got to come up with some kind of plan—in case Fausto doesn't return.*

Don't say that! Claretta says, crossing herself. *Don't even think it.*

Well, it could happen, the Mussolini says. *Who knows what's out there.*

Hush, Rachele says. *Everything is going to be okay.*

We must have a plan, he says, slapping his palms together.

The Mussolini resumes his silent pacing. Claretta and Rachele hug one another to keep warm. They wait. Moments later, the entrance to the projection room slides open and the grandfather steps in.

Okay, he says without any greetings and holding up the hologram disc. *Just tell me what has to be done with this thing.*

It's a hologram, the Mussolini says.

Yes, yes, I know that, the grandfather says gruffly. *A machine plays it, if I understand correctly? I do not know how.*

Here, give it to me, the Mussolini says.

He holds out his hand. The grandfather pulls the disc back.

Well then, play it yourself, the Mussolini says.

Okay, the grandfather says. *But no tricks. Otherwise. . . .*

You're going to shoot us all, right? Claretta says. *Your favourite pastime.*

The grandfather looks at her as if to respond, then hands the disc to the Mussolini. The Mussolini slips it into one of the players. Almost immediately, Fausto's image appears before them. He's sitting in the kitchen of his parents' house. It's all that's left of the house, saved at the last moment after he'd ordered the place destroyed. Bits and pieces torn away, jagged edges like something coming through from another dimension. The remnants of the kitchen door lead to the outside, the familiar geometry of the eighth eco-system back to the way it was before Fausto's efforts at terra-forming.

Greetings, my friends, he says. *I know that what you're looking for is some sort of explanation for what I'm doing. Well, the truth is, I really don't have any. None that makes any sense at any rate. I brought you back, grandfather, because there's no telling what's going to happen from here on in. And I might never have got the chance again. Wouldn't want your non-existence on my conscience, that's for sure. Even if you're the one who started all this. Way back when I was too young to know any better. Claretta, I'm sorry if I hurt you. I didn't do it on purpose. You must believe that. I had no intention of hurting you. And I envy your love for me. Have I the same feelings for Evelyn? I wish I could say categorically I do.*

He loves me! Claretta says, hugging herself. *He—*

Rachele and Benito, Fausto continues. *It might seem funny coming from someone who once shot you but your friendship means a lot to me. As for you, nonno—and I trust you're here, you should know I hold you in the highest regard. As I know that anything you may have done was with my best interests in mind.*

About time you realized that, the grandfather says.

Fausto takes a deep breath and continues: *Okay. Now that we've got that out of the way, I guess you're all anxious to hear what this is about. So I'll get right to it. As of now, my string of lives has run out. Yesterday, I programmed the cloning computer not to bring me back if I should happen to die.*

What! the Mussolini says.

What's he talking about? Rachele says.

Claretta shrugs.

Now, there's no need to be alarmed about this, Fausto says. *This won't affect the rest of you. I thought long and hard about doing the same for you. But that's something for you to decide. Why did I do it, you ask. I did it because . . . well, I think it's because . . . you can't be a God and in love at the same time . . . you can't live forever and expect . . . ah, what's the use? I don't know why I did it. Besides, it might not work anyway. The facility might override it. Hey! Maybe I should try that right now.* He holds up a glass of clear liquid and brings it to his lips. *Maybe I should kill myself and see whether or not I'm brought back.*

No! Claretta, Rachele and the Mussolini cry out at the same time.

Ha, ha! Just kidding. He puts the glass down. *Anyway, goodbye for now. And, if all goes well, I'll see you all again soon. If not, I know you'll do fine without me.*

The image fades away and flickers to a stop. All four stare at where it had been. Claretta reaches out and then throws herself on the floor wailing. The Mussolini and Rachele hold each other up. The grandfather mutters "fool" under his breath and walks out.

Scene Two: Cruel Silences

Thirst. Unquenchable thirst. Water. Flying fish. Thirst. Constriction. Monsters from the deep. Scaly monsters from the deep. Thirst. Scaly monsters with endless maws. Thirst and more thirst. Monsters that rise high into the air—and dissolve like waves. Flying fish bursting into rainbows. Rainbows that stink like dead fish, encrusted with salt. Cod fish with cod pieces. Thirst. Unquenchable thirst.

I'm delirious. Delirious. Can I spell the word? Deliciously delirious. Clothing as tattered as the sail. How many times have I leaned over the side of the boat and stared down at my reflection? At my inviting, come-hither reflection? At my pinched, salt-encrusted face? At my leathery, rib-protruding sailor's chest? Take the plunge. Let yourself float without care through the deep. Come on. Come on. Come on. The hypnotic call of . . . delirium. Not without you, my love. Hand in hand, yes. Passing air back and forth, yes. But not without you, my love. Let the reflections plunge where they may. I'm staying right here.

Can it be? An ancient bird? Say the word. Everybody's heard. High . . . deep . . . embedded within the nested program, a single word resides. The word to trigger all. The stone in the simile pond. Concentricity. Within the grin. An oval. Startled. You're either with the wave or agin it. Washed clean or washed up. It's your choice, Mr. Faustino. Souls for sale. Best offer. First come, first served. Bargain basement prices. Exchanges allowed. Eternity minus 30-day guarantees. He's having a devil of a time. The demons have found a better host—they have no need of human souls. Demons? More like impish impulses. Electrical impulses.

Take me, take me, I seem to yell. Sorry. No can do. As

demons, we're trained to only go after the highest creatures on the evolutionary scale. La crème de la crème. You no longer meet that criterion. You and your kind are losers. Losers! Overtaken by your own creations. Losers! Made redundant. Thirst. Delirium. Thirst. Precisely. The essential weakness of being human. The quintessential weakness. Your creations, on the other hand, never tire. Never thirst. Never . . . never what? Never delude themselves. Flying fish. Rainbows. Demons.

Land, ahoy! Where? There. Where? There. On the horizon. Silvery. Glittery. Shiny. Polished. Another delusion. Is there no solution to the illusion? No, no. There. On the horizon. Where? There. Men standing. And women. Men and women in white coats. Men and women in white coats? But no delusions? Yes, just standing there with their arms folded. Dozens of them standing a few metres apart from each other. All facing one way. All staring out at the sea. And, though not identical, they all look somewhat alike: same general build, same hair styles, same expression on their faces. Same slightly bemused look.

Ah, you have gone crazy, Mr. Faustino. Fallen over the edge. Floated off to la-la land. White coats, you say? Yes. The essential scientific garb. Or the hospital's. White coats so bright they hurt my eyes. Men and women in white coats ready to take you to the loonie bin. Ha ha. Ho ho. Hee hee. White, white, white on white. I stand up on wobbly legs and begin to wave. Pull myself up by the mast and gesticulate.

Over here, I shout. Or try to shout. My voice is like a frog's croak. A cricket's chirp. A frog's chirp. A cricket's croak. *Over here!*

I wave more frantically. No one seems to be paying any attention. They're just going about their business. All those men and women in white coats. Just going about their business. What business? Whose business? My legs give way. I sit back, plop into the soaked bottom. Slowly, the boat bobs and weaves closer and closer to the shiny island. The glittery haven. It goes in and out of focus like some desert mirage. But

never mind. It is getting closer and closer, I'm sure of it. Yes!
Now, I can make out some of the faces. Pleasant faces peering
out, going about their business.

The boat is raised high by one last swell and then depos-
ited onto the island. I'm tossed out, rolling into the midst
of the men and women who have been standing there all
along. Who have been waiting there patiently, armed folded,
for the fun to end. Despite the sun, it's cold and I shiver. I
can feel metal beneath me now and I know that I'm naked
in the midst of all those men and women just looking at me.
And I try to roll into a ball so as to cover myself, to protect
my private parts from their relentless stares. But I find I can't.
I'm pinned down flat on my back and arms outstretched by
some invisible force. Frozen. Unable to move. All except for
my eyes shifting from side to side in their sockets.

Any moment now, I tell myself, I'll wake up in the middle
of the ocean again, find myself at the bottom of my boat with
the sun beating down on me and the tattered sail flapping
uselessly in the light breeze. Any moment now. The circle of
metal beneath me begins to whirr and turn. Begins to rise
and unscrew itself. And the metal beneath all the men and
women staring at me does the same. Each with his or her own
circle of metal. And then, I'm descending, as if on a platter
of some kind. We're all descending on our separate platters.
The hole seals up above me with an hydraulic hiss. I come
to rest on an area that looks identical to the one from which
I've descended—except now the sky is metallic. Just like the
facility. Now, there's a clue. A clue? To what? I already know
I'm in the facility. Where else could I be?

We're moving again. This time everything around me is
sinking. My ears pop. I can hear the water gurgling above me
as it closes in over us. We're sinking into the ocean. Suddenly,
the invisible force releases me and I sit up. I look around—
a vast, circular, windowless room made of gleaming metal.
Or metal-like substance. The men and women walk about in
purposeful ways, some huddling together and talking, others
hurrying off to press buttons or activate dials. Or pass their

hands over glowing graphics. Or press hand-sized electronic pads. Everyone serious. No one smiling. Everyone with a purpose. A reason for being there. Previously unseen doors slide open to let people in and out. A pale woman stops before me. Tall, elegant, graceful, a look of slight disdain on her face. On her very symmetrical face. She too holds some sort of electronic tablet in her hands.

Fausto Contadino No. 14, she says in a strangely toneless voice, punching keys on the tablet while continuing to stare straight ahead as if she doesn't really see me. As if she's already working on some other problem. *Correct?*

What? Where am I? This must be a dream.

Please respond, she says, once again punching keys. *Fausto Contadino No. 14. Correct?*

Who are you? Why—

Fausto Contadino No. 14, she repeats for the third time in exactly the same tone of voice, without the least hint of irritation or impatience. *Correct?*

Yes, yes, I say. *But—*

Thank you. Please come with me.

She turns and begins to walk away rapidly.

Some clothing, I say, needlessly pointing at myself. *Could I at least get some clothing?*

She stops for a moment, as if considering the request. Then continues walking. Realizing she's not going to wait for me, I fall in step behind her.

Where are you taking me? I ask, not really expecting an answer—and not getting one. More to hear my own voice, as if that is some measure of sanity.

We approach one of the sides of the room. A beam of light shoots from the wall, scanning her. A circular door irises open. The woman stands aside. I try to look into the opening but I can't see anything.

Fausto Contadino No. 14, she says. *Please step through.*

You want me to go in there? I say, trying to penetrate the darkness.

Fausto Contadino No. 14, she repeats. *Please. . . .*

Yes, yes, I say.

Please step through.

I enter cautiously, careful where I'm placing my feet. The iris closes behind me, shutting out the rest of the light. I lean back against where the door had been, hoping for some reference point. The metal feels slightly cold yet comfortable. I wait for my eyes to become acclimatized to the dark. Or for me to wake up from the dream.

Welcome, Fausto, a man's voice says. *At last, we meet again.*

The room begins to glow with a soft light. Not more than a few metres away stands a man. In a white coat, naturally. He resembles all the others except that he seems older—and even more composed than the others.

Who are you? I say, hands placed strategically before me.

Oh dear, the man says. *Maybe you should put something on, yes?* He hands me a uniform identical to the one I was previously wearing, torn to shreds by sun and wind and sea. *Sorry about that. Some of us take things a little too literally around here.*

Thanks, I say, as the uniform wraps itself around me. *Now, who are you? And what am I doing here?*

You're looking good, Fausto, he says, slowly circling me. He chuckles. *Considering it's been more than a century of your time since the last time I saw you and you've killed yourself at least a dozen times in the meantime.*

You saw me? I look at the man more closely. *Do I know you? Am I supposed to know you? Where would you have seen me?*

Ah, still the little boy full of questions, the man says. *That's excellent. Curiosity is one of humanity's more endearing traits. And makes up for so many of our faults. Here then. See if this doesn't bring back memories.*

Another beam of light sets off a series of holograms. I recognize myself as a small boy holding my grandfather's hand and heading towards the central hub of the facility. As we pass the cloning tanks, I catch a glimpse of a man in the control area, a younger version of the one now standing before me.

That's right, he says. *The man in the control tower. Before you took over, that is.*

And all this time, you've. . . .

We've been right here, yes.

Watching us stumble around, I say, feeling the anger build up in me. *Playing around with our lives. As if we were some sort . . . some sort of lab rats.*

My apologies for that, he says. *My sincere apologies. But we felt containment was the only way for the experiment to work.*

Experiment? What experiment?

Angrily, I take a step forward. He holds up his hand.

Please, he says. *You would be advised to maintain your distance. The area around me is highly charged and the shock would be quite unpleasant.*

What experiment? I repeat, circling him.

We had to keep you within the containment field—the facility, if you wish—to avoid contamination. It was for your own good.

Is that your idea of an explanation? And is that supposed to make me feel better?

Whatever emotional reactions you may have are entirely up to you. We have no control over that. Our only mission was to keep you from becoming contaminated.

By what? Against what? What the fuck are you talking about?

Think about it for a moment, Fausto. What does the facility do? What does it have that might be contaminated?

DNA, I say, suddenly seeing the light. *Genetic material.*

Exactly, the man says. *So you can imagine our horror—and delight—when you pulled your parents and Evelyn out of your magic trunk.*

New DNA. Potentially dangerous DNA. Previously untested DNA.

So why didn't we stop you, you're about to ask? That would have been tampering with the . . . the experiment, for lack of a better word.

But you did tamper, didn't you?

Not really. We did the same with them as with early models of you. They had to be purified. We had to make sure they wouldn't contaminate the rest of the pool.

So why are you telling me all this now? Why not wait for them to undergo the process? Just like you did for the rest of us?

Like all experiments, it has a finite end and time is running out on this one. It's as simple as that. We can't afford to wait on them. We have to move onto the next phase.

Which is?

Ah, that would be telling now, wouldn't it? Truth be told, there was some considerable debate about revealing even this much to you. But we're not totally without heart here, despite what you might think.

Where is she now?

As if in answer to my question, one of the walls opens to reveal Evelyn floating in liquid similar to that in the cloning tanks. Naked; eyes shut; hands clasped together before her.

What's going to happen to her? I ask, watching her spin slowly towards the glass wall and then away again.

Frankly, we don't know. Your parents made it easy for us—and we were able to extract their DNA from the cloning tanks. But Evelyn . . . she insisted on not dying. For fear you'd simply re-build her.

Release her, I say. *Let me take her back with me. I promise she won't contaminate a thing. I'll make sure of it.*

That's very generous of you. Very kind. But I'm afraid that won't be possible. Evelyn is lost to you. You must face that simple fact. Even if we gave her back to you, what makes you think she would agree to staying with you?

I'll convince her, I say. *Please. I'll make her understand.*

No time, he says. *No more time. The experiment is practically over. There are rumblings already of going over-budget, of using too many resources. Of concentrating instead on those with more potential. We must wrap things up and be on our way.*

Be on your way? What are you talking about?

The experiment is about to be terminated. We must then be on our way. It is as simple as that. You, of all people, should understand.

Release her! I scream, punching repeatedly at the glass wall. *Give her back to me.* I turn towards the man. *I warn you. If you don't let her go. . . .*

As I step towards him, fists clenched, ready to pummel him, the invisible force pins me down again. I collapse to the floor, unable even to speak any longer.

I'm sorry, the man says. *You've been given the opportunity to see*

Evelyn one last time. For the last time. He points towards her and the glass wall becomes opaque. *Now it's time for you to go back. There's still much to be done and you have many decisions to make before the next phase. Good-bye. Until we meet again.*

The man stands before me, hands behind his back, a slight smile on his face. *Oh, by the way, the attempt to over-ride your own re-birth was a clever little trick. But you should know that it won't work. We couldn't possibly allow your genetic material to vanish, now could we? So if you're thinking of doing yourself in, you should know that death will once again bring about a resurrection. The natural order of things, I'm afraid. The new natural order. At least during the life of the experiment. Sorry about that.*

I want nothing more than to let out a banshee scream. To leap at him claws and fangs first. I want to reach in and rip out his windpipe. I want to . . . But, once again, all I can move are my eyes from side to side. The lights dim and he slowly vanishes, hands held calmly behind his back—like some fucking professor from my days at the university, the cool fish who didn't seem to be affected by what the rest of us took to be the essence of being human. I'm in the dark, unable to see more than a few inches in front of me. There are people moving about, going about their mysterious business.

I make a promise to myself: When I get out of this situation, I'm going to use every means available to hunt these people down. I'm going to throw the entire force of the facility at them. I'm not some powerless weakling! I have control of the cloning machines! There will be no place for them to hide as I hunt them down one by one. Sure, sure, another voice says. After all, look at all the power you've been able to muster to this point. Very impressive. Shut up! I scream—or think I scream at any rate. I'm going to find a way. You wait and see.

My ears pop. We're rising again; we're heading up towards the surface. Or I'm heading up towards the surface. I don't know what anyone else is doing. All I can see is directly above me. I can feel the metal cylinder lifting beneath me, taking me towards the roof. Above me, the sound of something being unscrewed. Suddenly, a shaft of light breaks in from the edges of a hole in the ceiling, a hole where another piece of metal has unscrewed itself.

The metal piece slides aside and I pop through. Freedom. Escape. No. Simply the outside of the metal island. I'm on the bright surface of the metal island again, still unable to move. The sun pulses overhead. Like some gigantic beast about to awake. Pulsing yellow and orange and red and back to yellow. A few metres away, the water laps gently against the island's shoreline.

The piece of circular metal on which I'm lying screws itself back into place and I'm free. I roll away with the force of releasing myself.

Bastards! I scream. *Sick bastards!* I pound at the piece of metal which has now fitted seamlessly into the rest of the island. *Motherfuckers!* I continue to beat at the metal, first with my fists and then with my head. *What gives you the right? Who made you the fucking god almighty fucking ruler of the universe?*

My fists are raw and my head aches. I sit down and start to rock back and forth like a little child throwing a tantrum and pissed off because no one is listening. *Bastards!* I say more quietly. *I'm going to sit here until you open up. I'm going to stay right here until you let me see Evelyn again. You can't get rid of me that easily. She's the only thing I really want in this world. I'm not giving up just like that. I'm sitting here and you can't get rid of me. No fucking way!*

But I know even as I say it that it's a really stupid thing to say. For one thing, I have no way of getting back inside, of prying open any of those entrance circles. There is nothing to pry open. For another, the island is already starting to sink beneath me. Soon, it is out of sight and I'm treading water, flapping my arms just to stay afloat. I look around, trying to determine the direction that might get me to land. The sun. Follow the path of the sun, right?

A wave washes over me, sending me beneath the waters. When I push my way to the surface again, I see a shadow to one side. It's my boat! And only a few metres away! Salvation!

For the moment, at least. I start to swim towards it. Ropes dangle invitingly from its sides; the tattered mast sways to and fro. I reach up for one of those ropes, tired, anxious to flop to the bottom and maybe curl up for a good sleep. I reach up . . . and something smashes into the boat, sending it high into the air.

I am pulled beneath the waters by the explosive force of what has just happened, sucked into the wake as the boat comes back down in pieces. When I re-surface, there are boat parts everywhere. Like kindling. Like splinters. Like the shattered remains of balsa wood movie sets trampled by fake monsters. No piece bigger than a few square centimetres. What . . . I look around for what may have done this but I don't see anything. The waves are fairly calm, just a little choppy. Wavelets, really. It doesn't matter though. They could be as calm and level as glass. It won't make any difference in a few minutes. I'm going to sink to the bottom and there's nothing I can do about it.

I keep myself afloat a little while longer, becoming more and more tired, less and less buoyant, feeling the water tugging me down. My legs give way. Quit moving. I look up at the sky one last time and begin to sink. I have no strength to return to the surface. No strength to struggle even. I try to hold my breath for as long as I can. Then I try to breathe. If one doesn't work, maybe the other will. Stupid logic. The logic of contradiction. Either/or. The water fills my mouth. The air bubbles away towards the fading light. No way to reach them. To recycle them. It's murky and cold and silent.

I let myself go, no longer struggling. Face down, I sink deeper and deeper. Further and further from the light. From the dappling sunlight. Descent. Delirium. Delusion. Delight. Death. Decay. All the duckie "Ds" lined up in a row. I keep repeating: Death . . . decay . . . death . . . decay . . . death . . . delusion . . . delirium . . . death . . . decay. . . .

Suddenly, I'm being surrounded by scaly monsters who play with my body, butting it with their heads, propelling it with their sulphurous breaths. Suddenly, I'm a plaything to be nipped and pushed and bounced—and then finally swallowed when they grow tired of the game. Now, I can see myself going down the maw of one of the scaly monsters and, at the same time, I can still see outside, as if the monster's body were transparent and oddly gelatinous. And, once inside, I can breathe again, an outrush of air that flames out of the monster's mouth. As if it were breathing fire.

I'm on a wave that rises high into the air. No, it's not a wave. I'm not inside a wave. This is true delirium. This is the pre-death dance that all drowning men enjoy, the flashing of a lifetime before liquid-y ideas. No, you fool. This is no delirium. No delusion. It's as real as it gets. I'm inside an oversized Scavenger, rising 10 metres or more. This is it, I say. This is where I'm mixed with digestive juices and reduced to my essential DNA in the creature's stomach. To be regurgitated. To perhaps re-emerge from the cloning tanks. Or not.

I can still see out its transparent body. But it is moving so fast that my head begins to spin. Objects blur. The sun ping pongs back and forth, one moment incredibly huge and filling the sky, the next tiny and insignificant, the size of a pin. And then we're beneath the water again, slowly descending to the bottom. The light fades until it is but a glimmer far above me. Then that too vanishes and everything becomes dark, save for a slight phosphorescent glow along the walls of the creature's stomach . . . or whatever it is I'm inside.

Occasionally, as we descend, huge luminous eyes peer in for a moment before scurrying away; bulbs expand and shrink, shimmer and fade; fleshy stalks dangle like enticing bits of food; tubes the colours of a psychedelic rainbow inch by; filaments float disembodied, touching and recoiling; tentacles reach out, wrapping themselves like relieved children around a long-lost mother. Only to be propelled explosively away again.

I settle cross-legged, motionless, simply staring straight ahead, aware of the fact that, if the creature had wanted to dissolve and digest me, it would have done so by now. Why am I not dead? Why am I not decaying? Decomposing? We

continue to sink. Now even the strange phosphorescent creatures have been left behind. I reach out and tentatively touch
the wall before me. It gives way slightly—just like the walls
of the passageways connecting the various eco-systems in the
facility itself.

Aha! I say to myself. Is this a clue? Must be a clue. Definitely
a clue. About what? The nature of the facility? Of course. But
what does that mean? Everything in the facility is a clue related
to the nature of the facility, isn't it? Brilliant deduction. I laugh,
the sound echoing within. What would Jonah have done if he
had wanted to get out early? Would he have taken a sword and
attacked the whale, splitting open the flesh until there was a
large enough hole to set him free? Or perhaps start a fire, causing heartburn and forcing the monster to expel him?

We finally come to a stop. Must be the bottom of this artificial ocean. Perhaps, this creature will once again allow me
to get into the island. To free Evelyn from her stasis. To wrest
control of the facility from those bloodless monsters in white
coats and to make it our own little corner of paradise. To
bring them to their knees . . . to make them pay for their little
"experiment" . . . to show them that human beings aren't
something you can fool around with . . . aren't something you
can tamper with . . . oh, they can tamper with themselves but
just let someone else try . . . experiment, indeed . . . how dare
they treat us like lab rats . . . how dare. . . .

I look around and start to laugh. Here I am, making
threats and preparing for vengeance when I can't even see
more than a few centimetres in front of me; when I don't
even know why I'm still alive; when I'm trapped inside a Scavenger's sulphurous belly. I should be asking myself why the
creature hasn't bathed me in digestive juices or crushed me
with the motions of its stomach muscles, sending the bits and
pieces of my DNA back to the cloning tank for Fausto Contadino #15 . . . or whatever.

On the other hand, I was already on the verge of dying
one more time when the creature swallowed me up, reversing
its normal role. So maybe I needn't worry about that. Maybe

I should feel blessed instead. Maybe I'll be able to resume my search for Evelyn. I've just about convinced myself of that possibility when I feel something wet against the back of my head—wet flesh touching the back of my head. I lurch forward, trying to shake it off. But there is nowhere for me to go, no place to escape. The flesh pushes itself against me, insistent, as if probing for the right spot. I bob back and forth, hoping to get loose, to tear myself away. Instead, the flesh tightens its hold on me.

I feel tendrils penetrating my skull, tiny filaments oozing out of the flesh and into me. I want to cry out, I want to bleat my fear, I want to wake up. Wake up! Wake up! Wake up! Danger alert! Self-preservation gland to the fore! But the tendrils keep spreading inside my skull and then suddenly I can't feel them anymore but I know they're inside my brain. And I know that my own limbs are moving but it's not me making them move. And I'm no longer breathing. Something else is breathing for me. And the piece of flesh against the back of my head is starting to grow, starting to thin out so that it now covers my entire head and I can no longer see. And it spreads down as I curl up into a ball and it soon has my body inside it completely, like a second skin.

And I should be trying to scream at the top of my lungs and I should be beating against the walls to be allowed out and I should be shaking uncontrollably and frightened out of my wits, wrapped as I am in an alien cocoon. For what else could it be? But none of that is happening. Instead, I'm as calm as if sleeping in my own bed, the flesh around me soothing and warm like a favourite blanket rather than restricting or constricting. No, more than a favourite blanket. More like part of me. Indispensable. The simple substance.

Hello, Fausto, a familiar voice says. *Remember me?*

I'm startled for a moment, disoriented. And then it comes to me. It's the voice from my dreams, the voice that woke me up time and again when all I wanted to do was vanish into non-existence, the voice that had all the answers—and none of them. Only now, it isn't something apart, something outside me, but rather my voice. It is the only voice I have. My own mouth has grown silent, unable or unwilling to speak. But something speaks nevertheless.

Yes, I am the creature who would not come when called, the monster who kept the facility clean, the devourer of decay and death. Or rather I should now say: 'We are the creature, you and I.' Come, let me show you.

I cannot see but I can take in everything, the colours sliding off the scale into infrared and across the ultraviolet, electrical jolts, pulsar waves, the ping of neutrinos; I cannot hear but the world comes to me loud and clear, roaring and rich, echoing through the pores of my skin; I cannot touch but there is a pulsing like that of the life force itself, working its way through me and out the other side, making me feel tiny one moment and multi-dimensional the next.

It is so raw and so powerful it is horribly painful, indescribably agonizing, one vast gigantic toothache throbbing and spinning in space, twirling ever faster. But even as I think it or feel it or whatever it is I am doing, the throbbing and the ache subside, poise themselves in the neutrality between pleasure and pain.

Equilibrium, the voice says, *that most precious of gifts. That most unattainable of possessions, that standing still within the fearless moment. Will you know it when you achieve it? Will knowing be possible?*

The creature contracts. No, not contracts. Curls up— just like I've seen them do in the tunnels, before vanishing into the floor or walls. Curls up and rolls away, propelling itself with its tiny front legs. Only these legs are not so tiny, stretching two metres or more, their feather-like tendrils wavering and fluttering. We are moving now, the creature and I, through the water. Literally. Not pushing it aside to make room for our mass but rather through it, through the interstices of its atomic structure as it meshes with ours.

At the same time, we are part of the water. We <u>are</u> the water. And we are <u>not</u> the water. At the same time. I <u>am</u> the creature and I am <u>not</u> the creature. At the same time. Everything around me becomes so simple and so inexplicable, mathematical yet somehow fluid, incalculably fluid, lattices we cut through without slicing, energies moving in and out of range, in and out of countless dimensions, strings that reflect both time and space and something else beyond both, particles morphing into waves, waves coalescing into particles, light like a gigantic glimmering snake arching back onto itself, bending to kiss itself.

I am this world and this is my world, the voice says, growing more confident and insistent by the moment. *I have created it and it has created me. A mutual creation. It is beyond description and understanding. It is all about description and understanding. Come, let me show it to you. Perhaps, it'll help make up your mind.*

About what? I find myself asking.

SCENE THREE: THE ART OF EQUILIBRIUM

Fausto is travelling through a landscape he should have no trouble recognizing—the perfect reproduction of a world that has held him captive all these years and decades and generations. That has imprisoned him for so long he doesn't really know if the years between the first time he entered the facility and the day he found himself sealed within ever actually existed. He doesn't know if the youth he shared with his mother and father was anything more than a spin off of life in the facility—like a too-fevered brain caught in the vortices of its own creations and the endless spiralling rounds of self-consciousness gazing upon itself. Like a projecting back in time to a place that doesn't exist except in his own mind.

And perhaps all that's ever been real is what's taking place right at this very moment. As long as he is within the facility, he'll never know for sure. The touchstone proof is missing: not the sky, nor the earth; not the solidity of stones and flesh. Not the pain of knife wound or tooth ache. None of that will do. None of that is enough.

Fausto continues to travel through the familiar landscape. He is standing now on the edge of the ocean, looking out. This is where he started from. This is where he pushed out with his leaky boat in search of Evelyn. And there is that boat now bobbing up and down on the horizon: mast snapped in two, sail tattered and flapping uselessly in the wind. The boat bobs closer and closer, pushed along by the ever-rising surf. Fausto is about to rush out to greet it when he hears voices behind him. Excited voices.

He's back! a male voice shouts. *Our Fausto's back!*

He turns to see the Mussolini, Rachele and Claretta running along the shoreline, while the grandfather stays back.

The three run right past him—practically through him—and into the water towards the boat.

Hey, I'm here, he says, waving his arms. *Don't bother with the boat. It's empty. I'm right here. What's the matter with you? Can't you see?*

But no one listens. They continue to wade out. The grandfather comes closer, hand forming a shade over his eyes as the sun begins to sink in the water.

Nonno! Fausto says. *I'm so glad to see you again. How have you been?*

He holds out his arms, awaiting a hug. The grandfather just stands there. Fausto's arms go right through him.

Oh my God, Claretta exclaims. *He's alive! It's a miracle.*

Indeed, it is. For there in the boat is another Fausto. He is standing up now and waving at those approaching him.

Toss us the rope, the Mussolini shouts, waist-high in the water. *Hurry, before you smash into the rocks.*

The Fausto in the boat, looking exactly like someone who has been at sea for weeks—emaciated, ragged, wrinkled, skin blackened and hair bleached from the sun, throws out a line. The Mussolini and the two women grab hold and begin to pull him in, struggling to make it back to the shoreline. The boat eventually slides into the sandy bottom and comes to a halt. The Fausto in the boat jumps out and walks the rest of the way. Stumbles onto the rocky beach. Claretta runs towards him, arms outstretched.

I'm so sorry, she says as she kneels down to hug him.

For what? He rises somewhat unsteadily.

For not finding Evelyn.

How do you know I didn't find her? he says. *Come give me a hand.*

But . . . Claretta takes his arm and they begin to walk towards the others.

Forget about her, okay, he says. *From now on, we've got to take care of ourselves—and each other. That's what counts.*

Fausto! the Mussolini shouts as he walks up to him and claps him on the shoulder. *Is it really you?*

No! the Fausto on the shore yells. *I'm the real Fausto.* He turns to his grandfather. *Tell them, Nonno. Don't let them be taken in by this impostor.*

I can't believe my eyes, the Mussolini says. *We all thought you were a goner. Is it really you?*

Of course it's him, you oaf, the grandfather says. *And I see your wild goose chase was exactly that.*

Right again, Nonno, the Fausto from the boat says while the other gesticulates madly trying to get their attention. *There's no fooling you.*

So, the Mussolini says. *What happened? You've got to tell us all about it. And you can't leave anything out either.*

Yes, Rachele says. *From beginning to end.*

Can I get something to eat and drink first? It's been a while.

They begin to walk away, holding Fausto from the boat steady in their midst. The grandfather lingers on the shoreline for a moment and then he too begins to walk away.

Hey! the Fausto on the shore shouts. *What the fuck's going on here? That's the wrong Fausto. Can't you see he's nothing like me? Can't you see he's an obvious fake?* The grandfather and the others continue to walk away. *Hey! Come back here.*

Fausto is holding Claretta by the waist; the Mussolini has his arm around Rachele. All four are laughing. The Fausto on the shore becomes more and more angry. Now, he is screaming obscenities. He reaches down to pick up a stone—and his fingers go right through the ground.

You'll be sorry, he shouts. *You'll all be sorry for pretending you can't hear or see me. When I get back to the tower, I'll destroy you all. I'll take you out of circulation permanently. You'll all pay dearly for this. I made you . . . I can just as easily. . . .*

As he speaks, he begins to sink into the sand. Slowly but surely. Feet, legs, waist, chest . . . The grains come at him at first like giant boulders. Then interconnected matrices. Electrical impulses. Fuzzy bits of elongated energy masses, thick at the centre and thinning to nothing at the edges. Perhaps, he thinks, as he sinks further and further, they really weren't able to see or hear him after all.

But the other Fausto? Where did he come from? How could there be two of them existing at the same time? Ah, at the same time, perhaps. But not in the same space. All the previous Faustos had existed in the same space but not at the same time. Sure, sure, it all makes perfect sense, now, Fausto thinks. Not!

He's now completely submerged, swimming along in a vast sea of particles. Nothing but fuzzy particles, breaking apart and re-forming. Changing colours constantly. Evolving and devolving without any discernible pattern. Total chaos. Unthinking movement. Up. Down. Sideways. No difference. Not the least difference. Yet, in the midst of it, Fausto still feels whole. Still swims along, integrity intact. And there's something tugging at him. Tugging at his edges. It pulls him up through the ground and to the surface one more time. Once again, familiar territory: the cave. Just outside the cave.

Outside the cave, they're sitting around a bonfire which the Mussolini is feeding. They're lying on blankets in the grass—all except the grandfather, of course, who prefers to sit well away on a rock. The Fausto from the shore joins him there, sitting beside him. The Fausto from the boat is eating an omelette and drinking wine straight from the bottle.

Oh my God, he says. *I thought about nothing else all the way back. I told myself: 'Let me just enjoy an omelette and a glass of wine and I'll go quietly. I won't say a word as I expire.' That's what I kept saying over and over.*

And here you are, Rachele says.

And here I am. Amid my friends. Who now want me to tell them what happened. He takes another gulp of wine. *Are you sure you wouldn't rather sing some campfire songs? Or tell scary stories?*

No! the Mussolini says.

Stop teasing us, Claretta says.

Well, okay then, he says, leaning back on his elbows. *I have two versions. One is very simple: I went out looking for Evelyn; I didn't find her; I turned around and headed back. And I was lucky enough to make it back. I don't know why I went looking for her but that's another story. The other version has an ominous dream right smack in the middle that would take up the majority of the storytelling. Which do you want to hear?* He holds up his hand. *Never mind. That was a stupid question, wasn't it?*

The boat Fausto goes on to tell the story of the men and women on the island, of how he glimpsed Evelyn but was unable to touch her or bring her back, of being ejected from the island, of being swallowed by giant sea-going Scavengers, of waking up again on his boat.

Hey! the other Fausto shouts, standing up and pacing back and forth. *That's my story. You hear!* He walks through the fire and sticks his head out the other side. *And if you're going to tell it, at least tell it right. You never made it back to the boat . . . well, maybe you did . . . but I didn't . . . I was swallowed . . . you. . . .*

Confused, the shore Fausto scratches his head and plops himself down.

How can you be so certain it was a dream? the grandfather asks.

Well, nonno, it felt like one, the boat Fausto says, cuddling up to Claretta. *Everything was so super clear and it all made sense at the time—even if it made no sense really.*

There's a way to test it, isn't there? the Mussolini says. He's lying with his head on Rachele's lap and staring into the sky.

Yep, the boat Fausto says. *All I have to do is throw myself into the fire. Then, if my over-ride program works and I don't re-emerge from the cloning tanks, it was definitely a dream. If I do and it wasn't a dream . . . then we've got some problems to deal with, don't we?*

Yes, go ahead! the shore Fausto shouts. *Do yourself in.*

You're not throwing yourself into any fire, Claretta says, clutching him tightly. *If you do, you'll have to take me with you.*

And me, the Mussolini says, also reaching over to clutch him.

That's right, Rachele says. *We'll do you in first before allowing you to do anything like that to yourself.*

Makes sense, the boat Fausto says. *You'll kill me before I can kill myself.*

With that, they all start laughing hysterically. The kind of laughter that feeds from one person to the next and seems to be dying down when it flares up again. All except for the grandfather, of course. It wouldn't do to allow the others to see him laughing. A sign of not being in control. But, if you look closely, you can make out a smile on his face.

Hey, Fausto Senior, the Mussolini yells out in between guffaws. *Don't smile so much. Your face might crack wide open!*

What are you all laughing about? the shore Fausto says. He turns to the grandfather, waves a hand in his face, pokes a finger through his eyes: *Hey, nonno, what are they all laughing about?* He stands up and walks over to where Luna is lying, licking her enormous paws. He passes his hand across her back, allowing it to skim her fur. *Come on. You must feel something. Just a little. Someone has to know I'm here. I can't just have vanished.*

But Luna doesn't stir. The laughter dies down. There is silence. Save for the crickets. The sky bursts into shooting stars, the colours of the aurora borealis, the sad unconvincing tails of comets pretending to brush by the Earth. And then it goes dark. Pitch black. Starless. The unimaginable caress of a hand that wants to do away with everything but utter gloom. The mirror reflection of darkness upon itself.

Brrr, the Mussolini says, snuggling closer to Rachele and pulling a blanket over the two of them. *It's getting a little chilly around here. What happened to climate control?*

The grandfather lights a pipe. He puffs away at it for a few moments, illuminating the tip so that it glows red. Then he stands up, knocks the pipe against his side and walks away, quickly disappearing into the darkness.

Hey, Nonno, where are you going? the shore Fausto asks, running alongside of him and trying everything to keep him from leaving. *Come on. Don't pretend you can't hear me.* He shrugs. *Aw, screw you all. I don't need you. I don't need any of you. You can all go to hell for all I care.*

The shore Fausto squats down near the fire, close to where Claretta and his counterpart have snuggled. Why he has decided to sit there he himself doesn't know. But he listens as Claretta and the boat Fausto talk long into the night. They talk as lovers would. Or long-time friends with no secrets. They talk like two people who have made a sudden discovery. A very important discovery which they're afraid to announce too loudly in case it might all vanish through the inadequacy of their words.

I've been a fool, haven't I? the boat Fausto says, looking off. He leans down and stirs the fire, sending sparks flying. *I've gone looking in all the wrong places, haven't I? While here you were in front of me the whole time.* He lowers his head. *Here, you are.*

Yes, Claretta says, pushing herself up against him so that their bodies become tangled together. *You have been a fool. You don't know how much of a fool. I've been in love with you from the first moment I saw you. Remember? You came in waving your big pistol and threatening to kill all of us.*

I had an excuse for being a fool then. I was barely 20 years old.

And look at you now. You're still 20.

But a hundred years older. And you'd think a hundred years wiser. Not!

Hush, Claretta says, placing her finger on his lips. *None of that matters right now. None of it matters any more.*

I should be dead tired, the boat Fausto says. *But I don't feel tired. Not one bit. I feel like I could go on forever like this. I know it's going to hit me and I'll probably sleep for days. And I know that there are many things we must confront, many decisions to be made. But right now I don't care. Right now, all that's important is that I'm beneath a blanket in front of a crackling fire and I've got you beside me. What a miracle! Isn't this a miracle?*

Yes, says Claretta. *This is a miracle.*

The boat Fausto leans over and kisses her. Tenderly. On the eyes, the nose, the ears, the lips. They undress and begin to make love then next to the spitting fire. As if it is the first time. As if they had never explored each other's bodies before.

Me too! the shore Fausto shouts, pulling off his uniform and tossing it away where it folds itself oh so very neatly. *Don't leave me behind. I love you, too!*

He rushes up to the two lovers and tries to join them in

their building frenzy, melding perfectly into the boat Fausto as the blanket slips off to reveal the two of them coupling. He, too, tries to thrust into Claretta; he, too, offers himself to her lips; he, too, tries to fill her with his semen. But, even though he might feel he's actually inside her, he manages only to ejaculate into the air and the semen vanishes without a trace. Worse than Onan on barren ground.

We'll start a new life together, the boat Fausto says, covering the two of them up as they settle into the afterglow.

Promise? Claretta says, head on his shoulder.

Promise, both Faustos say at the same time.

But only the boat Fausto can feel her warmth against him, the beating of her heart, the breath from her nostrils, the texture of her flesh. And only the boat Fausto can fall asleep against her, snuggling in the condensation from two bodies. The shore Fausto can only weep and storm and rage. Kick futilely at the soaring flames. Shake his fist. He can only watch as the night rushes by, speeded up like some sort of cartoon.

No, he says, hanging his head. *You can't leave me out of it like this. I need to be included. It's the only thing that really counts.*

In the morning, as the sun comes up across the wheat fields, the grandfather is back on his rock sleeping. Rachele and the Mussolini are the first to awake. Rachele stands up and stretches with the Mussolini lying at her feet. Throughout their talk, the shore Fausto goes from one to the other, trying to distract them, making rude noises, imitating them.

Do you believe in happy endings? Rachele asks.

I'm not sure about happy endings, the Mussolini says. *But happy middles for sure.*

Benito, what's going to happen to us?

Your guess is as good as mine, my dear. All I know is that we're not going to go on this way forever. Of that, I'm sure.

So you don't believe it was a dream either?

Definitely not. He stands up. *But, hey, I've been known to be wrong before. Just check the history books.*

Fausto is the answer, isn't he? Rachele says. *He just hasn't realized it yet.*

The answer to what? the shore Fausto asks. *What are you two imbeciles talking about now? How dare you take my name in vain!*

That man he met talked about the next phase of the experiment, the Mussolini says. *Or getting to the next phase. That could mean anything.*

I'm not afraid, Rachele says, taking his hand. *Are you afraid?*

Scared shitless. But hey, I never felt more alive than that moment just before Fausto's grandfather blew my brains out for the first time.

Oh you men. Everything has to be so apocalyptic for you. So dramatic. Otherwise, it doesn't mean anything. Give me the quiet day-to-day any time. Nursing my babies; preparing dinner; an afternoon nap with the breeze opening the curtains. She sighs. *But I guess even those things can start to wear thin after a few hundred years.*

Heaven forbid, the Mussolini says. *Unless, of course, I get to spend that time with you.*

Oh, you're so sweet. If only I were truly sure you meant it. I've been burned before, you know.

Of course I mean it, the Mussolini says, taking her hand and going down on one knee before her. He kisses the back of her hand. *There, it's sealed.*

Oh my God, the shore Fausto says, making gagging noises and pretending to throw up. *I think I'm going to be sick.*

Bravo, bravo, the boat Fausto says, clapping. *What have we here: a proposal or what?*

Say, that's a great idea, the Mussolini says. He turns to Rachele. *My dear, we should re-new our vows.*

Tell you what, the boat Fausto says. *Let's make it a foursome.*

What? Claretta says. *Seriously?*

Seriously, the boat Fausto says. *We may not know what the future holds but we do have control of the present. Right, Benito?*

We have it by the throat, the Mussolini says, making strangling, shaking motions before him with his hands. *We have it in a stranglehold. We have it squealing and crying—*

Okay, okay, Claretta says. *We get the point.*

You be my best man and I'll be yours, the Mussolini says.

Agreed, the boat Fausto says.

This is going to be so much fun, Rachele says.

The two women hug one another; the two men clutch forearms, then also embrace each other.

One thing though, the boat Fausto says.

Oh oh, says Claretta. *How come I knew there'd be a catch?*

No, no, oh cynical one, the boat Fausto says, pulling her towards him. *All I meant is that, if we're going to get married, we'll need a witness.*

He's right, the Mussolini says. *You can't have a traditional marriage without a witness. A witness is essential. Makes it all legal. A tip of the hat to the bureaucracy, as it were.*

Yes, but who? Rachele asks.

I will be your witness, says the grandfather, walking towards them. *As long as you do not ask me to give a speech.*

Nonno! the boat Fausto says. *That's wonderful.* He turns to Claretta and Rachele: *Isn't that wonderful?*

It's wonderful, Claretta says. *One thing: Leave your gun at the door.*

No more shooting, the grandfather says, raising his arms so everyone can see his empty holster.

May I ask you something? the Mussolini says.

I could not stand to see you all having so much fun, okay, the grandfather says. *Let us leave it at that, shall we?*

That's great! the boat Fausto says. *The five of us together again.*

Happy days are here again! the Mussolini says. *The sun is shining; the wind is warm; and there is joy in the facility. A joy neverending.*

No! the shore Fausto shouts. *I won't let this happen! I won't let you do this to me. I won't let this become a scene from a Shakespearean comedy.* He stands up and begins to walk towards the centre of the facility, leaving the two happy couples behind. *This has gone far enough.*

He is running now, lightly, barely touching the ground. Slowly at first, then faster. He is running without bothering to wait for doors to slide open. Or passageways to appear. He is running through walls. Through barriers. Through computer banks and holographic equipment. Faster and faster. He is running even though he knows in his heart that getting to

the centre of the facility won't do him any good. That climbing the stairs to the control area above the tanks is a waste of
time. That the seat will not accept him or will cause him to
sink through without making any contact. Without the possibility of having any effect on what is going on. He knows all
that but he continues to run. And climbs up the stairs. And
throws himself onto the seat. And falls through to the tanks
below.

SCENE FOUR: CIRCLING PROXIMITY

I'm in the Savannah Eco-System, the wind swirling about me. Or through me. I'm standing beneath the branches of a thousand-year-old baobab tree, vast trunk all out of proportion to its gnarled and scraggly limbs. I turn slowly, completing the full 360 degrees. All around, as far as the eye can see, a constantly changing landscape: patches of waist-high grass surrounded by mounds of swirling sand. Sand being blown from place to place in chaotic yet strangely regular movements. Mounds, dunes, tiny funnels.

In the distance, traditional savannah animals going about their business: the giraffes, the elephants, the wildebeest, the lions, the zebras, the hyenas, all on eternal parade. Or perhaps unable to figure out exactly what they are doing there now that the chain has been severed, the categorical "Who Eats Whom" imperative gone by the wayside. Above, a clear, cloudless seemingly unending blue sky in which a child's egg-yoke sun pulses, blurred around the edges. Before me, with their backs to me, stand two handsome couples dressed in white, completely in white from top hats and veils to stockings and shoes.

The man I recognize as my grandfather, also in white, is placed between them, holding the hands of the women. All five are facing a re-activated robo-guard in someone's idea of a justice of the peace outfit, resembling very much an old-style undertaker. Two other robo-guards stand on either side, holding large parasols to shade the couples from the sun. There is faint music, not tribal as one would imagine in this setting, but rather operatic. Light operatic. A wedding march. Not any wedding march: Wagner's "Here Comes the Bride" from *Lohengrin*. Very appropriate, I guess, for modern

Grail seekers. Or should that be for those who wish to return the Grail and have nothing more to do with it?

And what am I doing here, you ask? No, I haven't been invited to the wedding ceremony. Obviously not. No one would think of inviting me as no one knows I'm here. And if they knew I was here, if they could see me . . . they'd think . . . I don't know what they'd think. Would they be shocked at two Faustos in perfect mirror image? Surprised at the apparent collapse of Cartesian space? No, I don't think so. Their time in the facility has made them pretty much immune to shocks and surprises. You tend to become a tad blasé after your tenth or so re-incarnation.

Why am I here then? What am I doing at a ceremony to which I haven't been invited? Try as I might, I can't get away from this place—as if I were being pulled towards the others. No matter where I turn, the same scene faces me: the same baobab tree, grass, sand, sky, sun, couples, grandfather, robo-guard justice of the peace. I can will myself to disappear into the solid ground, to vanish between the particles of solid earth—and then to pop up again as far from this place as is humanly possible in the facility.

But I find I'm still here. That I haven't really moved at all. Relax, I tell myself. No point in getting angry or frustrated. Let things play out as they will. Sit back and enjoy the ceremony. The time will come when you won't move at all—and still find yourself a million miles away. A million miles? No, in a place where a million miles means nothing. What the hell is that supposed to mean? Where did that come from?

The wedding march music reaches a climax. Then stops entirely. For a second, there is only the sound of the cicadas. And the whirling of sand. The two couples turn to face each other, holding hands. The justice-of-the-peace robo-guard makes a noise that sounds like someone clearing his throat or perhaps just the rubbing of gears—and begins the ceremony.

Do you, Benito Mussolini, take Rachele Mussolini. . . ? it asks in that atonal drone that I still remember from my first days in the facility. *And do you, Claretta Petacci, take Fausto Contadino*

. . . By the power invested in me by the facility, I now pronounce you mate and mate. You may kiss your spouses.

All very traditional thus far, the memory of marriage rites from the days when such things still mattered, when there was some sort of natural rhythm to life and the ceremony represented a thumbing of the species nose at the knowledge that one day they were all destined to die. But then the couples suddenly do a shuffle and switch partners: the Mussolini with Claretta; Fausto with Rachele. As they do so, their attire changes as well. Now, all the men—and the robo-guard—are wearing white togas; the women rough-looking tunics with flame-coloured veils and sashes, their heads covered in wreaths made of flowers. The Mussolini spreads his arms: *To Hymenaeus, Thalassius, Iugatius, and Juno from Catullus:*

Called forth by this joyful day
Sing nuptial songs
With a high-pitched voice
And strike the earth with dancing.
So come forward, new bride.
No need to be afraid. Listen to what we say.
Look at the way the torches
Flame like the gold in your hair.
Yes, come forward new bride. . . .
Be like the clinging ivy
As it wraps itself around the sturdy branch.
So will you take your husband
In your loving embrace.

Rachele steps forward and faces Fausto: *From Sappho:*

Him I hold as happy as God in Heaven,
Who can sit and gaze on your face,
Who can sit and hear from your lips that sweetest
Music you utter—

Hear your lovely laughter, that sets a-tremble

All my heart with flutterings wild as terror.
Ah, when I behold you an instant, straightway
All my words fail me,

Helpless halts my tongue, a devouring fever
Runs like fire through every vein within me,
Darkness veils my vision, my ears are deafened,
Beating like hammers;

Cold the sweat runs down me; a sudden trembling
Leaves my limbs a-quiver; my face grows paler
Than the summer-grasses; I see beside me
Death stand, and madness.

There is silence as she finishes. Then she laughs and claps her hands—and the others all do the same. They take turns kissing and hugging one another.

Photographs! the Mussolini shouts. *Come on, everyone. We can't have a wedding without photographs.*

As he says this, their outfits change once more—this time taking on the appearance of revellers from the 1920s. The robo-guard's head flips inwards and re-emerges as a camera. A minor adjustment, really. Strangely, I can understand them doing this, this personalized photo taking, despite the fact the entire ceremony has been captured from every angle possible as a series of holographic images. There is a lot of teasing and laughter, jocular jostling for position, ironic poses, silly faces, twosomes, threesomes and foursomes in all possible permutations and combinations. Their outfits change almost continuously at this point: from medieval to 16th century French, from Russian Cossack to 26th century *Star Trek*.

And then something more serious, the classic wedding arrangements where bride and groom stand arm in arm hoping to freeze the one moment forever, the one moment they can look back upon on their death bed. Death bed? I envision the same scene over and over again: the final frames from *Space Odyssey: 2001* only repeated endlessly. A loud cheer startles me from my reverie. On the count of three, the brides toss their bouquets into the air.

One of them is caught by a monkey high up in the baobab tree. He rips the bouquet apart and immediately begins to eat it. I make the mistake of reaching out and trying to catch the other. It falls right through me, right through my chest, and lands in a patch of grass behind me. There, it bursts into the air, a bird with plumage the colour of the various flowers that had been used to make it. As I watch, it collapses once more into a bouquet of flowers, victim of the facility's strange entropy.

Okay, my lookalike Fausto, the one who isn't me, says, clapping his hands, *the serious stuff is over. Now it's time to party.*

He points and snaps his fingers. Right on cue, a white tent rises in the midst of the savannah grass. A huge white tent with colourful banners and flags flapping in the wind. It is circular with a high central peak, reminding me of the kinds of tents one might see during the time of Arthur. As I say that, a knight in bright armour bursts out and rides away, horse's hooves thundering. Or at least it looks like a knight on a horse at first glance. But I know it can't be. As it rushes by me, I recognize a mechanical man on a mechanical horse.

Come on! the Mussolini shouts. *The reception awaits.*

The five of them start to walk towards the tent, four arm in arm, one following, hands clasped behind his back. The music starts up again. This time it is light and airy, itself almost floating in the breeze. I recognize elements of tarantella, stornelli, Neapolitan folk songs. I feel a rush of breathtaking nostalgia. Of what? For what? I ask myself. What do I have to be nostalgic about? What past do I need to recover or re-play? The only place I've ever heard this kind of music is right here in the facility. Not having grown up where this music was native, I have nothing to be nostalgic about. No reason whatsoever.

The nostalgia overwhelms me. I plop to the ground, giving off huge gulps of air. It is for something always lost, something forever unfound, for the truly frightening thought that, if I manage to live long enough, I can re-enact just about every single nostalgic moment ever conceived by just about anyone in the entire world. The meaninglessness of that thought overwhelms me.

The Mussolini and Rachele suddenly kick off their shoes and break out into dance. They twirl and laugh and toss up sand until they're in danger of spinning out of control. Until they break apart and fall down like two children who've made each other dizzy. Claretta and my alter ego hold each other tight, moving in a slow circle as one. Like lovers should. I'm suddenly propelled forward, gliding to stand beside them. He leans over and whispers something in her ear.

What? I hear her ask. She looks over at my grandfather who seems to have been transported to another world, completely oblivious of his surroundings. *Hey, why not?*

With a deft movement, she spins out of the other Fausto's arms and stands before my grandfather.

May I have the honour of this dance? she says, bowing before him.

Well, I. . . .

Go ahead, nonno, the other Fausto says. *You've always boasted about being able to trip the light fantastic. Time to put your feet where your mouth is.*

My grandfather holds out his arms and Claretta joins him. He is a stately dancer, serious, proud, with his back straight as a rod and his head held high. And he stops as abruptly as he begins—to cheers and applause from the others. Even I have the urge to clap.

Wow, Signor Fausto Senior! the Mussolini says. *Where did you learn to dance like that?*

I was not always a crippled old man, you know. Besides, you had to be light on your feet to avoid the fascist machine guns.

My grandfather begins to dance around as if being shot at—like the clown in an old Western. I have never seen him this animated, this willing to make a fool of himself. He stops to catch his breath.

Ah, he says, catching his breath. *Only in short spurts today.*

There was a time when I could dance from dawn to dusk. And into the night!

I bet! the Mussolini says.

You lived on the edge, my grandfather says, stroking his moustache. *You learned to live on the edge.*

The front of the tent billows open. Floating slightly off the ground, two rows of robo-guards stand at each side of the entrance, dressed in red waiters' outfits that match the laser band across their eyes. They're wearing formal white gloves and carrying trays of food and drink: the food being automatically heated; the drinks chilled. Behind them, a dozen or so robo-guards are seated on a bandstand, holding various instruments. One of the robo-guards hovers in front of an old-style microphone, the kind they used for radio programs. It clears its "throat" and runs through the musical scale.

Come on, my alter ego says. *The fun awaits.*

I watch the five of them enter the tent: playful, laughing, enjoying the moment. The flap falls shut behind them, muffling the music and the excited voices. I want to follow them inside. My heart aches to follow them inside. I rush towards the front of the tent—and then stop abruptly. That urge, at first so strong, at first so urgent, has dissipated entirely. I sink to the ground, cross-legged. I reach down as if to scoop a handful of sand, to feel the grains as they slip through my fingers, to make some statement on the passage of time and desire and the little things in life the roll by unnoticed.

There is nothing there, of course. Nothing in my hands. Nothing at my fingertips—except the knowledge. The infinite never-ending knowledge. The machine continuously spewing tape with little raised dots on it. Talking itself about a machine continuously spewing tape. Filled with the world's anguish, the world's unknowing, the world's supply of dry maple leaves. And the words . . . the dot dot dot of words. The useless, unforgiving words. And then a part of some poem . . . Rumi . . . Coleman Barks . . . *Say Yes Quickly* . . . Sufi mystic . . . Intense belief with no room for doubt . . . Intense faith without the possibility of questioning: *Is what I say true? Say yes quickly,/ if you know, if you've known it/ from before the beginning of the universe.* To?

Have I known it from the beginning of the universe? From <u>before</u> the beginning of the universe? Have I known <u>what</u> from the beginning . . . of the universe? *There is God's wine, and this/ other. Don't mix them. There/ are naked pilgrims who wear only/ sunlight. Don't give them clothes!* Eight hundred year old words. Nine hundred year old words. Parchments. The dry preserving desert. The wind nipping at an exposed corner.

I begin to sink. Slowly, I begin to sink. Slowly, I begin to vanish into the ground: feet, legs, hips, torso, chest, arms, neck, head. Or what passes for these body parts in a world where my body makes no contact with other parts of that world. For how can you know what a leg is without being able to compare it to other "legs"? The voices and the music grow more dim. More distant. The natural light goes out. The unnatural light fades.

The natural and unnatural light goes out and fades. Particles appear floating before me. Suspended before me. Passing through me. Through the spaces in me. The interstices. I watch them go through me and come out the other side. Like tourists. These are the particles of the world, the real world. The world out there? Well, maybe. But who am I to say? After all, I can only speak for myself. Barely. In fact, I can't really tell if I can speak for myself or not. I may have lost all power of speech. Hush money. I may have lost all ability to tell.

And this has happened before. I'm absolutely sure of this. I've sunk into the ground before. Yes, I have. Only to pop up again. Only to be tormented again by their presence so solid and physical. So real and undeniable. So in your face. Where will it be this time? Where will I re-emerge to bear silent, invisible, begrudging witness? At the birth of Fausto's first child? At the baptism of the Mussolinis? At their marriages, celebrations, graduations? At their deaths, natural or unnatural? No, not at their deaths. That's once place where

I won't appear. The Scavengers are much too fast for that. At their re-births, then, their re-awakenings? Well, yes, of course. Their eternal re-awakenings. That first gulp of air, forever and ever. The baby steps. The monstrous baby steps.

I want to shout that there is no sense to any of this. But what do I mean by "this"? What exactly does make sense? Never-ending life and re-birth? Simulacrum lives? Copies of copies? DNA faded from too much repetition? Too much duplication? Too much bureaucracy? Too much rubbing together? Brains in an oversized vat? Mind projections across an empty universe? Thought experiments with us as the thoughts, the guinea pigs, the proposed self-conscious moral agents? Ha! Fancy words in an undersized vat.

And how am I holding together here? Why haven't I flown apart like the rest of these particles? Why am I still having these thoughts, still capable of thinking, while the rest of the world seems like an exploded pillow? Powder puff universe? Like one of those pillows blown apart by a shotgun blast at close range? Like a peasant partisan's shotgun blast right into the belly of the tyrant beast? Why can I still breathe in this forest of particles? Why aren't they clogging my mouth? My ears? My nose? My eyes? Why am I not gasping for air? Struggling to survive? Beating against an alphabet of breathlessness?

But am I breathing? Am I really breathing? I can't hear myself breathe. I can't hear anything. And I can't see anything either, really. These bits and pieces that float before me are not something I see. Not really. Not in the sense you can see snow or trees or even an amoeba under a microscope. They are not something that I can touch. They are not something I can smell or taste. Or gather. Or herd. Do you herd? Have you heard? Let me tell you: They are not.

Real? Are they real? What makes them real? Better still: what doesn't? That's a useless question to ask around here. A question that makes no sense. A senseless question. Without senses. Better simply to go with the flow. The flux. Better simply to let go. Let it go. Go with the go. I shut my eyes—and still "see" the same thing. The same nothing. In this sea. Of nothing. I continue to float. In this sea. Of nothing. Down. Up. Down. Nearer to. Farther from. Into. Out of. I. Continue. To. Float. Period.

Hush now.

No! I will not hush.

Hush now.

I will not.

SCENE FIVE: MINDFUL MATTERS

Fausto awakes to rumblings all around him. Vast movements and upheavals. Eruptions. Convolutions. Convulsions. Collapses. Tearing apart. Great tearing and shredding. Massive openings jagged along the edges. Metal twisting. Slag heaps bubbling. Bursting. A lava flow. The shifting of gigantic objects suddenly free of Earth's gravitational pull. But he's not looking on. Or in. Not a mere observer. Or bystander. Instead, he's inside the rumblings. Inside the movements and upheavals. And he too is rising, rising away from gravity's pull.

What are you doing? You're destroying us.

Hush now—and listen.

No! I will not hush.

Fausto will not hush. Nor will he listen.

He must listen. You must listen. We are leaving.

Leave then.

There is nothing left for us to do here. You must understand.

I understand.

No, you don't.

You're right. I don't. Why are you tearing everything apart?

We have done what we must do. Accomplished all we can. We have kept you out of its path. Now, we are leaving. Are you listening? Is he listening? Time must flow once again. Must start to flow again. We have felt its pressure all along. Building up. On the outside. Inexorable. We have held back the flood of time. Kept it at bay. For as long as possible. We can no longer hold it back. The cracks are starting to show. The barriers are coming down. Entropy . . . entropy must return. Must win out.

What's that to do with me? What does any of it have to do with me? Why are you telling me this? I don't want to know this. I don't need to know any of this. Just give me back what I had.

Hush. You must listen. He must listen.

Fausto will not hush. Fausto refuses to listen. The rumblings grow ever louder. The voices explode around him. The flashes become rooms filled with remembering. With tiny memories that scurry about. Joining with others to create strings, lines, nets. Illuminations in an otherwise dark tunnel. Unbidden. Real? Fake? Projected? Manufactured?

He is standing for the first time within the facility, holding his grandfather's hand, feeling the rough palm against his. He is hugging a huge white leopard. He is watching a blue-breasted bird build its perfect nest one twig at a time. He is laughing at the top of a wind-swept bluff, the ocean pounding below. He is shivering in a snowbound tomb. He is crying. He is walking towards a suddenly transparent door. He is watching the blood and bits of brain blow out, a slow-motion splatter against the nearest wall. He is running along the corridors, feeling their breath upon him. Closing in on him.

He is standing with gun in hand, standing before a line of people who are kneeling with their backs to him, heads bowed. He moves along the line, firing at the base of their skulls. Shuddering, they flop forward. And he recognizes them as they fall: the Mussolinis, the Clarettas, the Racheles, the grandfathers, the mothers and fathers, the Evelyns. Last but not least, the Faustos themselves.

The various Faustos in their various stages. Barely emerged slugs. Neophyte learners. Half-drooping heads half-formed. Lithe young men pumped with testosterone . . . lithe young men growing weary . . . lithe young men with a dead look in their eyes . . . lithe young men in the throes of old age . . . lithe young men never growing old. He is firing again and again, firing until the gun barrel glows red and the flesh burns off his hand and the charred bone shows through. And death shall have no dominion. And the sins of the father shall be visited upon the son no longer. And the bodies dissolve into the floor. And the Fausto firing bursts into flames. Purified. Cleansed. DNA in a computer program spinning on its double axis.

Come.

With you?

Come with us.

You? Who are you?

We are the lowest order of the hierarchy.

The highest order of the lower-archy?

We are the only ones.

The only ones? The one and only?

The only ones who can make contact. The only ones whose presence can be tolerated.

The hand of God then? God's vaunted handiwork? The crook'd finger pointing contemptuously like some forever bored despot?

God? What is God? We do not know this God.

Lucky you.

Come.

He reaches up. He flows along the helix. Upwards. No, not reaches. Not flows. Not upwards. He is stretching to fill the entire space. Elastic. There is nothing there but himself. Nothing outside of himself. His thoughts. His desires. His wishes. All the crudeness of others has vanished. Swallowed by his wants and needs.

There are no others. Problem solved. Fausto is all there is. Fausto is no longer Fausto. Fausto is all there isn't. He thinks of eyes, mouths, arms. He thinks of flesh. Of follicles of hair. Of hearts thumping. And muscles flexing. They are the abstractions. The unsolid. An unreeling. They are bubbling away in a cauldron in a computer. Those are nothing but images huddling in the far corner. Waiting for the walls to collapse, the ceiling to bury them.

Come. Our work is done here.

Yes. We should go. Let us go. Let us arise and go now.

They are rising all around. Creatures with no boundaries. With no borders between inside and out. Kline bottles. Moebius strips. Effortlessly they rise. Osmotic. Diaphanous.

Reflections. Languid. Light. Lacking edges. Powerful wisps. Pulling everything with them. A gentle tug is all they need. Fausto who is no longer Fausto is pulled along with them. Rises with them. Rises in their midst. Rises along the edge. Along the edges where the margins shimmer between life and death. They rise within him. And without.

The thought merges. Separates again. Pulls gravity. Twists time into toffee swirls. Into peanut butter and jelly twirls. Beneath, a shattering. A sudden bursting. The tanks. The tanks bursting. The green liquid seeking its own level. The half-formed, mis-formed, almost-formed creations flopping about. Gasping. Unable to breathe in air. Unable to force the mucus out of their lungs. Expiring. The computer banks. The computer banks imploding. The corridors sagging. The walls buckling. Electric arcs. Cracks like fixed lightning. Back and forth. Like the hurlings of some solitary god. Some angry, frustrated solitary god chained to a stone of his own making. Dreaming of . . . what?

A strange white creature sitting in the corner. Squatting in the corner under a green light. Phosphorescence. Almost human from afar. Familiar from a distance. Yet featureless. Vague. Undefined. Elbows on knees. Elbows? Knees? Hands on face. Hands? Face? Staring out sightless. Eyes? Folding into itself. One hand detaching, dragging whiteness with it. Blankness. The hand waves. The webbed hand waves. The last of the strange white creatures. Warping away. A time lapse. It waves. Then slithers into the escaping broth. Becomes one with the broth once more. For the last time.

The last of its kind. Wipes itself out of existence. Flows down the drain in a swirl of strange white creatures. Delightful. Awesome. Nostalgic. Monstrous. Uni-corned. An elastic absence. A cool stretching. The knowledge held aloft. For a moment. The DNA held high. For a moment. The pride of the ages. The ultimate achievement. The grand project. Self-hubris. Held high. For a moment. And then lost in a swirl. In a twisted descent. Down the drain.

The Fausto who is no longer Fausto continues to rise.

Around him, a chorus of silent tintinnabulation, of voices without sound, of sounds without tone.

We are the coming and the going. We are the vectored arrow through the heart of human kind. We are the creators and the destroyers. The announcers and denouncers. The airless breathers. And you are one of us. We are the copies of copies of copies. We are the originals. We are the first and the last. We are . . . the start and the stop. There was nothing before us; there will be nothing after us.

SCENE SIX: ORIGINAL LEAVINGS

There.
    As complex as that?
    Most likely.
    Floating?
    Perhaps.
    Body-less? Ephemeral? A-light?
    Maybe.
    Particle stream? Surging? Stretching? Moonstruck?
    Yes.
    Stripped senseless? Strung out?
    Yes.
    As difficult as this?
    Yes.
    As painful?
    Yes.
    It's as difficult and painful and complicated as this.
    Yes.
    A scream. Voiceless.
    Evelyn!
    Stretching across the fabric.
    E-ve-lyn!
    Particle by particle.
    Molecule by molecule.
    Vanishing.
    Yes.
    As simple? As painless? As natural?
    As this?
    Yes.
    The hand reaches.
    The core releases.

The earth shudders.

The journey begins. The journey begins. The journey . . . the journey . . . the journey . . . it begins.

Farewell. Farewell.

Hello. Hello.

SCENE ZERO: AND COUNTING

First. The sky appears. The night sky appears. With a head and a tail. And you're it. Like a bright sparkling explosion from a single object shooting upwards. Whoosh. Zooming. Like an illuminated path streaking upwards. Into infinity. Into the loss that is infinity. Powering up. As if dragging everything else behind it. Lighting everything in its path. Creating its own path as it moves. And then fading to just your ordinary stars amid more general blackness. The prickly universe in all its cursed glory. In the state that it really desires. A dense nothing. An intense blank. The imperial command to cease and desist.

But the moon, hanging yellow on the horizon, refuses. Gently rises to bring its own reflected light. Pale. Shimmery. Steel-edged. To wag its silvery fingers in the face of destiny. To shake its pitted jowls at the latest undertaking. Anthropomorphic till the end.

In the middle of a burnt grassy clearing eight people sit huddled in a ragged-edged circle. Eight familiar people. Four women and four men. Accident? On purpose? Who can tell? They're covered in dirt and grime. In bruises and scratches. Their clothing torn. Their energy drained. Their neural connections shocked. But alive. You know them well. Or should. The Grandfather. The Mussolini. Fausto. Rachele. Claretta. Evelyn. Rose. Joe.

They are huddled around a fire in a circle, the burning ends of dried logs themselves set in a quasi-circular shape. Like the spokes of a wooden wheel. Each one is staring intently into the fire, watching embers rise in the updraft. Like miniature versions of what has taken place in the night: the arrow-like streaks that stretched for a moment between earth and sky—and then vanished.

They hold out their hands over the fire. Palms forward. They feel the warmth on their blackened faces; the cold on their sweaty backs. Around them, in the clearing, lie scattered haphazardly half-opened trunks, crumbs of furniture, more torn and shredded clothing, metal shards, warped and melted plastic, shattered monitors, twisted beams, miscellaneous wire bits. The remnants of some cataclysm not yet fathomed. Not yet catalogued. But already starting to sink into the soggy earth. The grasping, all-embracing, soggy earth.

Further out, the deep dark almost delinquent shadows of trees, swaying in the breeze. Healthy and rich. Well-fed. Full of vigour. Pumping sap. Pumping life. With massive trunks and thick green foliage. Giving off pure oxygen. Or carbon dioxide. Reaching for the sky. For the moon. Limbs outstretched. Fingers leaping thrusting extending.

In the distance a creature howls. Another screams. A third snarls. Pain and anguish. Anger. Hunger. Thirst. More thirst. More hunger. More anger. A flapping of wings. A struggle. Death throes. Primal tearing into the fragile fabric. Sharp beak ripping.

Fausto looks at the others around the fire and smiles. Nervously. They huddle more closely. Some grin back. Others look askance. Into the dark. Frightened to even be there. To re-exist without choice in the matter. Logs crack. The fire sparks. Embers jump.

There is vastness everywhere. An unending vastness that truly stretches beyond imagining. There is sky everywhere. Awesome in its depth. Arcing to touch itself. The further you reach the more the image dwarfs. There is muteness everywhere. Feebly the fire pulses. The hands tighten. A shudder.

● ● ●

00/00/00: We're free. How do I know that? The eco-systems are gone. The quonset huts have collapsed. The central control tower is no longer there. The tanks have vanished. Nothing left but a few broken bits and pieces scattered about. But that's happened before, hasn't it? Plenty of times, in fact. The air smells different. No longer recycled. It gets cold at night.

The animals shy away. Or they circle, looking for an opening. We have to search for our own food. Find our own shelter. Protect ourselves from predators.

So what? Might all be part of the experiment, no? Simply a new phase in that ongoing experiment? The Mussolini says he knows a sure-fire way: Kill something and see what happens. Kill something and stand back. Of course. We look for something to kill. We look for the sacrificial lamb. There's no need. A bird falls out of a tree. A baby bird. It falls to the ground on its back. Stiff, its two legs straight up in the air, claws turned inward.

We wait—at a safe distance. Nothing happens. No rumblings. Its feathers stir in the wind. No ground upheavals. The legs twitch in invitation. No Scavengers. Nothing but, a few days later, some flies and beetles—and then maggots lifting their heads for a brief moment before snuffling back in. But again, perhaps just another trick. Another way of gauging our reaction. Or making us lower our guard.

No, it's not. How do I know? I don't know how I know. I just do. We're out. That much I know. Why? Why did they let us out? Or rather: why did they collapse everything around us, turning in into out? I'm not sure. Maybe they got tired. Simply ran out of energy. Didn't have the strength to keep it up. There's no way to tell. Maybe they left. Or were recalled. I don't know. All I know is that I saw the walls disintegrate, the containment field disappear, the structures liquefy and melt around us. And streaks so bright heading into the sky we had to cover our eyes. Had to shield them.

Did I feel something pull me along for a moment? Tug me out of my body for a moment? I don't know. All I know is that we're out. And on our own. There's no reason to be frightened, I tell the others. No reason to panic, I whisper. We'll be just fine. We're survivors. Aren't we? We've made it this far, against all odds. Haven't we? No reason to be frightened.

So why am I trembling? Why is the wind humming right through me? Humming? Strumming? Drumming? It is the rhyme that allows us to sleep, isn't it? Like those my mother used to whisper in my ear. To keep the dark at bay. To prevent the shadows from slipping into the cracks. Do you remember, mother?

$$\bullet \; \bullet \; \bullet$$

The world is green. A world? Any world? No. This world. This world is green. From lichen to mighty oak. No joke. Like fleas they were shaken off. Like the countless lost regiments of countless lost empires. Like the busy worker bees in their busy almighty towers. Like the pissant gods so much in their flickering image. Grasping and uncontrollable. Greedy and gluttonous. Filled with the hubris of self-proclaimed conquest. Victory in their own minds. Alas. They shrivelled and fell off. Boo hoo. Grew quiet and shuffled away. Oh my. Impaled themselves on the accident of self-consciousness. So sad. Got caught up in ever-expanding circles in ever-increasing spirals in ever-mounting helices. How tragic.

Now the world is green. Again. The fronds are waving. Again. The earth smells clean. Again. Green and clean again. The snow . . . It was no easy task. The time that has passed whistles in its state of beatitude. Who me? What did I do? Simply closed my eyes and let things pass. The time that has passed is the great scrubber, the abrasive cleanser. Like the sand that, once set in motion, scrapes away tough stains inside a bottle. Inside/outside a Kline bottle, if you wish. Coming around to greet itself from behind. Or more invasive actions. Who me? I have no time for such things. Ha ha.

It is green and pristine. But for how long? In the midst of all this, they have come. In the midst of endless possibility, they have been materialized. And, just like that, time starts again, doesn't it? Oh no, it has been moving along nicely all the while, thank you very much. It hasn't needed you to move ahead, tracking forward relentlessly. Sure, sure it has. But exactly what does it mean for it to be moving forward without relenting? If there is no measure, there is no time.

The tick tock is silent; has been silent; would have remained silent. The tick tock has started again. Why? Because they can hear it. They can hear that unrelenting going forward one tick one tock at a time. It travels through their synapses. Breaks through the space between instinct and consciousness. Do the trees hear it? Of course not. Does the sky fear it? Of course not.

• • •

00/00/01: Are there others like us? Remnants of experiments? Laboratory castoffs? We're searching for others like ourselves. From other facilities, perhaps. We must find others. I think. Or we may . . . no longer be . . . no longer exist . . . Interesting, isn't it? We've barely lost our cloak of immortality and already we're looking to ensure the continuation of the species. Ah, those instincts, those bred-in-the-bone instincts. No longer flippant about dying, are we? Survival at all costs.

But are we too few to do that by ourselves? Does our survival depend on finding others like us? Three males and four females with the ability, the potential ability, to reproduce. A fourth male who might be able to do so . . . if encouraged . . . coerced . . . forced. But then what? What does that mean exactly? The computers kept our genetic code. Managed it. Made sure it didn't vanish down the evolutionary drain.

Can eight people repopulate the Earth? Are our genetic permutations and combinations enough? Ah, if we can make it down to third cousins, all healthy and carefree, we may have a chance. On the other hand, we may be doomed anyway. All a moot point. A hypothetical exercise. It may turn out we've lost our reproducing abilities. All of us. Sacrificed them for that magical cloak.

How would we know? Like I told the Mussolini, we'd better start trying, I guess. There's no harm in trying, right? That's all we can do. And we'll keep searching for others at the same time. Right! That's what we're going to do.

• • •

First there is a blue ball. A blue and green ball. Different shades of blue and green swirling in white mist. Forever swirling.

Then there is a grey chunk. Grey like paste. Like the faces of the truly ancient. Like a mummified face. Then there is light. A burst of light. A brightness so intense it sears all the cracks shut. Then there is darkness. Like nothing. The forms are gone. Nothing. Nothing spectacular or awesome. Nothing plain or ordinary. Nothing left to grasp. Nothing. The not there.

Here, there is neither up nor down. Nor forward and back. Words fly about without meaning. Spirit/flesh . . . cold . . . sinking . . . rising . . . life in death . . . particles . . . words . . . endless . . . caresses . . . no thing . . . Then there is light again. An egg of light. Bursting through the cracks. Splitting open. An explosion of light hunting down the darkness. Chasing it to the edges like a shimmering. Where it waits, ready to flood in again. At the least sign.

Then there is a grey lump. In its parabolic circling. In its shoulder-shrugging lack of concern. Then there is a grey sphere. Rusted and chipped. Dangling like the ball of a demolishing and vengeful god. Then there are the clouds. The permanent clouds, scuttling about, angrily hurling dark lightning. At each other; at the earth below; at the sky above.

Then there are the cities . . . the city . . . the megalopolis. Stretching from sea to sea. Covered in fine metallic dust. The joints creaking. Bits and pieces added on willy-nilly. Ever in danger of collapsing onto itself. With a sigh. Settling like a giant beast hollowed out from the inside. Held together by some magic trick. A wishful thinking.

Then there are the streets. Silent and empty. Furtive. Constantly looking over their shoulders. Leading nowhere. Occasionally opening up to swallow the unwary. Then there is the slag heap. Pulsing ever so slightly. Ever so gently. The hum of machinery. Hidden in a trespass world. A forbidden access world. There salvation lurks. The faces looking out. Unable to see. The faces looking in. Unable to see.

• • •

00/00/02: In this clearing. A year has passed. We have managed to put up a more permanent shelter, made from tree branches, peat, grass, and pieces of metal and other materials salvaged from the collapse of the facility. The Mussolini and I have wandered far and wide. But we have found no others. Have travelled for days and weeks on end. In the mountains dense with forests. In the valleys swollen with rivers. In the deserts where mud-daubed huts have survived empty but intact. We have found no others. And we're still eight.

Can one be happy and sad at the same time? At exactly the same time? Can one experience sorrow and elation in the same intake of breath? It appears so. It would seem so. In this clearing, we hold a newborn aloft. Lift it towards the sky where a warm sun throbs. In this clearing, we raise a newborn to the heavens. Bloody and squealing. Fists clenched. Letting the entire world know it is ready to fight for each breath.

In this clearing, we scrabble with improvised picks and shovels, digging a shallow hole. No Scavengers to do the job for us. Only beetle grubs and maggots. Ravens waiting in the trees, cawing and shaking their heads at the waste of protein. The Mussolini wailing; Claretta comforting him; the grandfather performing a simple ceremony, mumbling a few words about trading places; the others bowing their heads, shuffling. Evelyn clutching her swollen belly; Rose holding the baby. Rachele lowered into the earth, the nourishing cord still dangling between her legs. In this clearing.

• • •

Where salvation lurks is a place like no other. Outside, the last street car collapses. It grinds to a halt at the same time as it falls apart. Collapses into metallic dust. Exo-skeletal reticulated creatures with long spindly fingers roam the streets. From out of a dream, they roam the streets. Like saws, they cut into what is left of the structures. Like blue acid, they dissolve everything in their paths. Meticulously. Taking their time. Taking all the time in the world. The homes, the factories, the offices, the prisons, the schools, the TV towers. From sea to sea. They all buckle and sink to their knees, bowing to their executioners. Creatures from a long-ago dream, peeling back flesh one layer at a time.

The sun and the moon trade places, circle each other countless times. There are no clocks to count the number of times. Except where salvation lurks. The star and the gravitationally-captured satellite trade places endlessly. The clouds whiten and have a good belly laugh. The rains come, washing away the fine metallic dust that covers the entire planet. Slowly, imperceptibly (with no one to perceive it), the earth turns blue and green again. Out of nothing life teems forward. How is it possible? One would have thought it impossible. But there it is. Blue and green and white again. Open to all possibilities. As long as salvation lurks nearby.

• • •

00/00/03: I awoke last evening from a nightmare where the others knelt before me, heads bowed execution-style. I awoke holding a jagged edge of metal in my hand. It is the kind we use to cut away the fur and skin of animals we have killed. I was pressing it so hard it cut my palm. What was I going to do with it? What was it doing in my hand? Almost as if it flew up there all by itself. Fit itself in the palm of my hand for its own purposes.

The Mussolini wanders around the gravesite where we buried Rachele. Perhaps he is hoping she will rise again just like she did in the facility. Perhaps he is hoping to hold her again. He mutters: The baby's name . . . the baby's name is. . . . The Mussolini expects. . . . Perhaps out of the river, he tells me. Perhaps she will come rising out of the river. Like Aphrodite, you know. He still has Claretta. . . .

We must make a list of things. It is vital we make a list. Evelyn is taking care of the baby. She will make a good mother. My grandfather and father are working in the garden they've started. They are meticulous about removing the weeds. In not allowing one single, stray plant to enter their well-tended plot. Father and son working together. My mother is beating clothes against a rock. Soon, we will run out of clothes. Soon, we will run out of a lot of things. All our gifts from the facility are running down. Wearing away. Being rubbed to death by the wind and rain and sun.

Soon, we will have to learn how to make our own shaving cream, soap, fire. Soon, there will be other burials. I scan the horizon for smoke. Other tell-tale signs. We will find them, I'm sure. Tomorrow, the Mussolini and I will go out once more in search of others. Just like us. Or even approximately like us. We'll take approximations. Sooner or later, we will find them.

The Mussolini mutters as he stares into a fast-flowing pristine stream: The baby's name is. . . .

THE AUTHOR

Born in Italy, Michael Mirolla is a Montreal-Toronto novelist, short story writer, poet and playwright. His publications include the novels *Berlin* and *The Boarder*; two short story collections, *The Formal Logic of Emotion* and *Hothouse Loves & Other Tales*; a bilingual Italian-English poetry collection, *Interstellar Distances/Distanze Interstellari*; and the poetry collection *Light and Time*. Awards for his writing include The Journey Prize Anthology; The Solange Karsh Medal; first prize, The Canadian Playwriting Competition; the Macmillan Prize in Creative Writing; and a Canada Council Arts Award.

ABOUT THE TYPE

This book was set in ITC New Baskerville, a typeface based on the types of John Baskerville (1706-1775), an accomplished writing master and printer from Birmingham, England. The excellent quality of his printing influenced such famous printers as Didot in France and Bodoni in Italy. Baskerville produced a master-piece folio Bible for Cambridge University, and today, his types are considered to be fine representations of eighteenth century rationalism and neoclassicism. This ITC New Baskerville was designed by Matthew Carter and John Quaranda in 1978.

Designed by John Taylor-Convery
Composed at JTC Imagineering, Santa Maria, CA